The Lost Fate
Book I of The Moirai Trilogy
L. W. Phillips

Dragon Scales Press

Also by
L.W. Phillips

<u>The Oneiroi Trilogy</u>

Dream Divine
Dream Healing
Dream Sacrifice

"A person often meets his destiny on the road he took to avoid it."
~Jean de La Fontaine

Trigger Warnings
Know Your Triggers Before Reading

THE LOST FATE IS a work of fiction that may contain triggers in the written word for some readers. Triggers are but are not limited to, the following: graphic language, consensual intercourse some may consider spicy, battle scenes, and death.

Often words are in their UK spellings due to the characters' origin.

Prologue
4010 B.C.

"He's coming, my lady," Muirgen rushed to The Morrigan's side, tossing her cloak beside her onto the bed of feathers and animal hides. "We need to leave, now!"

The Morrigan struggled to sit up, her hand instinctively on her abdomen, protective even in slumber. "Is he aware?" She asked her most loyal guard and maid.

The Great Queen never considered her guard a thrall. She wasn't her slave, but a friend—one who had stuck with her for over millennia, even vowed to protect her against the chief god and father of her unborn. Over the last nine and a half months, her friend had helped hide what she concealed from the world, and for that, The Morrigan owed her guard everything.

"My sources say he's angry, but that could be because you've been lost to him since Seikilos, my Queen."

After removing the sleep from her eyes, she conjured her leathers and fixed her hair into a single long braid, readying herself to ride. As she strapped a dagger to each of her thighs and a sword across her back, she remembered the day her love for her mate and king changed—the day she found out. Too bellyful with child to shift and fly, forcing her to flee on horseback, all while fighting the nauseating guilt that had become her companion.

"Why is he on horseback if he knows my whereabouts?" The Morrigan asked as she grabbed a sack and began shoving garments into it. She didn't have but a few items. Running meant leaving everything behind.

"My guess is he suspects but is not in full knowledge. Plus, he had a legion of soldiers with him last I heard," Muirgen strapped the remaining bags to their horses and helped The Morrigan atop her mare. "Hopefully, we will only have to stay hidden for another fortnight. Once you can shift again, all will be easier."

"If Dagda sees me, he will see my belly, and I refuse to allow him to know about his daughter. This child belongs to me." *He cannot find out,* she thought. Not even her closest guard and confidante knew the real reason she denied her husband his child. It wasn't the selfishness she spouted. It was what she had seen, and she needed to keep her child from seeing it.

Kicking their horses into motion, The Morrigan and her closest ally rode, sleeping in caves and hidden by her friends, the wolves, waiting for the birth of the most highly predicted seer to ever walk the earth. Less than a fortnight later, the babe was born. After a hard labor with sweat dripping from her face, The Morrigan looked down at the bundle in her arms and named her daughter Adair, Ford of the Oaks—the oracle who will predict their fall and bear a son who will beget a special one—the first of many.

"How do you know this?" asked The Morrigan.

"All the seraphim are discussing it. From what I gather, annihilation of all half-breeds is inevitable. Or at least those of us who were born of angel and human," Muirgen said as she rode along beside her and Adair.

"So, the goal is for all Nephilim to die? I can't fathom that happening," The Morrigan said.

"You cannot expect the Almighty to continue allowing such behavior. Just last month, I heard that a group of Nephilim and a few aquatic elves tortured a city because they felt like having fun after a hard day in the fields. God will never allow such things to continue for long. He gave a warning at the last Seraphim council meeting. Change or face the consequences. Unfortunately, a few thousand contaminants affect us all."

"Mama, I'm tired," the four-year-old riding with her wiped at her eyes. The sun no longer shone, having fallen so far behind the trees—time for her little Adair to sleep.

"Just a few more minutes, and we will stop where we can wash and sleep." The three of them were on the second day of a four-day ride to northern Scotland.

"When do you think this will happen?" The Morrigan asked.

"On the Almighty's timeline. All we can do is pray and trust he listens and, in the meantime, hope for some sense to come upon the several thousand who continue to create chaos," her friend said.

The Morrigan led the way once the trail narrowed, moving them single file. "Over that ridge, I see a flat spot. Let's bed down for the night." Once they found a place to rest, they dismounted and set up camp. She cleaned the dust and grime off her daughter's hands and face, fed the little goddess, and laid her down on a makeshift bed for the evening. After some time to herself, she would join her little princess.

Everything she had just learned worried her, making her gnaw on her lower lip, only stopping when the slight taste of copper filled her mouth. Goddesses, especially those as formidable as *The Great Queen*, should never have such imperfect habits. She didn't care. If her habits had not been flawed, she wouldn't have any. She stood up from tucking her daughter into her sleeping sack and wandered to the edge of the clearing, close enough to continue watching her little girl.

The last years with Adair had been the most ideal and special of all her years. She adored her daughter, but at night, when she dwelled on all that she had done, she ached for the only one who could relax her unsteady mind. Unfortunately, leaving her husband while carrying his child would mean she would never feel that comfort again. No one betrayed their king, especially his queen.

Chapter One
Jane Doe

Warrick

On the other side of the viewing window lay the unconscious redhead who had unknowingly thrown Warrick's morning into a tailspin. Tubes ran from her mouth and nostrils—countless lines stretched from under her thin blanket to machines that made various humming sounds and occasional shrill beeps that raised the hair on the back of his neck each time they blared. The irritating beeps were the most concerning. Whenever those little fuckers squalled, nurses ran into the room and started pushing medications through the lines as the patient convulsed. *What the hell happened to her?* Warrick thought for the hundredth time since finding her unconscious.

The morning had begun as every other morning. His alarm rang at 5:00 AM. Promptly at 5:10 AM, with his running gear donned, he took off on a five-mile, wake-his-ass-up, jog around the city and seaside of the beautiful Monte Carlo, Monaco. He always made a point of stopping by the construction site to see how things were progressing. The breeze coming off the Mediterranean as the sun rose, casting orange and red shadows over the water, made the morning course his favourite part of the day, even if he had to wake up so damn early. Unfortunately, this morning had been a little different for him and Warr Construction.

Damn, time dragged; it seemed like days since he found her. He looked at his watch and confirmed. Had it been only that morning? *Shit, there goes the beeping.*

Nurses ran from all directions into the room where *Jane Doe* convulsed—again. This time was different; she stopped convulsing on her own, and the line on the monitor slowed to a peak every couple of seconds. One of the scrambling nurses looked up and locked eyes with him, noticing that he was watching. She scoffed and rushed to close the blinds. Removing his view of the woman couldn't be a good sign.

Dammit.

He kept telling himself that he was hanging around to see if she woke so he could get answers. Not that she would be chatty when she finally woke up. Hell, after that last bout of seizing, he wasn't sure she would ever wake up.

His phone buzzed, and his personal assistant's name flashed across the screen. With a roll of his eyes, he answered. "Yes, Anna."

"Sir, your one o'clock appointment is here. I told her you had an emergency and needed to reschedule, but she refuses to leave until she hears it from you."

With another eye roll, Warr ran his free hand through his thick black hair. An act he had been performing since the ambulance picked the woman up and placed her unconscious body on the gurney, while sticking all sorts of objects into her mouth and veins. When they asked if he wanted to ride with her to the hospital, he hadn't thought twice about it. He jumped in. Now he was wondering if that had been a mistake. His hand ran through his hair again.

"I don't want her to have my number. Hand her the phone and stay close by. See her out once I hang up. When she's out of the building, I need you to pick me up some clothes from my apartment. Call me back, and I'll give you a list of what I need. Do not let that woman follow you."

"Yes, Mr. Harding."

He could hear Anna calling Lucia's name.

"Warrick, darling," Lucia said in her thick Italian accent. "How are you? I was told you had an emergency this morning. Had I known, I would have been there for you. Tell me where you are, and I will have my driver bring me to you."

That made Warr's lip curl. Lucia was his father's idea of a possible life match. She grated on his last nerve. "There is no need. Thank you, though."

"Nonsense. I insist."

"Lucia, Anna will put you back on my schedule for next week. This situation will take a few days," Warrick continued without breathing so that she couldn't interrupt him. "I'm needed. Have a great weekend."

He hadn't been lying. The nurse, who had closed the blinds and reopened them seconds ago, was walking toward him. Her face was grim, which made his heart race. He would puzzle out that reaction later.

"Monsieur?" the nurse asked in French.

"Harding. Warrick Harding. Is she going to be okay?" Warr returned his question in English, knowing she would adjust. Rarely did he run into anyone in Monaco who didn't speak some English. He also spoke French and Italian, but he would always be a stubborn Brit.

"She is stable for now. Are you her husband?" the nurse asked. Her French accent was so heavy that he almost felt bad for changing things up on her.

"Oh, no. I found her unconscious at my construction site this morning. She was lying outside the doorway of the onsite office."

"Do you have any information regarding her? Did she have a handbag or phone on her?"

"Not that I saw. I'm here to see if she will be okay and to find out why she was on my property. The police came in and spoke with me right after we arrived. You should ask them if they found anything." Warr looked from the nurse through the observation window to the woman lying on the bed, still comatose. "May I see her?"

The reason he wanted to was beyond him. Curiosity, he supposed.

"Normally, we only allow close family. In this case, she does need someone. Often, people in this state can hear things happening around them, which helps them fight their way to the surface." The nurse beckoned him to follow her into the sterile room.

When he stepped through the doorway, the intense, overpowering smell of antiseptic cleaners and alcohol swabs hit him. The constant humming was more pronounced, and he heard the low hum of a blood pressure cuff tightening around *her* arm. The monitor to her right read her blood pressure was 75/50.

"Isn't that low?" Warrick pointed at the machine.

"It is. So is her oxygen level."

He looked at the measurement; it held steady at 87. "Her head was bleeding so badly when I found her. Will she be normal after this?"

"She has swelling and some bleeding. She may have to go into surgery if they don't rectify themselves. Since we don't have any information on her, we are trying to wait and give her all the time we can before we intervene." The nurse checked the woman's IV line and typed something into the computer.

"I see," was all he said right as his phone rang. "Excuse me," he walked to the other side of the room, not wanting to leave, just in case they decided not to let him back in.

"Did you lose the pushing Italian wannabe bride?"

"Well, hello to you, too. Yes. She wasn't very nice when I refused to give her your personal cell number. If I may speak freely, sir?"

"Since when do you ask?"

"After hearing your panicked call this morning, I decided to be nice for the day." He could hear the amusement Anna was trying to smother. She was an excellent personal assistant. They had taken the world by storm the day he bought the property in Monte Carlo. Anna may be his PA, but she had the potential to be so much more. She lacked one semester of school. Once she was done, he would give her the coveted VP of Operations position. "If you don't tell Lucia to get lost, she will end up as Mrs. Harding. That woman is clever and bloody conniving."

"And my dad's new business partner's daughter. Don't worry. Once you are out of school, my plan is to go back to the States. You can marry her?" Warrick laughed.

"Funny. I prefer my women with less venom. I just got to your apartment. What do you need?"

"I'm still in my running gear. Can you bring me a pair of chinos, a button-down, a leather belt, and loafers? Oh, and my briefcase from the entry table."

"Is that all?" Anna asked.

"A sandwich and water."

"Do you have any information yet?"

"They believe she's slowly stabilizing, but her blood pressure and oxygen level are super low." Warrick looked at the machine as he spoke. Her BP held steady, but her oxygen was up to 89.

"I meant, have they found out who she is yet?"

"Not to my knowledge. The police took my number, but I haven't heard from them."

"Where in the hospital should I bring your things?"

"In the med unit, room 136," he said.

"You're in her room? Why?" Anna asked. He could hear her rummaging through his closet. "Also, why do you still have Allison's clothes?"

"I'm in her room because she has no one else here. The nurse thought it would be good if someone spoke to her. Something about the unconscious can still hear. And, for your nosy information, Allison told me to throw them out because she never wanted to set foot in my apartment again. I haven't had time to deal with them."

"I understand. Three months is not long enough to throw unwanted clothing out," Anna deadpanned.

"Just hurry with my clothes," Warrick said, watching the nurse busy herself with the mystery woman. "Don't forget my food."

Chapter Two

Overwhelming Need

WARRICK

The clock struck six in the evening, and the redhead had not woken, even though her oxygen had been normal for over two hours and her blood pressure had risen several points. The doctor said the bleeding in her head had stopped, and it looked like she was on the right track, yet she was still comatose.

Three raps on the door had Warrick releasing the fair-skinned woman's hand, which he had been holding for the last half hour. Unable to explain the pull he had toward the unconscious patient, he thought it best that whoever was at the door did not see him holding her or hear all the nonsensical words he had been reciting just moments prior.

"Come in," Warr said, projecting his voice so the new-comer could hear him over the machines' chatter. "Hello, Sergeant—have you found out anything?"

"Mr. Harding," the officer shook his head and looked from him to the woman lying unconscious. Warr knew the police-man was gauging the distance between him and the patient. The officer was British, like him; he could tell by his accent. "We haven't. I have a few questions for you, though. May I have a seat?" the sergeant asked and gestured to the chair stationed at the foot of the bed.

"Of course," Warrick rounded the hospital bed and shook the officer's hand. "Please."

"You said before you weren't acquainted with" the sergeant looked from Warr's face to the woman in question.

"That's correct."

"I'm sorry, but it just seems odd that you're still here, waiting by the bedside of a stranger. Don't get me wrong; that's very gallant of you, but it's unusual behavior. Are you sure you don't know her?"

"The nurse told me that if she had someone speaking to her, she might wake faster. So, since no one has shown for her, I decided that I would do the talking."

The officer nodded his head as if in agreement, but Warr could see the skepticism on his face.

"Tell me the story from this morning one more time. I want to make sure I wrote everything down," the sergeant smiled warmly and took out a recorder and notepad from a backpack Warrick hadn't noticed he was carrying.

"Sure," Warrick cleared his throat. He was becoming uneasy under the police officer's scrutiny. Taking the chair next to the man, Warr cleared his throat and began his tale. "Do you want me to start when I woke up or when I found her?"

"When you woke, please." The sergeant pressed the button on the recorder. Warrick looked at the device and tried to shake the uneasy feeling in his gut.

"I wake at five every morning, except Sundays, to run. I always run by the water and my construction site, no matter the rest of my route for the day; those two places do not change. This morning, when I started by the work site, I saw what looked like legs around the corner of the office trailer. No one should be on site that early. So, I ran to the front of the trailer to see who it was. When I rounded the corner, I was shocked at what I found. Before I went up to the woman, I called the police. Siri gave me the number when I asked." That had been a question from the sergeant that morning. *How did he know the police department's phone number?* So, he added that tidbit before the officer asked again. "While on the phone with the police, I confirmed they called for an ambulance or a SAMU. I was asked if I wanted to ride with her, so I did. The police followed us and questioned me at the hospital. She kept convulsing, so I stayed. When the nurse told me that speaking to her may help her to wake, I decided to do just that," Warrick said. He repeated his tale the same as before. The exact way everything had happened.

"Tell me how she looked when you found her," the policeman said.

"Her head was lying beside the concrete steps with her hair covering her face, and her feet and legs were straight. I could see blood on the bottom step and around her head, and it looked black, caked in her auburn hair."

"Did you touch her?"

"Only when the phone officer asked me if she was breathing. I moved her hair from her face and checked her pulse. She was breathing—barely, and her pulse was very faint. It took me several seconds to find it."

"Anything else you can think to add to your statement?" the sergeant asked.

"No. That's all I can think of right now. I'm worried about her. She was found on my property, and to my knowledge, no one has looked for her," Warrick admitted to the officer.

"If we discover anything, we'll contact you." The officer turned the recorder off and stood. "I will be by tomorrow. I'm sure you will be home or at work, so I'll call you with updates on her health if you want me to."

"That'd be great," Warrick said. He walked the police officer to the hospital room door as if he were walking out of his apartment.

The clock struck seven—time for the shift change. Thank goodness the nurse who clocked in was the same one on duty when *Jane* arrived in the trauma unit. She was the one who calmed him just over twelve hours ago, thinking he was family. Apparently, after finding a half-dead woman on your property, you look somewhat disheveled. He never told her he wasn't family. *I'll speak to her before I leave for my apartment,* he thought.

Fortunately, Anna had taken care of her job and his while he waited for the woman to wake. Unfortunately, more than a day of that juggling would be asking too much of his assistant.

Did her hand just move? It was not the only time he believed he saw the comatose redhead twitch—plus he thought he had heard her moan earlier. Staring at the hand he thought had moved proved a waste of time. After a few minutes, he returned to reflecting on her flawless skin. Not a mark or a wrinkle that he could see. She didn't seem to have any makeup on either. *How does she not have a freckle?*

"Mr. Harding? The night nurse startled him from his watchful musing. "I'm sorry. I didn't mean to surprise you."

"No problem," Warr rubbed his hands over his face, then rolled his head from side to side to rouse himself from his thoughts.

"Will you be staying the night? Can I bring in a cot and blankets for you?" the nurse asked.

"Oh, no. I'm good. I'll give you my number when I leave in case something changes."

"I'm sorry. I read over the chart a few minutes ago. It seems I had it wrong this morning. I thought you were *with* her," the nurse nodded toward the unconscious woman as if more than one woman were lying unconscious in the room.

"No worries. Please call me Warrick. No need to be formal. I found her on my construction property this morning. I just wanted to be around when she woke so I could find out what happened on my property. Even though I have no clue why she would've been at a closed construction site, I feel somewhat responsible for her."

"I see. Well, I can call you if she wakes tonight. Just don't get your hopes up. She seems content in her current state."

"Most likely, I was seeing things earlier, but I could swear I saw her right hand twitch. That's why I was watching her so closely when you came in," he told the nurse as he flung his duffel bag across his shoulder.

"I will keep a close eye on her this evening. As of now, I only have two patients," the nurse said.

"Here's my cell number. No matter the time, if there are any changes, please call me." Warr handed the nurse his business card and glanced at the sleeping beauty one last time before leaving the hospital.

Chapter Three
Accelerated Healing

Warrick

Warrick had forgone calling his driver and walked to his apartment. The June night air was perfect for a stroll to clear his head. Plus, he wanted to stretch his legs since he hadn't finished his run and had been sitting in an uncomfortable chair by the hospital bed all day. Memories of *Jane Doe's* body with blood all around her head had haunted him since he found her. After the nurse cleaned her up, he could see the beautiful woman behind the dirt and her lifeblood. Whatever took place, she had hit her head hard. *Why was she at my construction site?* The question of the day continued on a loop with the memory of her still body heaped by the office.

Arriving home, Warrick went straight to his kitchen and poured himself a glass of Merlot, rummaged through his refrigerator for some cheese, and headed to his bedroom. He needed a shower to wash off the sterile hospital smell, then some much-needed time to read through his emails.

Unfortunately, as he removed his chinos, a text from Anna caught him off guard.

Anna: Gabriel is requesting an early-morning appointment with you. Something about entering the yacht show.

Warrick: An excuse to find out why I blew his daughter off today. Put him on at ten. I won't be in the office until then.

Anna: Going to the hospital?

Warrick: Yes

14

Anna: You sure that's a good idea?

Warrick: Night, Anna.

Anna: Fine

Tossing his phone onto his bed, Warrick finally removed his pants and entered the shower. The hot water melted the disturbing day away.

The following morning, Warrick got up at 4:30 instead of his usual 5:00 so he could get his run started early and have time at the hospital. His sleep was restless, invaded by dreams of *Jane Doe* alive and well, then of her falling from the sky. The next scene woke him in a sweat, his heart racing. A visual of her head hitting the concrete steps, and the sound of her skull as it made contact, had him sitting bolt upright in bed. When his alarm finally went off, he was more relieved than rested. No more fighting for every second of sleep he could squeeze without nightmares.

After completing his five-mile run, he showered and donned a navy Cesare Attolini suit with a navy and red tie. He looked the part of the billionaire businessman that he was—now to prove it to his father's partner—after he visited the redheaded enigma, who continued to lie comatose in a hospital bed. The attraction to her was palpable. Over and over, he tried convincing himself it was because she was injured on his property.

He texted his driver, grabbed his laptop from the entry table, and checked his watch, making sure he had plenty of time to visit the hospital staff and meet with the doctor. Maybe there had been news, and they had just failed to contact him. He wasn't her kin, so it was plausible. After his restless night and his nagging dreams, he was more determined than ever to discover what happened to the woman he couldn't stop thinking about.

Warrick squinted at the odd way the lift to *Jane Doe's* floor made him feel. As soon as he pressed the floor number, his heart raced faster, and his hands grew clammy. *What the bloody hell is wrong with me?*

Three nurses greeted him, each making it rather obvious they liked what they saw. Luckily, the nurse he had spoken to the evening before was stepping out of *Jane's* room, giving him a reason to excuse himself from the flirts behind the nurse's desk. He pardoned himself and made his way to the one who had promised to watch *Jane* closely.

"How is she this morning?" Warrick asked. Even he could hear the anxiousness in his voice.

"Not much change. Her blood pressure is the same, but her oxygen is in the nineties without assistance, and the brain bleed is still under control. I'm going to get some bandages to change the ones on her head and arm. You can visit with her while I grab everything." The nurse turned to leave, then stopped and spoke over her shoulder. "It may not seem like it now, but speaking to her will help her find her way back."

Since he had her attention again, he asked. "Okay. I have a couple of hours, then I need to be at work. Will the doctor be in before I leave?"

"Most likely. It's rare the doctors round after ten," the nurse said.

"Thank you," Warr said as he turned, ignored the other nurses, and made his way to the hospital room. With every step, the need to make sure the woman was okay grew.

Anticipation was a bitch. He wondered what he was about to walk into. A comatose woman with extensive black and purple bruising and swollen red lacerations was his best guess. He wasn't sure how her appearance twenty-four hours after being found half dead would affect his thoughts the rest of the day and night. One thing was for sure—he dreaded what was in that room.

Slowly, he opened the door leading to the woman who had caused his sleepless night. From the doorway, he saw a small reddish stain on the gauze around *her* head, CPAPs in her nostrils, and various tubes continuing from her body to an array of machines. Her ivory skin wasn't as bruised as he expected. The parts of her skin that he could see, anyway. Overall, she looked better than she had yesterday. At least she looked more peaceful, no convulsing—yet.

"Mr. Harding," the nurse had returned with an armful of antiseptic and bandages.

"Yes?" Warr answered, not taking his eyes off *Jane Doe*.

"I realize you just arrived, but might I ask you to step into the hall while I change her gown and bandages?" The nurse asked, looking uncomfortable.

"And be visually molested by the nursing staff? I prefer not. I will turn my back," Warrick answered the nurse as if she had actually meant to give him the choice.

The nurse cleared her throat. "As you wish."

Warrick turned his back on the bed, where the patient continued her deep *sleep*, and answered endless emails on his phone. He hadn't responded to many of his nonstop messages when he heard a very slight moan. Jerking his head around, the nurse had *Jane* rolled to her right side, facing the doorway. Now, he could see much more creamy-smooth skin, with several unfortunate purple, green, and yellow contusions.

"Did she just moan?" Warrick had not only turned toward the bed—he was standing beside it. *When did I move?*

"Mr. Harding, please avert your eyes, sir," the nurse looked alarmed at his ogling.

"Did she moan?" Warrick repeated—something he was not used to doing.

"Yes, sir. That's normal with coma patients. Now, please give the fair lady some privacy."

Warrick reluctantly turned his back on the bed. However, he didn't leave the woman's side; his ears attuned to every sound behind him. He needed answers. Or so he told himself; that was why he was being overprotective of a person he had never met.

"Okay, sir. You may turn around."

"How are her injuries?" Warrick asked.

"Odd, sir."

Warrick quirked a brow. "How so?"

"Her head lacerations look like they've been healing for days instead of hours. Her bruising is yellowing, as it should be in a week, not just a day. She's healing remarkably fast."

Before he could respond, the baritone French accent of *Jane's* doctor rang out in the sterile room. "How's our *Jane* this morning?"

"I was just telling Mr. Harding that she is healing exceptionally fast. Her contusions are already yellowing, and her head laceration looks to be a week out from injury. Quite remarkable, I must say, doctor."

The doctor placed his stethoscope in his ears and listened to the woman's heart, lungs, and vessels. With wide eyes, he continued his assessment. "No convulsions since yesterday?"

"No, doctor. She did moan when I rolled her to her right side to change her dressings," the nurse said.

He pulled back the sheet and looked over her body. Since no one made him turn, Warrick looked over her as well. *Wasn't that bruise darker just ten minutes ago?* As the thought went through his head, the nurse gasped.

"It looks like she's healed since I changed her."

"How long ago was that?" the doctor asked as he made notes on the electronic pad.

"I was finishing up when you walked in. So," the nurse said as she squinted in confusion, "just now."

"I'm putting in for another cranial MRI. I'll come back for afternoon rounds. Please contact me if there are any negative changes between now and then," the doctor lifted his eyes to Warrick. "Mr.?"

"Harding. Warrick Harding," he filled in the blank for the physician.

"That's right. You're the man who found her," the doctor looked him up and down. Warr couldn't help but wonder what the good doc thought about a young suit finding an unconscious woman on his commercial property.

"I am. I stopped by on my way to work this morning, hoping to speak with you. Can you tell me anything more?"

"Just what you've heard here. The test I'm ordering will tell us more about her head injury. Has there been any discussion on what will happen once she wakes?" The doctor asked.

Warr cocked a brow. *Is he speaking to me?* "Are you asking me?" He found and saved her, and without knowing who she was or why she was on his property—why would he know?

"She'll need extensive therapy for the head injury. Until she wakes, we won't know how much, but she *will* need to be taken care of."

"Hopefully, she'll have family close who can help her," Warr answered. He had no idea what else to say.

"Has there been anyone looking for her?" The physician asked the nurse.

"No, sir. Not to my knowledge," the nurse responded while she busied herself changing out the bag of fluids.

The doctor typed on his pad. "Let's hope she can help us when she wakes, but Mr. Harding—after a person has been comatose for days from a head injury, they are often disoriented, sleep a lot, and have severe migraines. We can keep her for a few days, but only that."

He had no idea why the good doctor needed him to have that information—until another nurse came in to discuss the financials, since no one knew if she was a citizen. *Now it makes sense.* He also knew that he would allow no one else to take her unless they had proof of knowing her.

Chapter Four
Dodging and Awake

Warrick

Warrick arrived at his office with ten minutes to prepare for his father's persistent partner. Daddies often got upset if a man didn't see their precious darling daughters in the same light they did. This would be the third time something similar had happened because of his father's interference. He readied himself to remind the billionaire entrepreneur that it had been his father who had wanted him to take Lucia out, not him.

"Good morning, Anna. Has my father tried to reach me this morning?" Warr stopped to peruse the mail sitting on the corner of her desk.

"Unfortunately, I haven't had the pleasure of speaking with him this morning," sarcasm dripped from Anna as she continued typing, not looking at him. "Are you about to dump Lucia's father, effectively ditching her?"

"You really can't stand her, can you?" Warrick tried to hide his smirk.

"She's beyond annoying and pretends, or so I hope, to be an idiot. Indeed, no one is that bloody stupid. Plus, she thinks I'm here to serve her. So, no—I'm not fond of her." She continued without looking up from her computer. "Your three o'clock canceled. Do you want me to fill it?"

"No. I'll leave early and go back to the hospital. The woman is healing incredibly fast, so they have ordered another MRI. If the hospital or the police call, please patch them through, no matter who I'm with. Oh, and give me five minutes after Gabriel shows up before you let him through."

"That's interesting," Anna smirked, finally looking at him.

His eyes jumped from the papers in his hands to his nosy assistant's questioning eyes. "The hospital wants me to take care of the bill. I told them we would wait and see what the patient says when she wakes." He returned the mail to its original location and walked toward his office. "Remember, make him wait."

Anna buzzed his desk phone ten minutes later, letting him know Gabriel was there. He looked at his Rolex, marking the time. He had five minutes left to turn his immaculate dark mahogany desk into a cyclone of architectural drawings, work orders, schedules, and subcontractor applications.

Right on time, Gabriel strode through the door, escorted by Anna, while Warrick poured over the piles of documents as if time was of the essence and he had none to spare.

"Warrick, how are you?" Gabriel took two more steps into his office and made a show of looking around. He could guess the tycoon's thoughts.

What billionaire did such menial tasks? Blah blah blah.

"Have a seat, Gabe. Would you like tea or coffee?" He was sure his assistant had already asked, but he asked again anyway.

"No. When I looked over my calendar yesterday, I saw that I would be in the area and thought I would stop by and find out if you were entering the yacht show this time," Gabriel said, taking the leather chair across from the piles of work Warrick had meticulously placed moments before.

"Unfortunately, not. I don't plan to charter any of my boats next year. Once I return to California, the Amphitrite's new home will be Marina Del Rey. I will consider chartering the others once I leave."

"Interesting," Gabriel said. Then the silence in Warr's office became stifling.

"Did you need anything else, Gabe? As you can see, today is a busy one," Warr arched a brow, knowing he was poking the bear.

"Now that you mentioned it, there's a concern that I wanted to ru—,"

Before Gabriel's issue left his lips, Anna buzzed his phone. She never interrupted him, no matter who sat across his desk.

"Excuse me, Gabe. Anna knows not to ring unless it's an emergency."

Warr grabbed the phone and stiffened at his assistant's words—*Jane Doe is awake.*

Warrick jumped to his feet and buttoned his suit jacket while booting his father's partner out of his office.

"I'm so very sorry to have to do this, Gabe, but there is an emergency. Can I come by your office sometime this week to finish our conversation?" Without giving the man time to acknowledge his inquiry, Warrick continued, "Thank you for understanding." He gestured toward his office door, grabbed his briefcase and cell phone, and followed his guest out.

"Anna, call my driver," Warr nodded another goodbye. "Tell him I'll meet him on the first floor. No need for him to drive all the way up."

"Want me to come along?" Anna asked.

"No need. Once I'm done, I'll head home and finish work there. Starting in two hours, forward all calls to my cell. Hopefully, that will give me time to get my answers and see what I need to do about the hospital bill."

It took Warrick only twenty minutes to be standing by the beauty in the hospital bed. *Damn, she's divine.* To his left, next to *Jane's* head, stood the nurse, manually taking her blood pressure. The only thing running from her body was the IV in her forearm, allowing him to see the woman who, ironically, was awake from the coma but was now fast asleep.

"How long has she been out since waking from the coma?" Warr asked the nurse.

"She's just sleeping now. After waking to all this," the nurse gestured around the room, "she was disoriented and somewhat combative. We pushed meds to help calm her. That, plus her body is worn down from the coma, causing exhaustion. She will be in and out for a while."

Warrick didn't know what he was thinking. Of course, she would be exhausted and confused. In his mind, he thought he would walk in and introduce himself right before asking all the burning questions he's had since he found her battered body on his property. *Dumbass.*

"Have her MRI results come back?"

"When the tech placed her in the chamber for the scan, she woke from the coma. They could not do the MRI. Her doctor wants to wait until she understands what is going on before we force her into the machine. That equipment is narrow and extremely loud." The nurse gathered her things. "See this button? If she wakes while you are here, push it. We need to know."

Alone with the woman, Warrick felt a little apprehensive. Talking to her and holding her hand while she was unconscious was one thing, but while she was only asleep, it felt vastly different. He hesitated for only a second, then inched closer to her. It seemed that being uneasy about the situation would not keep him away from her. The draw to her increased every time he was near her.

She looked younger than he had thought. Her long eyelashes fanned out over her cheeks, and her brows were perfectly sculpted, even after days in the hospital. Between her high cheekbones and regal straight nose, he wondered if she came from royalty. One thought ran into another, and he almost convinced himself she was a princess who had been vacationing in Monaco and found herself in the wrong place at the wrong time. Grinning at his wayward musings, he was taken aback when her eyes fluttered, and her breathing went from slow and rhythmic to quick and irregular. His hand reached for the nurse's button just as her haunting emerald eyes popped open and looked directly into his—then shut.

Chapter Five

Where am I?

Jane Doe

Chirping sounds assailed *Jane's* mind. She felt a presence near her but could not pull herself from the darkness. *Dizziness should not happen when you are in an abyss.* Her head ached, and try as she might, she could not move. *Slowly,* she thought. *I need to move slowly.* With impressive concentration, she endeavored to move her toes—nothing.

Maybe my hands will work. Still nothing, but she could feel something latched onto her wrist, tight. Panic set in—*What in Hades' name is happening to me?*

With impressive strain, she forced her eyes to obey and open. As soon as her efforts manifested results, they immediately closed back. *Dammit!* She pushed herself harder.

Bright white light pained her eyes and shot what felt like daggers through her head as she tried to focus on the man standing over her. After several rapid blinks, *Jane* froze and tried to figure out where she was. It didn't help that her chest felt like something was sitting on it.

She pulled at her right hand to rub her eyes and was rudely confronted with the realization that she was strapped down to a—*bed? That's what was so tight around my wrist.* She felt the flutter in her chest speed up, and fear gripped her by the throat. Terror set in, so she screamed as loud as she could. With a throat full of what felt like sand, it wasn't deafening by any means. *Damn, that hurt.*

The man supporting sea-blue eyes reached beside her and pressed something as he cooed nonsensical words.

"You are okay. You're in the hospital," the man repeated until two women came in and put something in the line that led to her forearm.

What language is he speaking? "Voíthisé me!" That was the last thought before her eyes grew so heavy there was no fighting them back open.

Chapter Six

Back to Sleep

"Why did you knock her out again?" Warrick asked the nurses, who were busying themselves, making sure the restraints were still in place.

"She was panicking. Plus, you heard her—she was speaking gibberish. When a patient comes out of a coma, they are so disoriented that we have to allow them to wake slowly. She went from zero to sixty, so we made her sleep, and we will monitor her reactions when she wakes again," the nurse who had been watching over *Jane* said. "I promise, this is normal. She's," she pointed to the mysterious woman, "just moving a little faster than most."

"I think she was speaking some Greek dialect. None that I understand, but it sounded Greek*ish*." Warr shook his head more to himself than to the nurses. "I'll be here as long as it takes her to wake. I brought a book with me. Maybe reading to her will make her want to wake up. It's something I read online," Warr whispered.

"That sounds perfect, but you don't have to whisper. While reading, speak to her normally," the nurses then turned and left the room.

Warrick watched them leave, and as soon as he was alone with her, he lowered his mouth to her ear. "Wake again, gorgeous. I have no idea what language you were speaking, but if you can stay calm the next time you wake, I will wait before I call them." Warrick spoke in English, hoping she would understand his words.

He opened the romance novel Anna gave him when he asked what he should read to the unconscious woman, since he had already told her his life story and that of everyone he knew.

"I'm going to read you a story recommended by my personal assistant, Anna," Warr cleared his throat and began. "The Lost Heiress by Roseanna White." Warrick moved his chair as close to the bed as he could and propped his elbow up as he read aloud. He could feel the warmth of her body on his left arm and noticed that the anxiety he had felt from the fear in her eyes when she woke vanished with her nearness. Just as he announced chapter four, her eyes began fluttering again. It took him only a second to be on his feet, whispering in her ear to stay calm and everything would be okay.

Chapter Seven

Name?

Jane Doe

Fuck me, my head feels like a herd of centaurs has run me over. Why in Hades' name can I not open my eyes?

Jane's head felt heavy, and it pained her something fierce. All she could remember was a feast, dancing, and a bright light with people speaking in what sounded like modern French and perhaps *English?* Bright lights shocked her senses when she finally pried her heavy lids open. Blinking rapidly, trying to squelch the pain from the sudden, sharp light, she looked to her left where a beautiful man stood with concern plastered across his face. *Do I know him? He looks vaguely familiar.* Again, she pulled at her hand to find it fastened to the rails of the unusual-looking bed. *This I remember.* She narrows her eyes at the man. *What am I wearing?*

"Hello. Please don't scream," the gorgeous creature standing over her murmured. She understood his words, but they sounded off somehow.

"που βρίσκομαι; Όχι. Δεν είναι σωστό." *Jane* cleared her throat, then mimicked his language. "Where am I?" *That's it—modern English,* she thought.

"You're in the hospital. You've been here a few days—in a coma," Warrick answered. "Do you remember what happened to you?"

"No. Where is this *hospital* located?" *Jane* asked in a whispered voice. It felt like she had swallowed rocks. "Can you turn those off?" She looked at the harsh white lights above her.

"Sure. I need to call the nurse so she can check you. What's your name?" Warr asked just above a whisper.

"My name is—," She stopped and thought. *What in Tartarus is my name?* "I—I do not know."

Well, the admission did not shock her; however, it stunned the hell out of the human male. His mouth gaped at her words. "I really need to alert the nurses. If you don't know your name, there are more issues here than I thought." He leaned across her body and pressed a small, round object.

Damn, he smells amazing. What's wrong with my head? What in Hades' name is going on! *Jane's* thoughts assailed her mind as she watched the beautiful being stretch across her body, unable to move her arms.

"Try not to pull on those," the man pointed to her restraints. "I'm sure that doesn't hurt, but you've been through a lot and need to conserve your energy."

She lifted her brow. "Εντάξει," *Jane* replied just before the onslaught of what he called nurses descended upon her.

The furrow of the handsome male's brow at her agreement made her realize she had reverted to what felt more like her native tongue. She made a mental note to speak only English to him. *How is it I can tell he speaks English, but I have no idea what my fucking name is?*

One nurse rubbed something over her forehead, another operated a machine that connected to the device attached to her arm, and the third wrapped something around her arm that began to squeeze. It didn't hurt, but it didn't feel good either.

She noticed they spoke a different tongue. Listening closely to the women, she realized it had to be what humans called French. *Humans.*

Why did I call them that? She thought as one lady spouted numbers to the one who had touched the weird device to her forehead. *If they are human, what am I?*

She focused on using a language they could all understand; she tried for the one the man used with her. "Untie my wrists. I do not need restraint." To her surprise, her words came out assertive, even demanding.

All the women stopped their manic flitting and turned to look at her. The one standing at a machine, pushing little square things, responded in a thick French accent. "We will tell your doctor that you are now awake without panicking. When he gives us the order to remove them, we will. Unfortunately, until then, we have no choice but to leave them on."

"When will that be?" *Jane Doe* glared at the woman who had delivered the asinine reasoning. She was not a threat to herself or to them. For Zeus' sake, her head hurt too badly to do anything but lie there.

"He is making rounds now. It should be within the hour," the same—*nurse?*—answered her. *Wasn't that what the handsome man called these women,* she thought.

"Rounds?" *Jane* asked for an explanation.

"He's checking on each of his patients," the *nurse,* removing the band that strangled her arm, responded. None of them looked at her except to check her forehead and arm with mechanisms she knew nothing of—all so clinical. *What happened to me?*

Jane nodded in understanding, then turned to see the man standing over her in a protective stance, with his arms crossed over his chest and legs shoulder-width apart as if ready to pounce, watching the women bustle over her. His eyes flicked up to hers and softened as if reassuring her all would be fine. To her surprise, the look made her relax. *Who is he to me? Fuck, who am I?* Nothing around her was recognizable. She had no clue what was happening, only that she did not want them to make her sleep again—vaguely remembering waking once before. She needed to get out of the bright, sterile room and find out what was going on and why, in Zeus' name, she did not know who she was.

"She doesn't remember her name," Warrick informed the nurses.

"That is not uncommon right after a person wakes from a coma. Her memories will return, but I will let her doctor know," the same nurse replied.

Finally, the three women stopped bothering her and left the room, leaving the masculine individual, now propped against the wall, with instructions to call them if she had any *issues*. Slowly, the handsome specimen approached her. He advanced as if she were a scared animal, his hands held palm out, in a reassuring manner. Maybe he thought she would scream in fear or, worse, lash out in incensed rage. Neither would get her anywhere, so she tried to assure the man with somewhat of a smile that she would not do anything other than lie there like the princess she was. *Princess? Whoever I am, I think highly of myself.*

With that thought, the man stopped and looked weary. "Are you okay?" his deep voice rang out.

"Good as I can be shackled to a bed by people I do not know. Why?" *If I am to be shackled to a bed, at least he could be nak—Okay, so I'm a horny woman too. Good to know.*

"You just went from barely a fake smile to one that spread across your face. I'm curious," the man grinned.

Damn, he was gorgeous.

"Just some amusing thoughts I had. Who are you?" She asked as he started a slow stride toward her again.

"It's a long story. Maybe we should wait on proper introductions once the doctor verifies that you may hear all manner of news—good and not so good," the infuriating man answered.

"Well, can you at least give me your name?" She looked into his eyes, now mere feet from the bed, daring him to deny her that. "After all, you are in a room where I am strapped to a bed in a flimsy cover-up. Surely, that warrants the disclosure of your name."

With a twitch of his lip, the attractive stranger answered, "My name is Warrick Harding. You were found on my property and brought here."

"Why did I have to be brought to a place that tied me down? Why are *you* here?" she asked.

"To answer your second question. I wanted to make sure you are okay. For your first question—the doctor should see you before I answer it," Warrick said as he took the seat next to her. "I won't allow them to hurt you, and I understand that you have no reason to believe me, but I tell the truth."

"Are you the one who has been telling me stories?"

"You remember that." Warrick looked at her with curiosity in his blue eyes—the *eyes of a god.*

"Just now. Your voice triggered the memory. What I believe is a memory anyway." Just as she stopped speaking, a loud knock at the window startled them both. Warrick stood and walked over to see what had happened, leaving her to sit up straight in panic with her wrists locked by her sides.

"Is that a crow?" Warrick asked aloud.

"Not sure what a crow is, but why did it hit the glass?"

"No clue. It's lying dead on the outside windowsill. Crows are very rare here. They are typically intelligent, solid-black birds. Odd, it hit the window so hard." He turned, walked back, and retook the seat next to her bed. "While you were sleeping, they said you may be able to hear people talk, and speaking to you could help pull you out of the deep sleep. So, I read a book to you in hopes it would help."

"To claim not to know me, you have gone out of your way to help. I may not remember who I am, but I know that no one does good things for those they have no ties to, without reason. What is your reason, Warrick?" *Jane's* eyes narrowed on the striking man. *He has a reason to help me and is not altruistic. Is he the reason my head rings in pain, and I am currently tied to this poor excuse for a bed?* She gave the restraints a slight tug.

Instead of pushing him, she waited. She watched as the man stood, ran his hand through his black hair, then walked back to the window, where he stared so long she was sure he would never answer her question. Clearly, he didn't want to explain himself, or if he did, he didn't quite know how.

"Every morning, I go for a run. Most of the time, I go to my construction site to see the progress. It allows me to look at my creation without answering questions or addressing problems. The other morning on my run, I found you on my property. You were unconscious. At first, I thought you were dead," Warrick turned and looked at her, and she felt herself flinch at his words.

Gooseflesh pebbled her arms. She looked down at them, not remembering such an odd feeling. *He thought I was dead. What happened to me?*

"When I got close to you, I felt for a pulse. I called for help and rode in the ambulance here, where you have been in a deep sleep since."

"What happened to my head?" She was determined to find out, and the anxious man seemed her best bet for answers.

"There was a lot of blood, so I know you hit your head. How? No one knows. Why were you on my site? That's what I hope you can tell me," he ran his hand back through his hair.

"What have they done to me, other than tie me down?" she gestured toward the door.

Chapter Eight

Rapid Recovery

Refusing to tell the redhead the exact state he found her in, afraid it might trigger another freakout, Warrick answered with fragments of the truth. "They treated the injury to your head and gave you fluids through the IV," he pointed to the IV and watched as she looked down at it.

"What is a coma?" she asked.

Well, so much for skirting around things. Warrick rubbed his hand down his face while thinking of a way to explain a coma while downplaying her injuries. "It's where you—,"

A slight tap-tap at the door saved him from explanation when her doctor stepped in. "Ah, the mysterious Jane Doe is finally awake." The Frenchman walked to her bed with a clipboard in one hand and waved the other as he spoke.

"Are you the doctor making rounds? The one who can tell the nurses to remove these Zeus-forsaken manacles?" *Jane's* stern countenance and odd verbiage had Warrick's head cocking to the side.

"Yes, that would be me. Let me look at you and confirm you are well enough to have them removed."

The redhead's brows shot to her hairline. "Well, binding a woman without permission seems a little rude."

Unperturbed by his patient's words, the doctor removed the stethoscope from around his neck and listened to her heart and lungs. Warrick watched as her eyes enlarged and then squinted at the doctor's ministrations. It was evident that she was not accustomed to this or had forgotten what it was like to have a doctor check on you.

"Let me look at the bruising," He tugged at her gown.

"You will not," *Jane* looked wide-eyed and scandalized by the suggestion. "How dare you touch me?"

"I'm your doctor. I must make sure you are healing properly."

"First, I want answers. What happened to me? Why am I here, and why am I tied to this makeshift bed?"

The doctor looked at him for advice. He arched a brow and shrugged. How was he supposed to know what to do? She didn't know him either.

The doctor looked back at the fiery redhead and cleared his throat. "You were found at a construction site by Mr. Harding. It looked as if you had taken quite the fall. You hit your head hard against concrete steps and suffered many lacerations, which caused a brain bleed. Had Mr. Harding not found you when he did, you could have died. Because of the head injury and the coma, you are experiencing some memory loss. We call that loss post-traumatic amnesia. Your brain should rectify itself within a fortnight, if not sooner." As he spoke, he loosened and removed both bindings from her wrists.

"I see," she said as she rubbed her wrists. "When may I leave this hospital?"

"I would like to get a brain scan, but since you are healing at an unprecedented rate, I suppose you can come back for that. Being in a regular bed will help bring some normalcy and hopefully your memory. The nurses told me everything, and it isn't uncommon to lose memory when you first wake from a brain injury. I want to keep you here overnight, and if you continue to do better, I will see about you leaving midday tomorrow. Sound good?" The doctor looked between Jane and Warrick for his answer.

Why the bloody hell did he look at me? "May I speak with you in the hall, doctor?" Warrick asked as he rounded the bed.

"Sure. I will be back in the morning to see your progress. Take care and get plenty of rest this evening," the doctor said as he followed Warr to the hallway.

"Where will you send her if she leaves the hospital tomorrow? She can't remember anything." Warrick asked the doctor as soon as they entered the hall.

"If she doesn't remember anything by morning, she will be sent to a home. Most likely she will have her memories back soon."

"Likely? What if she doesn't?" Warrick asked.

"She'll need to work to pay for her room and board; otherwise, there's not much we can do," the physician shrugs as if it's none of his concern.

Warrick ran his hand through his already mussed-up mane. Nervous habits and all. "She can stay with me or my PA until she can remember who she is. Hopefully, that will be sooner rather than later. What should I do to facilitate that?"

"Since you signed her paperwork, it shouldn't be an issue. She can be discharged under your care. Can you sign this, stating what I discussed with her? I will let the nurses know that she is no longer on a diet and can slowly start eating like normal," he said, handing Warrick the clipboard with handwritten notes.

Living primarily in the United States since his late teens, he found all this a little antiquated. Warrick signed the notes, without a signature line, and gave the doctor a half-smile as he handed the paperwork back. "Are there any instructions I should know before I take a stranger with amnesia home with me?"

"Once discharged, the nurse will give them to you. I will write orders for her to see a therapist in a week. She will also need to see me at my clinic next week. Here's my card. It's nice of you to take care of her. Just remember, as unusual as all this is to you, you have your memories. She doesn't even know who she is." Clapping Warrick on the shoulder, the Frenchman left him standing in the hallway, wondering what in the hell he'd gotten himself into and why he cared.

Chapter Nine
Moirai

The Fates

"Stop pacing, Clotho." Lachesis, the eldest Moirai, rubbed her temples as she tried to figure out where her sister had disappeared. Two days before, the three of them had attended the wedding of the eldest Oneiroi, Phantasos, to the Nephilim, Amanda. That is where they last saw Atropos. One minute, she was flirting with one of Amanda's mortal friends, and then she was gone.

Clotho stopped her mindless wandering and stared at her sister. "I can feel you, hear your thoughts, but I can no longer hear or see hers. I can't stop pacing. How can I sit down? It has been two days with no words. We have never been apart like this. The longest ever was hours at best." She continued pacing before the three thrones. Every time she passed the middle sister's throne, she glared at it as if Atropos would appear if she looked hard enough.

Lachesis was the oldest of the sisters by mere minutes, but she had always held that mantle—the one who took care of the others and decided how to handle the most mundane tasks. Watching Clotho fret was almost as bad as Atropos' disappearance. Both broke something inside of her. For the first time, she didn't have the answers.

"We need mother," Lachesis admitted.

"What about Father?" Clotho asked.

"For now, we need a clear head to help us. When Zeus finds out she is missing, he will rain lightning down on every realm he resides over. No mortal or immortal would be safe," Lachesis said, as she slowly stood from the throne she had sat on since her sister went missing—two full days ago.

Chapter Ten

Unwanted Guest

Warrick stood just inside his apartment's entryway. For a man who prided himself on strength and endurance, he was exhausted. In a few hours, it would be three days since he found the lovely mystery on his construction site, and he still knew no more about her than he did when he found her.

"Dammit," he muttered to himself. He'd forgotten to call Anna. Checking his watch, he saw it was just past 11:30. She would still be awake studying. He walked over to the bar cart and poured two hefty fingers of Macallan—liquid courage and all that—as he pressed her number. Anna was about to give him hell.

"Hey, it's me," Warrick said as he walked to his bedroom with his phone pressed to his ear. "Yes, I just walked in... What the hell are you doing in my apartment? Not you, Anna. Lucia's here. I'll call you back."

"Darling, don't be like that." Lucia rose from his bed, wearing only a tiny sheer black lace thong. "I've been waiting for over two hours. Can you tell I'm chilled?" She looked from her breasts to him.

He strained to keep his eyes on hers. She was a bitch, but he was still a man, and she was built to please all the senses. "I repeat, why the fuck are you in my apartment? How did you get in?" He snarled at the manipulating bitch.

Standing toe to toe with him, Lucia pushed her hands under the shoulders of his jacket and pushed it off him. "You know I have my ways. Now, why don't you get comfortable and let me take care of you?"

Grabbing her wrist, Warrick's words came out like a growl, "You broke into my apartment, Lucia. Get dressed and leave before I call your father. I'm sure he'd love to know his daughter was throwing her naked body at a man after she broke into his home."

"Warr, you don't mean that."

"Damn if I don't. If there is one thing I value over anything else, it is my privacy, which you just invaded. What will it be? The police or your father? Pick."

"Fine, but after my papa finds out how you've been treating me, life as you know it will become very glum." She flipped her hair and retreated to the en-suite, where he hoped she would find her clothes.

Fuck! He tossed back the Macallan in one go.

Less than five minutes later, his unwanted intruder was gone. Ten minutes later, he finished the phone call with Anna, who scrutinized all his decisions over the last forty-eight hours. She felt Jane Doe should stay in a home that didn't belong to him. *What if she's right?*

He made a quick once-over of his apartment, making sure Lucia hadn't left anything she needed to return for. Satisfied, he jumped in the shower and then tried hard to fall asleep.

Vibrant red hair tumbled from his hand as he released it to trace both hands down the flawless milky skin of her back to land on either side of her hips. With her ass in the air, he pushed into her tight cunt one last time.

Blinking rapidly, Warrick sat up in bed, with his heart racing and his sticky hand still wrapped around his cock. He had never woken, mid climax, let alone masturbated while asleep. *What am I, a fucking teenager*? He knew of only one redhead who could elicit such a reaction, and she was lying in the hospital with no idea who she was.

"Siri. What time is it?"

"*4:42 AM*," the voice answered.

He left his bed, knowing he wouldn't fall back to sleep. He washed up and dressed for his morning run. Once he was done, he would work for a few hours, then head to the hospital. Most likely, he would return in less than twelve hours with a redhead in tow. After his *dream*, Warrick wondered if Anna was right. Maybe the beautiful enigma that was Jane Doe shouldn't stay with him.

As he rounded the bend to his construction site, Warr saw a man standing beside the fence. He wore white linen pants and a navy button-up. He looked very much out of place standing at a construction site at five o'clock in the morning. *Odd.* Without preamble, Warr jogged right up to the man.

"Can I help you?" Warr asked.

The man slowly turned to face him with a half-grin. "Hello, I was just admiring the structure going up here." The well-dressed stranger had an American accent.

"Morning. My name's Warrick." He held his hand out to the stranger. When the man's hand grasped his, a strange jolt of sickness, followed by complete euphoria, hit him. He had to restrain himself from yanking his hand free.

"This is my work site. We are building state-of-the-art business offices on the first seven floors. The top five floors will be individual apartments." Refusing to have a thirteenth floor was a sore spot for his father. He thought his son was ridiculous. Warr was the only superstitious person in his family.

"It's quite nice," the man said.

"Are you vacationing? I mean, from your accent, I can tell you aren't Monegasque," Warrick questioned. "You sound American.

"Something like that. So, where are you from, Warrick?"

It didn't go unnoticed that the man failed to answer him and asked a personal question in return. "I'm from the UK. Are you interested in my structure or Monaco?" Warr tilted his head to the half-finished building as he tried to get a read on the man.

"My daughter, Amanda, just married the man of her dreams," the man smirked at his own words. "I was thinking they would love the view from here. I'm looking for the perfect wedding gift."

"At five o'clock in the morning?" Warrick couldn't help himself. Their entire interaction was strange.

"I just landed and decided to take a look around. I saw the view and the new structure going up. Convenient, we ran into each other." The man's lip twitched, making Warrick wonder if their interaction was not a coincidence. "Are you taking payment for the apartments now, or waiting until they are finished?"

Interesting. Warrick could not believe this. The sun was barely over the horizon, and he was speaking to a stranger about purchasing a floor in his building. Yes, there had been others who claimed interest, but this man was a little more eager than one would expect in the middle of a project, especially since he hadn't seen mockups of the finished building.

"You haven't seen the projections, mockups, or pricing, and you're curious if I will sell now? I don't have a card on me, since I'm in the middle of my run, but if you would meet me at my office in two hours, I would be happy to go over the logistics. If you're still interested, I'm sure we can come to an agreement."

"Sounds good," the stranger smirked.

"My office is on—," the man finished his address before he could. *What the fuck?* Warrick looked into the man's strange eyes and reached his hand out to shake. The sickening feeling was just as potent as the first time. "By the way, I failed to get your name."

"Alaric Fanel," the man said, stepping back. The stranger assured him he would see him soon, then strolled off, hands tucked into his pants' pockets.

That was the oddest interaction Warr had ever encountered, and after meeting Jane Doe, that was saying something.

Warrick had not informed Anna that he had scheduled an appointment early that morning, so she wouldn't be there to greet the puzzle that was Alaric. After finishing his run, he threw on chinos and a Henley. He dressed for the hospital and the inevitable release of the even larger mystery with auburn hair and dazzling emerald eyes. *Did I just think that? Shit, Warr, get your thoughts straight.* He arrived at his office fifteen minutes early to open up and prepare for his guest.

Moments after pulling out the schematics and the digital presentation, still in its planning stage, he heard the elevator.

Chapter Eleven
A Watcher

Jane Doe

Tossing and turning, *Jane*, as they were calling her, could not get comfortable. Her mind reeled with questions. She knew beyond a doubt that she was not meant to be here. Stranger than that, she had an unnerving sense that the *humans* — why she continued to think of the people as such—were not her peers. *They are not like me.*

The more her mind turned, the more pain that shot through it. It felt like trying to figure things out made her situation worse, physically and emotionally. Ironically, the only comfort she had felt since waking in the strange place was when the gentleman, Warrick, was beside her. She was certain she hadn't known him before ending up in the *hospital*. After all, he had said so, but she had no idea whether anything that was told to her was the truth.

Easing off the makeshift bed, *Jane* slowly made her way to the window, her legs trembling with every step. She had to stop twice, gripping the wall to keep upright. It was unnerving how weak she felt. Surely, she wasn't usually this frail. Finally, hands clasped tightly around the windowsill, she looked across the property toward the sun rising over the horizon. With its rays of bright yellows and oranges peeking over the sea, *Jane* thought it the most magnificent sight ever. Feeling something roll down her face, she swiped it to find a tear had leaked from her eye. What an odd reaction to the beauty before her.

A hot tingle, much like a small bolt of lightning, ran up her spine. She whipped her head around to see a mesmerizing man in the viewing window watching her. His eyes were so blue, they rivaled the beauty she had just witnessed at the sunrise. The grin that tipped the corners of his mouth was not as captivating. Yes, his smile was perfect, but it lacked kindness. She blinked, and he was gone. *What in Hades' name just happened?* At that thought, a croaking call came from the window. She spun back to look, gripping tighter, wading through dizziness, to see a giant, much larger than the crow from the day before, inky black bird. It stopped cawing and stared at her. *What is going on?* A blistering pain shot through her head. With one hand securely fixed on the windowsill, she grabbed her head with the other and screamed.

Chapter Twelve

Everything is New

WARRICK

After the very productive, although bizarre, meeting with Alaric, Warrick was about to be eight million dollars richer. The mysterious man purchased the eleventh-floor apartment for his daughter and her new husband—*what was his name?* If memory served him, it had been an ancient Greek name. Why couldn't he remember it?

Locking his Audi, Warr went up to *Jane's* room to see if the hospital was ready to release her. An unusual fluttering in his stomach had him on edge. He needed to get the day over with. As before, the nurses waiting behind the desk were of no help. They couldn't stop ogling him long enough as he tried to ask when she would be dismissed.

Giving up, he shook his head and walked straight to her room. The nurse, who had been the only one to help the day before, stopped him as he pushed *Jane's* door open.

"Mr. Harding, may I speak with you before you go in?" She looked at the floor, meek, not at all confident, as she asked to speak with him.

"Sure," he followed her to the chairs on the other side of the elevator.

"About three hours ago, Jane screamed. When we reached her, she was propped against the wall below the window. When asked what happened, she said the man and pointed to the observation window. With her next breath, she gestured to the window above where she was crouched and delivered one word—bird.”

Warrick blinked. He could feel his brow pinching together. *What the hell?* “What does any of that mean? We heard a bird hit the window yesterday. Could she have been talking about that?”

“Possibly. The doctor believes her brain is trying to, what was the English word—reset? Yes, reset. She was most likely projecting pieces of memory and seeing what was in her mind and not with her eyes.”

“I see,” was all he could come up with after such an odd encounter. “Will she be okay to release? I don’t think I can care for someone in that state of mind. Don’t you think she needs more educated help?”

“I asked the doctor the same questions,” the nurse answered in her best English. “He thinks since she asked for you during that episode, being with you will help more than being with strangers.”

“I *AM* a stranger to her. I only met her when she opened her eyes.” Warrick was on his feet, running his hand through his hair, pacing. He had just met her, that was true, but it seemed like he had known her longer.

“We know, but she seems to have connected with you. He has dismissed her. We were merely waiting for you to check her out. I have paperwork for you to sign and a list of dos and don’ts. I just wanted you to know that things like what just happened could continue, possibly get worse before they are better.”

Warrick watched the nurse stand and straighten her scrub top. She gestured for him to follow, so he did. Every step felt like wading through wet cement. *Fucking hell.*

Once inside the room where his new roommate stood, Warrick's mouth went dry. She was stunning. On his directive, Anna had sent over a set of clothing for *Jane* to wear home. The redheaded beauty stood in form-fitting, low-cut jeans and a navy tank top. Her auburn locks hung in full, long waves around her shoulders. *Wow!* Memories of how he woke with his cock in his hand to dreams of her flashed through his mind. *That's all I need. Scare the poor woman with a hard-on right before I take her home with me.* He chastised himself.

"You look lovely. There should be a closet full of clothes and shoes by the time we get to the apartment," Warrick said.

"Thank you," Jane responded, a blush covering her cheeks.

"Can you sign here and here?" The nurse asked, holding a clipboard before him, effectively pulling him out of his trance.

"Uh, sorry. Yes." Warrick took the paperwork and signed without reading what he was signing for the first time in his life, focusing more on controlling his body than on whether he had signed his life away.

"Thank you, sir. Here are her instructions and the phone number to schedule an appointment with the neurologist who has been overseeing her care. He wants to see her in two weeks."

Warr heard only half of what the nurse said, his eyes trained on Jane. She all but floated over to him, her bright green eyes locked on his. He couldn't see any scrapes or bruises. Her clothes must have covered them all.

Clearing his throat, he shook himself out of the trance her presence had caused him. *Fuck me!* Once beside him, he placed his hand on the small of her back, not expecting the jolt of electricity through his arm or the smirk on her face. *Did she feel that, too?* Warr guided the enigmatic woman out of the hospital, then removed his hand only to place her in the passenger seat of his car. As soon as their connection broke, the loss caused an ache in his palm, like he needed to touch her, even though he couldn't.

Warr slid into the driver's seat and did a double-take. *Jane* looked extremely nervous. Her eyes were wide, and her breath shallow. He watched as she ran her trembling hands all over the dashboard, then tentatively glided her fingertips over the buttons and controls. She even reached over him and touched the steering wheel. If he didn't know better, he would wonder if she'd ever been in a car before. He watched as she cocked her head to the side when her window rolled down and grinned when she reversed it with the touch of her finger. *Was this strange behavior because of her amnesia?*

"Are you okay?" Warrick asked.

Jane jumped, even though his voice barely registered within the confines of the vehicle. "Yes, why do you ask?" She started looking in the back seat with excitement in her eyes.

"Do you not remember riding in cars?" Warrick asked.

Her bright green eyes darted straight to his, and he could tell she was trying to remember, but what shocked him was the awe he saw on her face. He was almost certain she thought she was riding in a car for the first time.

"No. I remember what cars are, but I don't remember ever being in one. I'm sorry," she said. Her words came out robotically.

"No reason to apologize. You can't help that your memory isn't working properly. Hopefully, you will be as good as new soon. Now, let's get you home." Leaning over, Warrick grabbed her seatbelt. She smelled of lavender and warm vanilla. His eyes locked onto hers as he pulled the belt around her. He felt her tense when his hand grazed her hip as the buckle slid into the lock. *Fuck.* Setting back in his seat, he casually adjusted himself and started the car.

Getting into the apartment took longer than usual. *Jane* took everything in as she had the car. She touched every surface she could, and from the way her head whipped from one thing to the next, Warr could tell she was consuming a lot of information at once. He thought about how strange it would be to lose all of his memories and see everything anew. On the elevator, she grabbed his arm, holding on as if her life depended on him. When the chime rang out, alerting them they had arrived at the penthouse, he had to all but drag her from the lift.

She stood by his side, twisting her fingers and biting her lip, as he unlocked the apartment door. All the lights were automatic, so as they walked through his home, they lit the surrounding area without being touched. After sixty seconds with no one around, the lights turned off automatically. This surprised her, and he couldn't help but watch her fascination. The next thing that caught her attention was the refrigerator. Warrick had grabbed them both a bottle of water before showing her the layout, and her face lit up when she realized it was cold, from a steel box in what she called the strange room. Watching her prowl around his apartment was akin to what he would expect from a child. Everything was new to her.

As requested, *Jane's* closet was full of clothes and shoes. The illuminated drawers on the left side of the large walk-in held lingerie, which Jane held up and inspected with a critical eye. He didn't see a problem other than that the garments held his attention a little too long. On the right side, the drawers held accessories. A few necklaces, two watches, and a couple of bracelets. She ran her fingertips over every article of clothing, inspecting each piece. When she finally had her fill, she cleared her throat and looked at him.

"You did this for me?"

"I asked my assistant to set things up for you. Unfortunately, I don't know what you like to eat, so I thought we would order in this evening," Warrick responded to the look of awe on *Jane's* face.

"Order in? I'm not sure I understand the expression. Thank you for doing all this. I feel that I am intruding horribly on you."

In a subservient action, she lowered her head, making *him* slightly uncomfortable; however, his dick twitched at the motion. *Down, boy.* This arrangement was definitely going to make his life difficult.

"I will have food sent to us already made, and it's my pleasure to have you here." *Oh, if she only knew.*

Chapter Thirteen
Mother of Moirai

CLOTHO

Silence had enveloped the Moirai mansion, and all the servants were afraid of what came next. The only exception was the click-clack of Clotho's footsteps whenever she resumed her pacing. Exhaustion and fear had her body so worked up that she didn't know how to process the emotions rolling through her. Everything was off. She sat on her throne and stared at the two other seats of power to her right. Reserved for her eldest sister, Lachesis, the middle seat sat empty. She went to speak with their mother. The farthest seat on her right made her tear up. Something she had done only once or twice, and then only as a child.

It had been three days since Atropos had gone missing—seventy-two mortal hours. Mortal time had always gone by quickly until the last three days. Never had the phase of time beat rhythmically through her body. After all, human measurement meant nothing to the gods. Immortals never kept timepieces or clocks. The gods had no need of human calendars. Until now, her sister's disappearance had led her to view mortal schedules differently. She now counted every second—she now knew the date on their calendar. *Where is my sister?*

Unable to sit, Clotho once again stood from her throne and resumed her pacing. She wasn't just roaming around aimlessly; she started chewing on her fingernails. "What in Hades' name am I doing?" *Horrible human habits.*

After she made a few rounds circling the thrones, Lachesis finally appeared with their beautiful mother in tow. Themis was Zeus's second wife, supplanted by Hera, the Queen Bitch herself. Her daughters never understood their father's infatuation with the evil temptress and often sided with anyone who wanted to thwart her. Both goddesses were stunning, but their mother was on another level. Her beauty was as close to Aphrodite's as one could be without being her blood relative. With her long black hair, a stripe of auburn, and a distinct stripe of blonde, and her stunning dark grey eyes, she looked like the deity she was. Most of all, she was kind and trustworthy, unlike many of the immortals on Olympus. She was the goddess of divine law after all. The embodiment of justice and order for all beings, she never chose sides, even for her loved ones.

"Mother!" Clotho threw herself into her mother's arms. "Atropos is missing. It has been three days since we saw her."

"Oh, darling, do not fret. We will find her. Now, your sister told me the last place she was seen was at the wedding of the angel's daughter and Phantasos. Was there anyone attending with whom she had a problem, or they with her?" Themis asked her daughters.

"That's just it. No one truly likes any of us. We are The Fates Three after all. Since Atropos is the death fate, out of the three of us, she is the least liked," Lachesis answered. "There's not one being that hasn't been affected by her scissors."

"True, but all immortals understand that is her lot to bear. They may not like what she stands for, but they recognize someone must suffer the post. Harming her would mean someone else would step in, and that person might be a worse Fate for everyone. If someone took her, it meant they had issues with her that went beyond her station. Think. Who has a vendetta against your sister?" Themis sat on the far-right throne, steepling her hands.

Both Fates sat in their respective chairs, pondering their mother's question. After several minutes, Clotho saw Lachesis shift around in her seat. And when she looked over at her sister, she saw her brows raise just as the thought ran through her own mind. *Phantasos, Amanda, and Alaric. Alaric! The Warrior Angel. He has a problem with her.*

Chapter Fourteen

Nothing Makes Sense

Jane Doe

Left to her own devices, Jane looked around the room with the critical eye of one who wanted nothing but, unfortunately, needed everything. The room was small compared to–*what?* She had no idea. She ran her fingertips over the soft duvet cover while imagining who had been in the room before her. *Did Warrick rescue many women?* What puzzled her the most was why she was in what he called his *guest room*. Did he not want to share a bed with her? Didn't men want to sleep with women? She didn't know, but her innate sense told her that most men would want her in their beds.

As she took in every piece of furniture and artwork on the walls, her attention fell on a particularly strange decorative piece. Large, solid, black, and shiny, it held the center point of the room. Fascinated by its oddity, it drew her in. Gliding her hand over its surface, she jumped when a man's voice, followed by children laughing, came from it. Slowly, it shifted from solid black to people outside, sitting on grass. *What in Hades' name?* Jane looked behind it—*nothing but a wall.* Straining to understand what she was seeing, the word television popped into her mind. Captivated by the view and the humans, she sat on the bench at the foot of the bed and watched the family. Presumably, the father of the two little ones tossed one into the air as the other yelled out that they needed a turn. After tossing and catching each child several times, he claimed they had exhausted him, fell to the ground, and lay spread-eagled on the grass. A moment later, a lady came to lie beside him. The two littles ambushed their parents, leaping atop them and screeching a battle cry. That's when a rap on the door startled her.

"Are you ready to eat?" Warrick asked.

Shaking herself from the trance the television had placed her in, she responded, "I will be right there."

Jane's nose led her to the table by the window, where makeshift containers held their evening meal, and the handsome Warrick sat waiting for her to join. The food smelled divine, and she couldn't wait to devour it. Her stomach growled, and she felt her cheeks heat. *Did that just happen?*

"It sounds like dinner arrived just in time. Please have a seat," Warrick said, gesturing to the chair across from him.

He had changed into a tight-fitting shirt and short pants. They hugged what she could see of his left thigh. It was enough to make other parts of her hungry. *For Hades' sake, what is wrong with me?*

Without speaking, she followed his motion to the chair and sat. Everything about the situation made her uneasy. She had to eat, so what about sitting at a table to eat was making her anxious? *Something else to ponder.* Noodles and vegetables cooked in a sauce she didn't recognize were the first to catch her eye. Her mouth watered. The only problem was that she had no idea what to do. Looking up at her host, she saw him watching her. With a warm smile, he took the bowl closest to him and spooned some onto the plate before him. He then grabbed another bowl and did the same. With understanding, she followed suit.

A peaceful few minutes went by as they ate in companionable silence, until Warrick cleared his throat and decided to ask questions.

"Is your room to your liking?" he asked, just before he lifted his glass of red wine to his lips.

Eyes so blue, the image of an ocean ran through her mind as he locked onto hers over the rim of his glass. She shifted in her seat to relieve a bit of the ache growing between her thighs, she answered. "It's quite nice. Your home is lovely."

"Have you had any breakthrough in your memory?"

If possible, her rigid spine went even tauter with his question, and she had no clue why. Clearing her throat, she dabbed her lips with the cloth napkin and answered. "I have not. In fact, I find myself questioning if my memories will ever return."

"It's just been a few days. The doctors believe you will have your memories within a couple of weeks, if not before. I'm sure they will return soon," Warrick replied.

"It's just that––," she stopped mid-sentence, almost spilling her anxiety all over the beautiful man across from her. The last thing she wanted was for him to think of her as insane. Anyway, even if she trusted him enough, how would she explain that she doesn't believe all the wonderment of her surroundings is solely because of her amnesia?

"Just that––what, Jane?" Warrick asked with his head cocked to the side, waiting for her to elaborate.

"Oh, nothing. I was thinking aloud," she took a larger-than-necessary sip of her wine. *Liquid courage and all.*

Warrick set his chopsticks down and gave her all his attention; the result was both unnerving and a little thrilling. Every bit of his crystal blue, deep-set eyes trained on just her, waiting for an answer. *Damn.* She knew he saw her unease and suspected her visceral reaction to him by the slight lift of one side of his mouth.

That smirk made her shift around in her seat some more. *Not sure I will make it through this meal.*

"I know you and I just met and have been plunged into an unorthodox union, of sorts. Hopefully, you will learn that you can tell me anything, and maybe if you talk about your situation, it will spark a memory." Warrick said.

She looked down at her plate and back to the man watching her, knowing he waited for her to pick up the conversation. The flames in her cheeks grew stronger from his scrutiny. How does she tell him that nothing about here, there, anywhere since she woke feels natural? *Nothing.*

One more sip of liquid courage and a couple of nibbles to her lower lip, and she decided. She would trust him not to judge her—*and fuck...what if he does?* She began with her concerns, without allowing her mind to dwell on that "what if" anymore.

"I'm not sure how to explain myself, and I have the sense that I have never had to. So, bear with me, please. What I'm about to explain may not make much sense." She fidgeted a little before she began. "When I woke up, I had to think about what was being said and in what language. I understood both your language and the nurse's. One of the oddest things I thought was that they were in modern tongue. My head ached so bad that I had to make a conscious effort to speak so you could understand me. I still have to mentally correct a few words before I verbalize them in your language. Even stranger is that I know the words for so many objects around me, but it's as if I have never seen or at least touched them before. If it were just the loss of memory, wouldn't I at least feel that the world around me made more sense? I look at you and think human. I look at myself in the mirror, and that term doesn't fit." Jane stopped rambling and looked up from her where she had been moving her food around just long enough to see if her dinner partner was dissecting her. He was looking at his wine as he swirled it in his glass, listening, so she continued.

"For example, when I looked around the room you gave me to stay in, I thought the solid black, shiny piece of art was unusual. So, I ran my fingers over its surface. When people manifested on its surface, I jumped and was fascinated. The word *"television"* popped into my head, but I have no impression that it's an ordinary object for me. I was mesmerized by it. Now, as I look just from my seat, I see two more. They must be typical of this world. I'm sorry. I'm not making sense." Jane dropped her napkin and caught her face in her hands. Muffled words came from between fingers. "I think I've lost more than just memories."

Chapter Fifteen

Raven?

Warrick

Warrick thought the flush on *Jane's* cheeks when embarrassed was adorable, making the memory of his dream surface. *Not what needs to happen right now.*

The concern in her voice worried him. He knew very little of post-traumatic amnesia, only that her memories may not return for days, possibly weeks. Neither her healthcare workers nor the internet ever elaborated on how she would perceive herself or the world around her. It certainly seemed trite compared to what she was experiencing. What he knew was that for now, she needed a friend and not the horny adolescent he became the moment he saw her eyes open. Before she opened her eyes, he saw a broken woman injured on his property; now he saw a stunning woman who captured his attention like no other, and he didn't understand his sudden visceral connection to her.

"You just woke from a coma caused by a brain injury. Please do not think I would ever judge you for what you're going through, or think that because of your experiences, you aren't normal. I've never experienced amnesia. Give yourself some grace. What seems odd today may very well feel normal tomorrow. Take this one day at a time." Warrick took another sip of wine, then continued. "You know—my mother was a big advocate of journaling."

"Journaling?" Jane asked.

"Yes. She believed that when people wrote down their feelings and daily activities, they came to understand themselves better.

I must admit, I've journaled during hard times, and she has a point. Anyway, if you would like, I could give you a notebook to journal your thoughts and feelings in while you're on this journey," Warrick said.

"That sounds nice. I would like that," Jane said.

"Give me a moment. I have a notebook in my office that you can use. It's nothing fancy, but it should do for now." He rose from the table, feeling her eyes on his back as he walked to his office.

No longer in the same room, he could replay some of her words. The most interesting part was calling everyone but herself human.

Once dinner was over, Warrick had no clue what to do. He knew she must be exhausted. Instead of asking *Jane* to watch a movie or anything that could cause her stress, he told her to enjoy her evening and dismissed himself to his office, where he spent more time contemplating his new roommate's reaction to the world around her than he did on work.

Unable to use critical and abstract thinking while Jane consumed his concentration, he chose an easier work diversion, opening his calendar to his tasks for the next day. There, he was reminded of the upcoming fundraising gala he had to attend. *Ugh.*

"I hate these pretentious events," Warrick said aloud. "I wonder if Jane would consider going with me?" *There I go again,* he thought as his phone rang. "Anna," *thank the Lord, maybe now I can work.*

After an hour of debating flooring with his assistant, he decided it was time to retire to his room, needing some time to wind down and read for fun, and not to strengthen his investment portfolio.

It happened in a flash, so fast he wondered if he was seeing things. When he turned to stand from his leather desk chair, the outline of an enormous bird sat outside his window. The ledge was relatively small, and the bird was rather large. *Weird.* With a blink, no more large bird. *What the fuck?*

Chapter Sixteen
Harbinger

The Morrigan

How can this be? Three days ago, the Morrigan felt the shift. Her grandson was with one of the Greek Fates—a goddess. An immortal. A member of the Greek Pantheon. After all, she and her daughter, Adair, had endured to keep him from their world. Never allowing a relationship between them to manifest, never speaking with him, never holding him as a child; oh, the pain they had endured just to keep him from the divine world that was now invading his mortal home. *How did this happen?* She lifted from the window in flight, determined to get answers, but first, she needed to speak with her daughter. She had known better than to try to circumvent destiny—for the second time.

Chapter Seventeen
Pain

Jane Doe

Jane was a little taken aback that Warrick wanted to work. After all, one would think, it being her first night in his home, he would want to get to know her. He had been so agreeable and attentive during their meal; surely, he found her attractive or at least someone with whom he could converse. She had seen herself in the mirror. How could he not be attracted to her? *There I go, thinking well of myself again. We just met. Why am I so attracted to him?* She mentally chastised herself. Turning in a circle, deciding what to do next, when the glass doors leading to the balcony caught her attention. A city of lights lay before her, and she wanted to see more of it. Finally, she figured out the metal mechanism, slid the door wide, and walked onto the balcony to revel in the beautiful glow of the city.

Far out, she could see a black abyss and, from the smell on the breeze, she knew it came from the sea. The word Uncle came to mind, along with several sharp pains. Closing her eyes, she rubbed her forehead, trying to dispel the discomfort. As fast as the aches hit her, they left just as quickly, as if they had never happened. Shaking the moment off, Jane walked to the lounger and sat, drinking in the beauty before her. The city curled around the blackness, hugging it close. The urge to visit the lit structures lining the sea before her was strong. The salt air and dazzling lights sparked the light touch of a fleeting memory. More like a vision, which she had no clue if it was an actual memory.

She and two other women, one blonde and the other with hair as black as night, stood beside a large body of water, much like the one before her, except that the sun shone brightly. And with that memory came another jolt of pain.

Again, she grabbed her head and rubbed it to ease the ache—*for Hades' sake*—this one wasn't letting up. She didn't remember ever having a pain, let alone one so vile.

"If to recall memories hurt like this, I should hope never to remember anything." Talking to herself, she continued trying to relieve the agony just above her brow by pressing the heels of her hands into her forehead and squeezing her eyes shut.

"I'm sorry, I knocked, but—are you okay?" Warrick stood just outside the sliding door.

Startled, but unable to show it, Jane continued to press her head. First, his scent hit her senses—sandalwood and something she didn't recognize. *He's getting closer.* Feeling him sit down beside her and unable to open her eyes, her anxiety spiked. The heat of his body radiated off him, consuming her. Seconds later, he was touching her shoulder. Her body shuddered at the contact.

"Jane, should I call for the car and take you back to the hospital?"

Worry coated his voice. *Wonderful, he sees me as weak.* "No, I just get headaches sometimes, that's all. It will dissipate shortly." Lies, all lies. She had no clue whether or not she got headaches. She didn't remember.

"You look like you're in a lot of pain. Can I get you a painkiller?" Warrick asked, now rubbing light circles between her shoulder blades.

"You have something that will end this torture?" Jane slowly opened her right eye halfway. And widen it even more when she saw how close beside her he sat. His hand was large and warm, making her thoughts run wild. *What in Hades' name is wrong with me?*

"Yes. I have pills that will hopefully take the ache away. Only problem is it takes about half an hour to work."

He rubbed those thought-provoking circles further down her back, causing heat to follow. *I'm in horrific pain and still eager for the touch of this man.* She again wondered what kind of person she had been before the memory loss.

Finally, she received his attention, and she must now ask him to leave to get a pill to stop the insufferable pain. Honestly, it had to be the most infuriating moment of her life. Or so she assumed anyway.

"If it's not much trouble and you think it will help, I would most appreciate it," Jane said, holding her head. She wished that not only would the pain subside, but he would return and sit down beside her again—and if she were fortunate, he would continue rubbing her back.

"I'll be right back," Warrick said.

She felt his warmth leave, along with his comforting touch. Warring against itself, her body had been in both agony and arousal. Now, the torment amplified with him gone.

Thank Zeus. Much faster than she could have hoped for, Warrick returned with water and two of those pill things he said would help.

"Swallow these," Warrick said, placing the white miracle workers in the palm she held out to him.

"I swallow these whole. Are you sure?" Jane looked down, with increased pain, at the two cylinders in her hand.

"Yes. I'm sure."

Doing as he said, she swallowed back the medication. Their fingers touched when he grabbed the glass from her hand, and her body warred with itself—again. *Something is off.*

"Want me to help you back inside?" Warrick asked, still hovering above her instead of sitting beside her.

"No, but thank you. I believe I will lean my head back and breathe in the salty air. Hopefully, the painkiller and fresh air will help me. Would you like to stay out here with me?" She asked, hoping her plea did not sound as desperate as her traitorous body felt.

"Sure. I'll stay until you start feeling better."

To her chagrin, he sat on the lounger beside her instead of resuming his spot on hers.

"Thank you, Warrick. You have been very kind to me," Jane said, just under her breath.

Chapter Eighteen

Past Meets Present

The Morrigan

The Morrigan flew to the Plain of the Moytura to search for her daughter, Adair. Most believed the divine fled the sacred lands after the final battles between men and gods. Thousands of years later, and the gods are still present. If one knows what to look for, the realms of the Tuatha Dé Danann can be found.

Landing in the middle of the ancient stone circle, wind whipped around her as she transformed. Her rich black feathers turned to ivory skin, and her fowl-shaped body became the luscious curves of a beautiful woman. A button nose replaced the large, curved beak, and she traded the ebony plumage on her head for auburn curls that fell down her back. With a smile, she covered her nakedness in a long, flowing, forest green dress with billowing sleeves. With a bodice trimmed in gold, it cinched at the waist with a leather rope that ended with an ancient chaplet.

The circle was steeped in history. A world before man knew Christ. The one where giants roamed the earth beside her and her fellow deities. It had been several centuries since she had been in the circle. Memories of her dearest friend flooded her thoughts. Muirgen had always kept her safe. No matter that she was the daughter of a fallen and a mortal, she had been a faithful ally. One tear slipped down her face; that was all she would allow. Her desperate need to find her daughter was the only reason she returned to this stone circle. It was time. The first premonition had come true.

Observing each stone carefully, she glided her fingertips over each one's rough surface. When her palm heated, she knew she had found the entrance. Just like she knew her eyes were glowing white. She could sense him—her husband—the king.

She reached for the chaplet hanging from her waist and pressed the cold metal beads to the stone's surface. The infusion of Dagda's blood into the beads would allow her entry. For a brief moment, she wondered if he remembered giving them to her.

When she blinked, she was looking across the lush green moors of ancient Ireland. Again, memories assailed her mind. This is where she had lived for thousands of years. She fell in love, married Dagda, and had several babes before escaping with her last one. After centuries of keeping her daughter from Dagda, he found them. Now, neither had much to do with her—except for twenty-nine years ago when Adair came to her, desperate for her help—and that had been futile.

Thousands of years had passed since she had been in Dagda's kingdom, but standing on the other side of the veil, it felt like yesterday. She rubbed her breastbone where the ache from the memories was taking up residence. She pretended that her selfishness made her flee from her husband, not that she saw that the babe in her womb would predict the fall of the gods—the fall of Dagda.

Foolishly, she thought that if she never allowed her daughter to know of their divine world, she wouldn't speak her predictions aloud, and they would not come to fruition. Out of fear and irrational thought, The Morrigan believed she could keep her daughter from being a seer, or at least convince her that her visions were mere dreams and nothing more.

Her daughter was kind and loved all creatures, much like Dagda, and unlike her. Adair had a kind soul like her father, not the harbinger of death that those on the battlefield knew her to be.

As it unfolded, her daughter did have second sight, and the day she shapeshifted into a crow at age fifteen, there was no hiding her divinity. Adair's predictions came true, even though The Morrigan misinterpreted the *fall*. Instead of death, all the divine beings, creatures, and seraphim were cast into separate realms. The Almighty was done with his humans being toyed with.

Dagda still ruled the Tuatha Dé Danann, and her daughter hated her for keeping her away from her father for centuries. She could, with little effort, count the number of times she had seen her youngest daughter since the Irish king learned of her, making do by watching over her grandson instead.

The lad, Warrick, was much like his mother, especially in looks. They both had jet-black hair and radiant blue eyes, inherited from Dagda. Their smiles—those came from her—so did their sneers.

As she looked out over the striking land she once fought upon, still clasping the beads, a supplication fell from her lips. She closed her eyes and hoped her plea would work.

The tingling sensation of the divine started at her fingertips and spread to the hair at her nape. Before her eyes, the city of her peers emerged from the mist hanging low to the ground. And before she blinked twice, Dagda stood before her. His imposing body had not changed. Over two meters tall, on a frame coveted by all deities, Dagda was breathtaking. His hair was as dark as her raven feathers, and his eyes were as brilliant blue as the beaches of Albania. Even now, her heart skipped when she looked at him. *What I would give to have his affections again,* she thought. Unfortunately, no matter how kind a god he was known to be, he would never forgive her for keeping his daughter from him, no matter the reason.

"What are you doing here?" Dagda's baritone voice radiated through her body. "How did you get through the gate?

"I come to speak with Adair. It's important. I would not be here if it weren't." The Morrigan crossed her arms, mirroring his stance; hers was to keep her heart from breaking, while his was to keep her at bay. She gave her why, but not her how, hoping he would let it go.

"You dare?" Dagda narrowed his eyes.

"I dare. As I said, it's vital I speak with her."

After several minutes, her estranged husband relented. "Very well. She is here. Follow me." He turned, clenched fists at his sides, and started toward the mansion. Speaking over his shoulder, he said, "Keep up."

Tall as she was, it wasn't easy keeping up with the mammoth of a god. She contemplated shifting into her wolf form but decided against it. Curiosity danced across her mind. Never had she thought he would allow her to see their daughter so easily. *What's he up to?*

It took them several minutes to arrive at Adair's door, each second reminding her of what she and the god in front of her once had. She'd had many lovers over the years. Monogamy was rare among immortals. Had they not separated for thousands of years, she would have never taken another—what she had with Dagda was more than sex. It was passionate, and she had once loved him more than life. At that moment, the truth of their situation lay heavily on her shoulders. When in her realm, she could pretend differently by not thinking of ancient times. Unfortunately, the past stood in front of her, and her heart ached for him.

Dagda knocked on Adair's door. She moved to stand beside her *husband*. The warmth of his body engulfed her senses, and her palms itched to touch him. She would only have to extend her hand millimeters. *Control.* She internally berated her need for him after so long. Thousands of years had not dulled her intense desire for the god. He was all divine male. His looks, strength, and integrity were all the same. *Bear it*, she told herself.

Unfortunately, not all of her memories were positive. The last time she had been this close to him, his eyes swirled red, and the veins in his forearms popped with the strain he placed on his muscles to keep from wielding his infamous club—a weapon capable of killing or raising the dead. The day he found she had kept his daughter from him for hundreds of years.

His eyes on her skin filled her with desire, but all she saw from him was contempt. He was no longer straining to keep from pummeling her. Regrettably, love and longing were no longer present in his dark blue eyes either.

The creak of the heavy iron door pulled The Morrigan from her rambling memories and regrets. Her eyes focused back on the present and landed on her stunning daughter.

"Adair," her daughter's name came out like a gasp. The shock of seeing her child after so long brought those regrets back ten-fold with layers of self-loathing and heartache.

Adair stood in the chamber's doorway, glaring at her. She had forgotten just how dark her daughter's hair was, so black it looked blue in the light spilling from the room. Her eyes weren't like Dagda's; they were exact replicas. She looked no older than her early twenties. Not a goddess who had lived thousands of years and bore children well into double digits. A small crow sat atop Adair's right shoulder, and after an uncomfortable minute, the crow cawed and made a couple of clicking sounds right before it said, *Who in Donn's name is it?*

"Dia duit, Adair. Smart bird, calling out the god of the dead's name," Morrigan finally answered. "May I come in? I wouldn't be here if it weren't important."

She heard the breath exit her daughter's lungs in resignation. *She must have been holding it the whole time.* Adair took a step back and held the large door open, and The Morrigan stepped in front of Dagda, who seemed rooted in the spot as he took in their exchange. This was the first time all three had been together since that night. The one that changed her relationship with her daughter.

"Thank you," The Morrigan said, stepping fully into her daughter's quarters.

"I will go. Call for me when you need her to leave," Dagda said, speaking only to his daughter. He thought Adair would be ready for her departure and would need him to force her out. That sentiment made her woeful.

"No, Father. Please stay." Adair said.

"As you wish," and he stepped into the room.

Adair busied herself by placing the crow into a large enclosure, smoothing out her skirts, and visibly stealing herself some courage with a few deep breaths before sitting beside her father.

It had not gone unnoticed that Adair put a table and as much space between herself and The Morrigan. How she wished things were different. If she could go back and change what she did, she would without hesitation. Ultimately, her sight had been correct, but the truth played out much differently than she thought it would. The only death was of her heart. *So far.*

She closed her eyes and mustered the courage to tell Adair that a Fate of the Greeks was with her youngest born—the son she had helped hide had been found. *Damn prophecies.* If nothing else, she hoped her daughter would see that she, too, listened to sight, and instead of allowing things to play out as they should, she tried to impose her will and stave off destiny. They had both been mistaken.

"I assume you must know that I keep watch over my family. All my children, grandchildren, and the ones they have begotten.

I have been watching over Alasdair. The mortals refer to him as Warrick." The Morrigan began her tale.

Adair's face turned pale. "Is he—," She looked down at her fingers, which lay in her lap, trying to bring herself to ask the question. "Is he alive?"

"He is. But the truth has come to pass. Almost four days ago, I felt the shift and knew it had to do with Warrick. I morphed into raven form and found him standing over a woman in the hospital. As soon as I saw her, I knew who she was—,"

"Who?" Dagda asked, interrupting her brief pause.

"She is the Greek Fate, Atropos," The Morrigan said.

"The thread cutter?" Adair asked, her face becoming paler.

"Yes. Many know her as *The Inflexible One*. She is the Moirai with the most power; that of death," The Morrigan continued.

"How? How did this happen? Does he know?" Adair was on her feet, wringing her hands, fear written all over her face. "He's powerless. I should have never—,"

"What? What did you do?" Dagda, on his feet beside his daughter, took her shoulders between his hands and turned Adair to face him.

Chapter Nineteen
Migraines

Jane (Atropos)

Before Jane opened her eyes, the light spilling into her room was evident. She could see the glow behind her eyelids. *It seems the pain is gone,* she thought, and slowly peeled her lids open to see the day for herself. Breathing deep, thankful the discomfort had subsided, she pulled herself up in the bed and stretched. Mid-mouth agape in a yawn and arms stretched above her head, she noticed the large man, his head slumped, chin to chest, in the armchair in the corner of her room. *Warrick?*

Dressed unlike she'd ever seen him. He wore—*nightclothes*? Or that was the only explanation she had for the thin, short-sleeved top and baggy pants he wore. At least he looked comfortable, all but his head. Easing out of bed, she quietly walked over to him. Not knowing if he was a gentle giant while asleep, she gently shook his shoulder and then backed away, just in case. It took three more shakes for him to stir.

Blinking a few times, Warrick raised his head and then closed his eyes when he saw her. With eyes still shut, he ran his hands over his face and said, "I didn't mean to fall asleep. I thought I would be back in my room way before you woke."

"May I ask why you are crumpled in the corner chair?"

Now, looking at her but still seated, he explained. "After the medicine took effect, you wanted to lie down. I helped you to your bed. Once your head hit the pillow, you were out. The pain must have exhausted you. I worried about the migraine returning, so I changed clothes and watched over you. Unfortunately, you caught me. I meant to be gone before you woke," Warrick said, clearly embarrassed to have been caught sleeping in her room.

Unable to hold a stern look, Jane felt her grin spread wider. "That was sweet of you. Thank you."

Warrick stood, and it was his turn to stretch. His thin shirt rode up to show skin, and Jane's desire spiked—*for Zeus' sake.*

"How are you feeling?" he asked.

She wondered if he could sense her sudden arousal. "Much better. I'm sorry you felt you had to stay up and watch over me."

"No problem. You just got out of the hospital from a head injury. I wanted to make sure you were okay. Give me half an hour, and I'll have breakfast done."

Before Jane could respond, Warrick fled the uncomfortable situation, leaving her to start her day.

After breakfast, Jane found herself back in her room. She pulled a book from the bookcase and went to the balcony to read. The book entitled *Destiny* had caught her eye. *Odd, no author to speak of.* With a slight huff, she opened it and began reading. When she turned the page to a chapter labeled *Moirai,* pain seared through her body—not just her head.

The book fell onto the cement as she bent over, clutching her head. Her eyes seared with burning agony. A vision of herself standing beside the same two women from her prior memory of the sea was her first recollection. Then flashes flooded her mind, one after another in rapid succession.

Her hand cut threads repeatedly.

The two women held the strings between them.

A large, imposing man sat upon a very intricate throne.
A beautiful woman held a pair of scales and a sword.
The last thought was of her falling through the air before everything went black.

Jane woke, lying on her pillow, her head aching, and Warrick pacing her room. She watched as he rubbed his hand through his hair every other turn. After several turns from one side of the room to the other, he looked up and noticed her watching him.

"Jane. Are you okay?" He rushed to her side, fear spread across his face, his hair sticking up in all directions.

She couldn't help but notice how striking he was while in protective mode. It made her happy somehow. "Yes. I think I had flashbacks. A book in my room caught my eye, and when I began reading it—well, I suppose it triggered something."

"I found you passed out on the lounger. Your body twitched a few times as I brought you in here about ten minutes ago. I didn't see a book," Warrick said, looking more concerned for her than when he paced her room.

"Are you sure? It had a title, but I couldn't find the author's name." She stood from her bed, bracing herself to keep from falling right before Warrick pulled her to his chest.

"I don't believe you should be standing so soon. I'll go look, lie back down," Warrick ordered.

His arm around her sent chills down her spine and gooseflesh across her arms. She briefly wondered whether he had any physical reaction to her. Doing as he said, she climbed back onto the bed and propped herself against the pillows.

"There's no book out here," Warrick called to her from the balcony.

"There must be. Wait," She looked over to the bookshelves, and there it was, in the exact spot it had been when she first retrieved it to read. "It's there," Jane pointed to show him as he walked back in from outside. "But how can that be. The last thing I did was read. The book should have been with me."

Warrick looked at her, worry etched across his brow and pity in his eyes. "I think you should rest. I'll call the doctor and see if he is up for a home visit."

"Really, I'm fine. I probably read and returned it, and because of passing out, I don't remember. There's no need to disturb the doctor." She didn't want to see the doctor.

"You passed out, Jane. You most certainly are not fine," Warrick raised his voice a fraction more than what she liked.

"Please refrain from taking that tone with me. I know this is not normal, but I did just get out of the hospital. Please give me a few more days before you contact the doctor," She begged.

Warrick watched her for what seemed like minutes when, in reality, it was seconds, then sighed in resignation. "Fine, but if you pass out again, before you wake, I will have already called the doctor, and you will wake in the car on the way to the hospital. I apologize for making you upset, but you didn't see yourself lying lifeless on the lounger. The only other time I was ever that worried was when I found you on my property. Now rest, and I'll bring you tea and biscuits." Warrick turned and left her room.

Jane looked from the bedroom door to the balcony's sliding doors and wondered how the book got back on the shelf. While contemplating the enigma, two black birds landed on the terrace. One on the lounger, the other directly in front of the glass door. It watched her as she eyed it. When she tilted her head, the bird did the same. Slowly, she eased off the bed and made her way to the glass doors, and she could have sworn the bird shook its head at her. When she reached for the door handle, both birds took flight. *Maybe I am going crazy.*

Chapter Twenty
The Angel?

The Fates

Mother, I believe we should tell Father. It's abnormal for me and Clotho to not feel Atropos' presence and hear her thoughts. Something bad has happened—as our king and our father—he should be informed.

"I am not saying to keep this from him; we should just have more to say when we do," Themis said.

"We," Lachesis pointed between herself and her sister, "have decided that the Angel may know where she is."

"Why would Alaric know?" Themis asked.

"Other than he's an angel—he had a minor issue with our dear sister several years ago. Phantasos fell in love with Amanda after we warned the Oneiroi not to. Fate foretold of problems with their union, so we pushed hard, warning him at every opportunity. Atropos liked Phantasos since they were young. Her problem with them being together had more to do with jealousy than destiny. Alaric recognized that and promised she would learn a lesson. That was seven human years ago, so we have not concerned ourselves with it. Maybe he knows more about her going missing than we think. If not, we continue to ponder. What can it hurt?" Clotho explained.

"So, my daughter may be missing because of petty jealousy that took place almost a decade ago?" Themis asked, her back going straight with indignation.

"Time is of no consequence for us, and especially not for seraphim. It could be a millennium, and it would make no difference to the angel. She tried to keep Phantasos from Amanda, leaving her vulnerable to Ares. That is not something a father forgets. And, we could be incorrect. Alaric may not know who or what took our sister. You asked who has an issue with Atropos, beyond her station, and that is the only being we can come up with—not to mention it was the wedding of the Oneiroi and the Nephilim where she went missing," Lachesis responded to her mother.

"As much as I hate for my daughter to be harmed in any way. I see your point. She should never have interfered with Phantasos out of jealous rage. Did you three know Alaric's daughter was immortal, a Nephilim?" Themis asked.

"No. All we knew was that her thread began to fade, and once her demigod status was revealed, it vanished completely, meaning it could never be cut. We didn't know Alaric was a War Angel, and she was his daughter. Even the Moirai cannot see the future or the past of a seraphim," Clotho answered.

"His power supersedes ours. He kept her signature covered since her birth," Lachesis continued. "Now her powers are only second to his in all the realms, except that of the One God. Confronting the Angel or his daughter should be done with extreme caution."

"If my memory is correct, Alaric resides on earth with his wife—Hawaii, I believe it is." Themis bit her lower lip in concentration.

"Yes. He teaches humans at the adult level. In fact, I would go so far as to say that you, Mother, would enjoy a visit. From what I gather, they have a school of law where he works," Lachesis grinned widely at Themis. She knew her mother could not resist gaining more knowledge of mortal law.

"Really?" Themis grinned back. "Well, I suppose it is I who should speak with the Angel. After all, I am Atropos' mother."

"He will feel when you materialize on the island. You should go straight to him and ask for an audience. As long as you are just a concerned mother and do not go in prepared for battle, all should be well," Clotho said.

"If you hear of anything before I return, send Hermes with a message. I should return soon." Themis vanished.

Chapter Twenty-One

Monte Carlo

Warrick

Three days had gone by since Warrick found Jane unconscious on the chaise lounge outside her bedroom, causing him to be in constant fear for her safety. So, he started treating her like an invalid, stalked her every move, and worried incessantly about everything from what she ate to when she slept. He was sure she was ready to strangle him. His need to protect the woman was all-consuming, and he didn't know what else to do but dote on her and keep her safe. Unfortunately, he had only one day left to be her nursemaid before Anna went from calling every half hour to showing up and dragging him to the office. He knew he had to return to the world of business and construction, but after everything that happened, he wasn't sure he could leave her alone.

Succumbing to his new roommate's wants, Warrick would surprise her with a shopping trip. Jane had all but begged him to take her out to see the city, but he had been reluctant. So many what-ifs ran through his mind.

For the last couple of days, Jane had helped him clean up after their meals, giving in to something that made her feel *helpful*, as she put it. While doing chores alongside her, he realized he enjoyed having her in his home. He had never had a woman over for more than a night, except for Allison. She had been his only exception, and that had ended in disaster. Plus, he and Allison had never washed dishes together. In fact, he wasn't sure she knew how. He may have been worth more than even the gods could offer, but work was something he never shied away from; whether physical or mental, he was a workaholic. Even the mundane everyday tasks, he did himself.

Once the dishes were dried and put away, he told *Jane* to go get dressed in something comfortable, emphasizing shoes for walking long distances. He adored the slight tilt of her head, wanting to ask questions, but just grinned and went to change. He waited by the door, already dressed comfortably, since he knew where they were going.

"I hope this means I get to go outside of this building today," Jane said as she approached him. "Are my shoes satisfactory?"

"You look lovely. And to answer your question, you are. Actually, you are going to be outside and inside of several buildings today, including my office," Warrick placed his hand on her lower back, feeling the warmth radiate to his elbow, as he pressed the down button for the lift. He continued to guide her into the elevator with the palm of his hand, only lowering it when they were side by side, heading to the parking deck. The smile on her face made the trip worth whatever could happen.

"Jane, I have a little favor to ask of you," Warrick began as he opened her car door. She looked at him as she climbed into his Audi with questioning eyes, so he continued. "I have a fundraiser in a week. Would you consider being my date? I know it's rather last minute, but—,"

Before he explained his late request, she answered. "I would love to."

He couldn't help the smile on his face. "Thank you. We'll get your dress today." The smile on her face made his heart swell with pride.

After two hours of nonstop shopping and tons of laughter with his redheaded companion, Warrick helped her back into his car. "Next stop, my office."

"Thank you, Warrick, for taking me out. I needed this," Jane said, looking from him to the road. When he glanced over, he noticed her flushed cheeks.

"No need to thank me. I'm not normally much for shopping, but today has been enjoyable. You got several nice dresses and shoes, and I bought a new suit. Win, win," he glanced from the road to briefly look at her again, unable to keep his eyes off of her for long.

She was stunning, and he grew fonder every second he spent with her. Her behavior was often obsolete, but very elegant. She reminded him of the royals he had been around during political parties. When she laughed, he felt his chest tighten. It had only been a week, and what he was feeling troubled him. He had never been one to trust or care for a person so quickly. Most of the time, he was hyperaware that the women in his circle wanted to be seen with a billionaire and hoped to marry one. Jane didn't seem to care about his money or prestige, and damn if that didn't make her even more attractive.

Between the warmth of her forearm against his on the console and her bare leg from mid-thigh down, he was having a hard time focusing. *What were the reasons I shouldn't be lusting after this woman? Oh, yeah, she doesn't even remember her own name.*

Focusing on the turmoil within instead of what Jane was looking at, his dick twitched when she sighed out of nowhere, effectively getting his attention. She was looking at the statue on the other side of the street. She twisted in her seat to continue looking at it when he parked, and the pencil skirt crept up two more inches. *Fuck me.* He rubbed his hand down his face.

"May I take a closer look at the sculpture?" Jane asked, still turned in her seat.

"Yes, give me just a second, and I'll walk you across. The traffic gets heavy this time of day." Warrick replied. He had to rein in his desire before the entire district of Monte Carlo saw his arousal.

Once out of his car and in control, Warrick walked to her side and opened the car door. As he took her hand, he saw her eyeing his crotch when she stood. This set every part of him alight with heat. *Shit. Did she notice why I took so long to round the car?* The smirk on her face told him it was a good possibility.

Warrick had never paid much attention to the statues of any city he visited, but the one that had caught *Jane's* eye was on the route he ran every morning—Heracles, or as the Romans called him, Hercules. The statue stood proud at the corner of the intersection, with its right fist wrapped around a large club and a lion at the demigod's left side. Strapped to his back was a shield with carvings depicting the battle scene of his invasion of Troy. Minimal armor covered his marble body, showing off the Argonaut's muscular form. His legs were like tree trunks, and his chest was that of two and a half men. He stood 3.2 meters or ten and a half feet, all according to the plaque.

"Is he not magnificent?" Jane stood at the foot of the vast statue. She walked around it in awe, and Warrick found he didn't like the wonder in her eyes. *It's a fucking statue, dumbass.*

"If you like that sort of thing?" Warrick answered, not quite understanding why he was allowing the statue of a demigod to get under his skin.

"That sort of thing?" Jane's questioning eyes glanced over at him.

"Mythological beings. Do you like mythology?" He tried to turn the conversation away from his sudden disdain for the statue. *Am I jealous of a damn statue? For fuck's sake, what's this woman doing to me?*

"Mythology?" she asked. Then her eyes darted around in thought. "Myth, not real. This is a statue of someone that isn't real?" Jane asked, rubbing her temple and wincing.

The amnesia seemed to have erased more than he thought. Not knowing whether a mythological being was real was odd to him.

"How's your head? Are you okay, or should we head back to the apartment?" Warrick asked.

"I'm okay. It was just a sharp pain, but it's already subsided."

"To answer your question about the man in marble," he pointed his thumb behind him. "No. He is from stories passed down from generation to generation, to explain things like good versus evil, why wars were fought, and to teach lessons. They are just parables with unique, larger-than-life people," Warrick answered, continuing to contemplate why he didn't like *Jane's* curiosity. No woman had ever made him *jealous* of a fictional man.

"That's a shame," Jane finally turned from the hunk of marble to look at him. "Now, you were going to show me your office." She reached for his hand, and when he slid his fingers between hers, his body reacted as it did when she eyed his crotch. *Fuck me.*

When he turned to cross the street, he noticed a large black bird had landed atop the statue. *Another black bird? Odd.* He thought as he pondered whether he had ever seen one in Monaco before. Turning to face forward, he continued to hold *Jane's* hand as they crossed the street, into his building, and even in the lift. He didn't want to let her go, and she didn't seem to mind. The palm-to-palm contact felt natural.

Warrick pushed the button for the third floor. "This is one of my buildings. It's only three stories, but it houses my Monaco office, and I rent the rest to local small businesses. Once the new building is complete, I will sell this one."

"You said one of your buildings, and you are building another. Do you have more?" Jane asked as the lift doors closed.

"I do. I have a fifteen-story office building in Los Angeles, and I own a large portion of a thirty-story building in Manhattan," Warrick responded as the doors opened onto his floor, where Anna stood waiting for the elevator with large eyes. He looked at his and *Jane's* joined hands and up at Anna. *Great. She's about to give me shit.*

"Good to see you, Anna. This is *Jane. Jane*, this is Anna, my PA." Warrick didn't have time for Anna's smart mouth. Instead, he introduced them and got to the point of his visit. "I came to get everything I'll need over the next few days. I've decided to work from home until next week."

Anna's brows shot to her hairline. "What about your meetings tomorrow and Thursday, sir?"

She called him, *sir. This is not going to be good.* Anna was like him—well, the way he usually was. She worked all the time, and nothing came between her and her job, especially not relationships. Anna had lost many of her relationships over the years because of her dedication to Warrick Enterprises, of which Warrick Construction was a subsidiary.

"Please have my father and Gabe come by my apartment tomorrow, keeping their same appointment time. Reschedule Mr. Marks for Monday afternoon. Ask if the bank can do a conference call," Warrick answered, never releasing *Jane's* hand.

If the situation were about someone other than himself, he would find amusement in Anna's wide eyes and open mouth as she tried to comprehend his words. Unfortunately, he was the one who provoked his assistant, and the backlash would not be nearly as fun. She stared at his hand joined with the woman who had consumed his every waking minute.

"Are you okay, Anna?" he bit his lip to keep from grinning, knowing he was stunning her even more.

"Yes. I'll have your schedule fixed before this evening. Is there anything else, sir?" Yeah, she was not happy with him. Anna feared the repercussions of having *Jane* in his home after being hurt on company property. Her brain injury spiraled the situation into unknown territory, and Anna was convinced someone was looking for a large payout. He felt different, not that he hadn't considered it. After spending so much time with the redhead enigma, he was convinced that *Jane* was nothing but honest. *The only problem is how she will feel when her memories return.* The nagging question popped up when he least expected it.

Warrick noticed *Jane's* head moving between him and his PA. He also caught the narrowing of her eyes when Anna spoke. How he wished he could read her mind, because he was sure she was reading the room wrong.

"No. Thank you for holding down the fort while I help *Jane*," Warrick grinned at his assistant.

"No problem. How are you feeling, Jane? Has your doctor given you a timeline for recovery?" Anna turned her full attention to what she considered the problem at hand. He had never seen Anna being catty.

Chapter Twenty-Two
Staggering

Jane (Atropos)

Jane watched the back-and-forth between Warrick and the beautiful woman he called his PA. She tried to piece the relationship together without knowing what a PA was. What she knew was that Anna did not like her, and the only reason she could think of was jealousy. *It's my hand he is holding.* The possessive thought ran through her mind, catching her off guard.

"I haven't seen the healer since I left the hospital. Regrettably, he wasn't able to tell us, since everyone is different," she raised their clasped hands in a show of who the "us" was. "Only that they may not return."

"So, you're saying your memories may never come back? That sounds scary. How do you deal with that?" Anna asked, and *Jane* could see the skepticism behind her question.

"It's difficult. I don't know what I would have done if Warrick had not been kind enough to help me. Not remembering things about myself feels like my brain is waging against its owner. How long have you and Warrick worked together?" Jane turned the interrogation back on the assistant, looking between her and Warrick for her answer.

"Several years now," Anna turned toward Warrick's office, beckoning them to follow. "I've worked with him at all of his locations, and he and I built the Monaco sites from the ground up."

"That's nice." She watched Warrick take in their conversation before he let her hand go and asked her to sit on the visitor's side of his desk as he gathered paperwork. Anna stayed in the doorway with her arms crossed over her chest.

"Thank you again, Anna. You should come over tomorrow night and have dinner with us. This was *Jane's* first day outside the apartment, and I bet seeing people other than just myself and the housekeeper will help her healing process," Warrick said as he rummaged through files.

"Would it be okay if I brought a date?" Anna asked.

Warrick popped his head up and looked at his PA with what *Jane* considered curiosity, or—*was he now jealous?*

"Of course, but I had no idea you were dating someone. Who's the lucky girl?" Warrick asked, then returned to his hunt for files.

Wait. What? Was her date a girl? Maybe she didn't have to be upset over their exchange after all.

Jane tossed and turned all night. A feeling of unease started when she left Warrick's side on the couch, after their movie, to prepare for bed. The sensation of someone or something watching her began the second she entered her bedroom. Needing a distraction, she turned the television to a show she had been watching about Greece. Several people in the hospital had mentioned she had a thick, old-Greek accent, so she wanted to know more about the land from which she had inherited her lilt. Surely, it was a step in the right direction. Unfortunately, nothing she saw on the show sparked a memory.

After a dozen sighs and switching from lying on her left side to her right multiple times, Jane decided that a drink might help. She ventured into the kitchen to prepare a warm cup of tea and a biscuit. She hadn't donned a robe since Warrick would be asleep, and what she needed was to shake off her uneasiness and move around while upright instead of destroying her covers any further.

Walking down the hallway, she heard sounds coming from the living room. As she rounded the corner, she could see the light from the TV and indistinct murmurs of people on the screen. She looked around and saw Warrick had fallen asleep on the couch. Tightness in her chest led her to his side. He was mesmerizing. Thick black hair stuck up in all directions, and his stubble was longer than usual, defining his sharp jawline. With his eyelids shut, she could tell exactly how long his eyelashes were lying atop his cheekbone. The large man looked peaceful and younger than when awake. His arms were folded across his broad chest, well-defined muscles even in slumber. Oh, she wished she could touch him. If he only wanted her as she did him.

As the thought left her, Warrick stirred and blinked open his eyes. They were so bright blue that she could tell their color just by the light the television emitted. She watched as those eyes, without shame, took her in from her head to her toes. That was when she remembered she was wearing only a thin camisole and panties.

Jane's face heated as she stumbled over her words. "I'm sorry. I couldn't sleep. So, I decided to get some tea. Then I heard noise in here and—,"

Before she could get out her excuse for standing over him while he slept, Warrick pulled her by her hip down onto him. Those blue eyes boring into hers had her tingling all over, and when his hand clenched her hair and pulled her mouth to his, she moaned. In seconds, they were nothing but lips, tongues, and teeth frantically devouring each other.

He sat upright, her still on his lap. Surely if she had ever experienced such before, she would have remembered it. He was all-consuming. His smell, his taste, his—*is that?* When he pushed up against her heat, he answered her unspoken question. Yes, that was his erection. She was making him this way, and that made her feel powerful.

He pulled his lips from hers, just centimeters, but it felt like miles. "I've wanted to do that since you woke up in that hospital."

"Curious. I've wanted you to do that since I woke up in the hospital," Jane smiled, then lowered her mouth back to his.

Warrick removed his hands from the thick strands of her soft hair, clasped her camisole at its delicate lace hem, and asked, "May I?"

With her slight nod, her eyes trained on him, she raised her arms above her head and melted when his devilish half grin confirmed where the night was headed. When he lifted her top from her body, she felt the cool air on her already erect nipples that ached with need. He noticed and latched his warm mouth onto her left one and pinched her right one between his fingers.

"Fuck, Warrick," she leaned her head back and groaned.

"That's the idea." She felt his smile on her breast when he spoke. He ran his tongue from between her breasts, up her neck, and back to her mouth.

"Eros, have mercy, that feels amazing," she moaned.

Chapter Twenty-Three

First Time

Eros? Wasn't he the god of sexual desire? Warrick continued his divine servicing of *Jane's* body but wondered about the odd mythological phrases and words she often used. She was definitely different from anyone he had ever known—but damn, she tasted amazing. Never had he felt so fixated on a woman. This wasn't only about trying to bury himself deep inside her; it was about consuming her body and soul, and while doing so, wrecking the memories of other men that were eventually going to come back. He was determined that when her memories surfaced, he would be the only one she remembered devouring her because she was the only woman he wanted.

Her little moans had his erection so hard that the only control he had was animalistic at best, driven by instinct. Before he realized what he was doing, he stood and her legs wrapped around him like a vice, keeping their mouths together as he set off for his bedroom. His hands gripped the junction where her ass and the backs of her thighs met, and when his fingers skimmed wet heat, he almost stumbled. *Fuck me.*

Once inside his room, he sat her on the edge of his bed. Kneeling in front of her, his face was met with wet, lacy panties that matched the camisole they left on the couch. Unable to help himself, he leaned forward, ran his nose up her slick knickers, and inhaled her scent. The smell of pussy always made him weak in the knees, but hers, well, hers smelled like sweet arousal and lavender. With his tongue, he lifted the gusset of her underwear and allowed only a brush of it to the edge of her lips, causing her to pull his hair and demand more. He couldn't help his triumphant grin. She was so wet and writhing under his mouth. He needed to taste more. Kissing her through the material, she rewarded him with more moans of pleasure.

"You react to me so well, gorgeous," he said as he gently bit her clit through her panties.

Curling his fingers around the thin material, he dragged it down her legs—her pussy fully bared to him made him feral with need. *Friction, I need friction.*

"You are stunning," Warrick told *Jane* as he drank in her naked body. "Can I have you tonight, *Jane*?"

"Yes," she looked him straight in the eyes and demanded. "Don't you dare stop."

Warrick stood and walked to his bedside table, pulled out a sleeve of condoms, and tossed three onto the bed beside her.

"What are those?" she asked. He blinked.

What the actual fuck? Is she serious? The curious look on her face said she was very serious.

"Condoms. I wear them over my erection while we fuck." How else was he supposed to explain it? He needed to get inside her. Sooner rather than later. Explanations were not coming to him—all of his blood was in his dick.

"Why?"

Warrick was unprepared to answer such strange questions about protection, and her not knowing concerned him. "For protection against diseases and pregnancy. Have you never had your partners use protection before?"

"I can't remember doing this—I'm sorry." She closed her legs and scooted back on the bed, wrapping her arms around herself as much as possible. He had embarrassed her and needed to fix the problem since pre-cum was dripping from the head of his cock.

"That's okay. Please don't worry yourself. I'll use one and protect you and myself, even though I've been tested and I'm clean." He could see the confusion on her face, so he explained without slang. "Clean means when a doctor checked me, they confirmed I was disease-free. So, as long as you are, these are more for protection against pregnancy. I know you haven't been using birth control pills, but since you cannot remember your medical history, we don't know if you have an IUD or another form of contraception in place."

"Okay. I don't know what most of that meant, but I understand that by using those," she pointed at the foil squares next to her, "I won't end up with a baby."

He watched her relax. *Damn, she's cute.* "Yes. That's correct." Well, ninety-eight percent effective, but he wasn't about to say that out loud. His only immediate concern was being inside her, not debating how well rubbers worked.

When she gave him a sheepish smile, he knew all was good and grabbed the neck of his t-shirt and pulled it over his head just before crawling across the mattress toward her. It took less than a minute to have her dripping with need again, and before another verbal lesson in sex could come up, he was sheathed and at her entrance.

"Fuck!" Just the head, and she was so tight he knew a hard push would be painful for her. "You are so warm and so fucking tight."

"Don't stop," Jane panted and writhed beneath him, and if she wasn't careful, he wouldn't be able to hold back from thrusting to the hilt.

On her command, he gave her another couple of inches. The only time he had ever experienced such a tight pussy was in his sophomore year in college, and his girlfriend had been a virgin. *Surely not.* Warrick raised his head and looked into her eyes. "*Jane.* Are you a virgin?"

"Like I told you. I don't remember ever doing this, but whether it's because of my amnesia or the fact I've never done it, I'm not sure."

"If you're a virgin," he was having trouble holding still because she felt so damn good, "then this is probably going to hurt some."

"I don't care, Warrick. I want you—now." She trembled, and he fought to keep from burying himself balls deep. A thin layer of sweat coated his whole body with the effort it took to keep steady.

With a slow push, he sank himself to the hilt. *Jane* gasped and drove her fingernails across his back. He stilled, allowing her to adjust to his size. White spots filled his vision when he looked down to see if she was okay. Both were panting—he, to keep from ravaging her, and she with fullness and pain. When he pulled back and looked down, the condom glistened with her arousal and streaks of her virgin blood. *She has to be at least twenty-five. How is she still a virgin?* He heard the rattle of art and knick-knacks as the earth shuddered. Her eyes flew wide.

"No need to fret, baby, we get minor quakes here on occasion. Nothing unusual. Are you okay?" Warrick asked as he kissed each of her closed eyelids and brushed hair from her face. "I won't move until you have adjusted." Damn, he had never experienced such a connection. His chest ached to see the pain on her face, but he needed to be with her deep inside her. There was no choice. *Mine.*

"I'm good." Jane said as she writhed underneath him showing him that she was ready.

With slow, languid thrusts, he moved inside the most beautiful woman he had ever met. It didn't take long before bliss replaced her discomfort. The little whimpers and moans she made had him wanting to claim every part of her. Not just her body, everything. *Mine.* How would he let her go once she remembered who she was? *I won't. She's mine,* the mantra continued with every beat of his heart.

Chapter Twenty-Four
Mothers

THEMIS/ADAIR

Humans, goddesses, or creatures, it made no difference—all loved their children with a vengeance. It didn't matter that Themis was the goddess of Divine Law and Order, the goddess of justice, and the second wife of Zeus. Her primary reason for existence was the title of Mother of The Fates and Horae, and one of her daughters was missing. Going into the den of a lion was one thing, but to step toe-to-toe with a war angel, most would consider suicide. And that was precisely what she was about to do—because she was a mother, and the angel knew where her daughter was. She felt it in her bones.

After leaving her other daughters on Olympus, she materialized on the doorstep of the angel's home in the human realm. She stood with her hands on her hips, waiting for Alaric to open his door. She knew he felt her presence, and he did not disappoint when the door opened.

"Goddess, how can I help you?" Alaric grinned at her, continuing to stand just inside his doorway.

"Are you not going to invite me in, Angel?" She needed to be inside, where she could feel her daughter's signature if she was even there.

He held the door open and gestured for her to enter. "I'll ask again, Themis. How can I help you?"

"We both know why I am here. But to play your little game, where is my daughter?" Themis asked. She couldn't feel Atropos' presence, which increased her anxiety. *What if he had nothing to do with her disappearance?*

"Which daughter? Don't you have six? The Horae and the Moirai." Alaric smirked.

"For Zeus' sake, you know which one—Atropos."

"She is where she should be, Themis." Alaric's eyes turned from mischievous to serious in a blink.

"And that is?" She felt her body tremble with fear. She mentally recited the mantra: *He is good and would not hurt my child.*

Alaric touched her shoulder, immediately calming her racing thoughts. "Your daughter needed a lesson in humility, and she needed to understand that just because she was given an essential station in life—one that affects all races of beings—does not mean she should control everyone's God-given right to free will. She overstepped her bounds by interfering in Amanda and Phantasos' relationship. She did it out of petty jealousy." Alaric's serious eyes were now glowing, and she could see the aura of his true identity. "Your daughter is—,"

Before he finished his sentence, an immense tremor shook the foundation of the immortal world. His glowing eyes enlarged, and a sincere smile spread over the angel's face. "Your daughter is well, Themis. And that feeling we both just had confirmed it."

"What does that mean? Where is she?" She could hear the fear in her own voice. *What just happened?*

"I have placed your daughter with the person she should be with. Trust me, though—no one will understand this for centuries. Many will try to stop it. I've put in place what must be. Atropos is on earth and will soon be in many realms. Telling you not to interfere will be a waste of my breath, because there is nothing you can do."

"You speak in circles. Where on earth is my child? She is a Greek Fate—the one who cuts the threads of life. Beings of all realms despise her for the mantle she holds—the one she was never given a choice in. The human realm is not the place for her. She should be with her sisters and safe on Olympus." She begged the war angel to heed reason.

"What I've set in motion comes from above. No one, not even Zeus, will be capable of stopping it." She felt his challenge. She knew the angel did not lie.

"What was the quake we just witnessed?" Themis demanded.

"It was the bond of the next *fix*. In due time, all will understand. But, as with everything that came before, trust will be the issue. Know that Atropos will no longer feel the need to go beyond her station to harm anyone. She will know true love and sacrifice because she will live it. Now, I was about to leave for a conference in Monaco. You should let the Greek Pantheon know that their thread cutter is alive, well, and doing the work she was meant to do. Once you find her—and you will—remember that I told you not to interfere."

Themis blinked and stood in the bedchamber of her home on Olympus. The Angel's dismissal was powerful, and his words were concerning. *What has he done?*

Time between realms works independently. Not one mimics the other. Ten days in one realm could mean minutes in another. Moments in the realms of the Tuatha Dé Danann equaled a couple of days in the human realm. The Greek and Roman pantheons were the closest in time sync with the human realm. Why? Who knew but the Creator himself? Because of the time difference and as Adair mustered the courage to answer her father's question, a shudder passed through the Celtic realm.

"What was that?" Adair asked, looking between The Morrigan and Dagda for answers. She, being the strongest of seers, had never had to ask another what was happening. She always knew before anyone else. This time was different. There had been nothing to see. The realm shook, and from the looks on her parents' faces, they were just as confused.

"It felt like the realm shook," Dagda stated, in his rumbling, ancient Irish accent.

Her mother closed her eyes for a second, and when she opened them, the sclera had taken over. Her irises and pupils were no longer visible. Solid white—she was now an oracle. It was the same thing Adair did when purposefully looking for something. However, for her, that was rare. She saw things on a continuous loop without trying. Being only partly in her own world and mostly in everyone else's was why she fractured after leaving Alasdair in the mortal realm. The moment she turned from him, the world opened up without her trying to see, driving her almost mad. It was that insanity that drove her to seek help from her father.

Over seven millennia had passed, and Dagda did not know of her existence. When she entered Tuatha Dé Danann, half-crazed from clairvoyance, demanding to see her king, her father took her in, and the rage toward the love of his life began. When he learned that his lost daughter had borne several children, he rejoiced to have them in his line of succession. How would she tell him about Alasdair?

The Morrigan blinked three times, and her irises returned to the beguiling emerald green with hints of amber. Her mother was pale, and for the first time in her seven and a half thousand years, Adair saw panic on her harbinger's face. Adair shuddered in fear.

"Mother, what did you see?" Adair stood, holding her breath.

Eyes still glossy, Morrigan answered. "I saw the child of Fate—the child of Death. Two powerful gods from royal lines combined into one seemingly innocent babe. One so powerful that if turned bad, all will be lost." Then, for the first time, she witnessed The Morrigan, the Phantom Queen, and Harbinger of Death, pass out.

Chapter Twenty-Five

Centaurs and Headaches

Atropos (Jane)

Roman shades blocked the sun from the dark room Atropos found herself in. She could faintly make out the outlines of the massive windows and *his* scent. Oh, gods, her head ached. Memories surged of chirping machines, blood-soaked hair, Phantasos' wedding to the Nephilim, and falling from Olympus. She sat up, allowing the sheet to pool around her waist. Forgetting she was bare-chested, she felt the air on her breasts, but her concern was with the torture she felt in her head. She pulled her knees to her chest and squeezed her temples. *I fell. I was injured.* Every memory flash caused immense pain that radiated from the back of her head to her eyes. Even her teeth hurt.

"Jane, are you okay?" the deep male voice said from the darkness.

She felt him. The soft hair and heat of his chest pressed against her side. He was the first man she had ever touched other than a hug from her father when she and her sisters were young. *My sisters.* Sharp pain had her tighten further into herself—pressing her palms against her temples.

"Please answer me, Jane." She could hear the distress in his voice.

Somehow, she managed to nod. "Yes. It's my head."

Sensual heat came off his hand in waves as he gently stroked up and down her back. When his lips caressed her shoulder, she knew it was out of concern and not him trying to seduce her.

My virginity. It's gone. Do my sisters know? Another wave of pain shot through her brain. It felt like it bounced from one side of her head to the other, begging to be let out. She wished she could let the agony go; what she would give in that moment to release the pressure. *What have I done?*

"I'll bring you something to help." She felt the absence of his touch and the bed shift.

Waterfalls, meadows of lavender, centaurs guarding her home, three thrones, endless threads all took their turn running through her broken mind. The pressure had to be the flood of memories vying to be noticed. She was thousands of years old with memories of them all. *Could this pain last that long?*

"Here, take these." She felt the bed dip and warmth return.

She managed to free only one hand from her head and took the tiny white tablets with water. *Now that I know, will human medication help this?* Next, she felt a cold cloth pressed to the back of her neck.

"Please don't be upset with me. I took the liberty of contacting the doctor. He will be here in less than half an hour," Warrick said.

She could hear the worry in his voice and knew if she were to argue, he would be ready for the verbal battle and win. Atropos couldn't tell him the truth. She wasn't able to speak. With every beat of her heart, the pain intensified.

Not only were the memories of being a goddess poured into her mind, but the memories of all the threads she cut bore down on her.

"I'm going to get you something to wear for when the doctor gets here. I'll be right back."

It was a miracle that the doctors had not discovered that she was so different from the humans they healed while she was in the hospital. *What if he can tell now? I need to get out of here.* She tried to open her eyes. Black and yellow spots were the only things visible. She wasn't going anywhere. *How did this happen?*

With what the physician called a shot of relief, Atropos could finally release her head and relax a little. Cold tingling in the back of her head let her know the torture was waiting patiently to return once the medication left her system. *Could this be my chance to leave?* Her eyelids became heavy. So heavy, she couldn't keep them open, no matter how hard she fought. Still in Warrick's bed, sleep consumed her.

Jane woke still in Warrick's room, with a slight headache and disjointed dreams. Unfortunately, whatever those slumbered visions were of, she had no memory. She tried to stretch and realized that two arms were encapsulating her. His touch had her recalling what had just happened between them. A shift she didn't understand happened deep inside her chest.

"Do you feel any better?" Warrick's deep, sleepy voice sliced through her thoughts.

"I feel okay. You?"

Warrick chuckled. "You woke in so much pain you had to be knocked out, and you're asking me how I am." He kissed her temple and pulled her tighter against him. "You are selfless."

What is he talking about? "Knocked out?" She questioned. "What do you mean?"

"When you woke, unable to look up or stop squeezing your head in agony, the doctor gave you an injection to stop the migraine," Warrick said.

"When?" That was all she could get out when a shudder of dread shot up her spine.

"You've been unconscious for close to eleven hours. You slept the day away. And because you can now hold a conversation, I believe it was for the best." Warrick laid her on her back and leaned over, looking into her eyes. "Do you not remember?"

Jane swallowed before answering. With a whisper, she replied, "No. I don't remember."

Warrick continued looking into her eyes. He traced her cheek with his fingertip and looked concerned, with the deep crease between his eyes. "What is the last thing you recall?"

She felt the flush start at the top of her chest and steadily climb to her hairline. "I uh—I remember being with you." She looked away; even in the dark room, she didn't want him to see her embarrassment.

"I'm glad that was memorable. If you had forgotten, not only would it have been humiliating—living together would be awkward as hell when I crawled into your bed naked."

She couldn't help but giggle. He had a way of making her feel comfortable. "So after—uh—we—uh," she was having trouble verbalizing what they had done.

Warrick pulled her on top of him, directly over his, *gods help me,* semihard cock. She was thankful to be wearing a t-shirt and shorts.

"Say it, Jane. After we, what?" She could see the smirk on his lips and the amusement in his eyes.

"After we had sex," she bashfully covered her face. He removed her hands. She felt him harden.

"Don't hide from me, Jane. I want you to always be uninhibited with me, especially when we are in bed together."

Jane bit the inside of her lip and looked down at the man who had saved her. "What happened to me?"

Warrick sat up, with her still on his lap, and moved the hair away from her eye and tucked it behind her ear. "You woke in severe pain. I thought you would break your teeth as tight as you gritted them. I gave you pain tablets, but I knew they wouldn't be able to touch the agony you were in. So, I called the doctor. He made a house call and injected you with pain medication, hoping they would work. Now here we are."

"I have no recollection of any of that."

"He wants to see you in one week if you continue to have headaches." Warrick continued to stroke her everywhere except the spot where she was growing the need to be touched.

She wiggled against his erection. His eyes narrowed. "Behave," he scolded.

"It sounds like I'm good for now," she smiled down at him. She couldn't help but search for friction. *What is wrong with me?*

"As much as I want a repeat of last night. The physician just saw you, and I think you should rest without me pawing at you," Warrick said, rubbing his hands up and down her back.

"How long?" she asked.

"What do you mean?" Warrick pulled back and winked. "Let's wait a few hours. You just woke. I want to make sure you're better first. Yes, I know my words contradict what my body is saying, but I'm determined to listen to my brain right now. Lay here," Warrick turned the television on. "Watch TV, and I'll make you something to eat. Rest." He kissed her on the forehead, and she watched as he exited the bedroom. *His bedroom.*

Chapter Twenty-Six
Soup Talk

Warrick

Rummaging through the pantry, Warrick looked for something Jane could eat after having such a rough time. He decided on homemade vegetable soup. Since the soup would take a long time to prepare, he pulled together toast with butter and a thin layer of Marmite, hoping to curb her body's need for immediate nutrition and stave off another migraine.

His mother had migraines, and watching her battle them since he was a boy wasn't easy. Knowing the redhead who had crawled under his skin had the same issues made him determined to fix it—or at least make her as comfortable as possible.

After slicing the vegetables and pouring in the stock, he plated two slices of spread toast, a few pieces of fresh fruit, and ice water, then took them to Jane, who was still in his bed. Where he had decided she would stay.

"This is just the appetizer," Warrick said as he placed the tray over Jane's legs. "I'm making homemade vegetable soup, but you need something on your stomach now, so," he waved his hand over the food.

"Thank you, Warrick. You didn't have to do this. I feel fine. I would have—,"

"Don't you dare finish that sentence. It's been a long day and a half, and you need rest. Don't argue," Warrick insisted, trying to hide his smile. "After you've eaten your toast, I would like for us to talk. If you don't mind?"

Studying her enlarged eyes, peeking over the bite she was in the middle of, confirmed she knew about what. "Sure." Jane chewed—slowly.

Knowing she was dragging this meal out to keep from speaking with him, Warrick smirked, grabbed the TV control, "May I?" and leaned against the headboard. He had an hour before he needed to add anything else to the soup. She could take her time and avoid their talk.

Her overwhelming smell of lavender made his dick twitch, reminding him of the way she smelled when he was between her thighs. *How does she continue to smell amazing after hot and sticky sex, sweaty sleep, and the headache from hell? She needs to relax.*

"Where are you going?" Jane asked when he rose and rounded the bed.

"While you're finishing up, I'm going to run you a warm bath."

"I thought you wanted to talk."

"That can wait until after you've done a little more relaxing. Besides, I'm sure the activities over the last twenty hours have made you sore." The immediate blush across her cheeks had him fighting not to grin or boast.

He completed the soup's final touches after settling Jane into the jacuzzi. The recipe came from his grandmother, and as a little boy it always made him feel better when he was sick.

Making the soup reminded him he needed to call his mum. He knew his mum loved him; he had little doubt. He supposed his father did too, but he was so self-absorbed that unless you were talking about investments, construction, or real estate, he just wasn't that interested. Did he provide a pleasant life for himself and his mother? Yes. Did he care what they did all day—absolutely not. He hadn't spoken with his mother in a couple of weeks and supposed he should see how she was.

Remembering that he had left his cell on his bedside table, he quietly went to retrieve it. When he opened the bedroom door, he heard a slight humming, followed by singing. *Is that the Seikilos Epitaph? Interesting.*

He wondered whether she realized what she was doing. Clearly remembering all the words to the oldest known ancient Greek song had to mean she was gaining some recall. After grabbing his phone, he leaned against his bedroom door listening to her. She turned the upbeat song slow and methodical. Each word was expressed as if she needed the listener to heed her words—her warning to enjoy their remaining time. Chills ran down his arms.

"I love you too, mum," Warrick said just before he hung up the phone and noticed Jane standing in the doorway of his kitchen wearing nothing but a terrycloth towel.

"How long have you been standing there?" Warrick asked.

She was still dripping, so he thought she couldn't have been listening long. He didn't care if she overheard his conversation with his mother, but the call prior to the one with his mother wouldn't have been a conversation he would want her to hear.

Lucia couldn't seem to take no for an answer. She called and insisted he meet her and explain the radio silence. He reminded her that the last time he had seen her, she had broken into his home and waited for over an hour, naked, and he made her leave. She hung up. No, that wasn't one he wanted Jane to overhear.

"For just a minute. That was your mother?" Jane asked as she padded over to where he stood. "The soup smells delicious."

"Yes, that was my mum. She knew I was going back and forth to the hospital, but she had no idea you were living in my apartment. And the soup has about an hour before it is ready, so why don't you get dressed?" He couldn't believe he was telling her to put clothes on. "I'll wait for you in the living room." From the tilt of Jane's head, he guessed she couldn't believe he was having her put clothes on either.

Warrick paced the living room, trying to decide how to start a discussion about virginity when the croaking sound of a giant black bird on his terrace stopped him dead in his tracks. "What the hell. Is that—yes, it is. I haven't been going crazy."

Slowly, he walked over to the glass door. The raven watched his every move, tilting its head from side to side. Once he touched the latch, the raven took a couple of hops toward him. With the door open and nothing but fresh air between him and the enormous creature, his heart raced with excitement. Its eyes were so unusual. Who knew ravens' eyes were green and so humanlike? Its feathers looked as if they would be silky to the touch. Its crooked beak had to be nearly ten centimeters long. How could such a creature exist in this area? Ravens weren't indigenous to Monaco. Neither were crows—and he had been seeing black birds everywhere since—*that day at the hospital. One crashed into the window.*

A slight noise came from the living room, and the bird peered around his leg, so he looked to see what was behind him. Jane stood beside the couch, her hand over her mouth, eyes wide as saucers, looking at the feathered giant at his feet. "Is that—,"

Before Jane could fully ask her question, the raven took flight, and she grabbed her head. "Shit, Jane." Warrick ran to her side, leaving the door open.

"Jane, are you okay?" *Not again.* "This can't be happening again so soon." He guided her to the couch.

"Yes. I just had a stabbing pain shoot through my head from my eye to here," she pressed her hand to the crown of her head. "It's gone now. I suppose it was leftover from earlier. Was that a giant black bird on your balcony?"

"Yes. Wasn't it magnificent? What's even stranger than it allowing me so close, they're not supposed to be here."

"They don't allow birds around your apartment? That seems hard to control." Jane continued to rub her browbone.

Warrick chuckled. "No. That was a raven. Ravens and their smaller counterparts, crows, don't live in Monte Carlo. I thought I had been going crazy, seeing large and super large black birds everywhere."

"That is strange. How do you think it got here?" Jane asked. She had finally stopped massaging her head. Looked like their conversation would happen after all.

"I've heard some people keep ravens as pets, although I've never known anyone who's done it. They can live in the forested area of Monaco, but not around here. From what I gather, they are brilliant animals and can be taught to speak." Warrick picked her feet up and slid under them to sit beside her. If he was going to ask invasive questions, he should make sure she was as comfortable as possible.

"Really? Are you—how is it they say it on TV? Are you pulling my leg?" Jane's smile was wide. He could tell she was proud of herself for knowing the idiom.

"It's what I've read," he shrugged. "Now, how are you, really?" Warrick began massaging the arch of her right foot. All bird talk needed to end. He wanted to get to know her better.

"I'm good. It really was just one sharp pain. My head isn't hurting right now. What did your mother say about me living here with you?"

Warrick wasn't expecting to answer questions; he was prepared to ask them. "She's a little concerned, but I put her at ease."

"I'm sorry I'm making things hard. Hopefully, I will start remembering soon. It's almost been a fortnight," Jane moaned when he pressed his thumb into her arch, cutting off her apology.

"I wanted to talk to you about last night before we fell asleep. Before you woke in so much pain," he glanced from her cute toes to her face, and indeed she was flushed from the mere mention of the only time he'd been buried inside her.

"Uh—okay," she audibly swallowed, and he decided she was adorable when embarrassed.

"When I pulled out, the condom was coated in your delectable wetness and—blood. I know you were a virgin. Why would you give such a gift to me?" Warrick asked, still rubbing her feet, trying to provide some comfort. Now that the question was out, he decided he didn't want her to be uncomfortable anymore. He teetered on the edge of playful and sincere, sometimes wanting her to flush with embarrassment and other times, like now, he tried to protect her from it.

Chapter Twenty-Seven

Not So Fast

Jane (Atropos)

Jane looked everywhere but at the man holding her feet. He stopped his massage and waited for her to answer. The only problem was that she didn't have one. She suspected she was a novice in the flesh. *What would he do if I just got up and went to my room?* Having intercourse and speaking about it were two vastly different things.

"I'm not really sure how to answer your question. I suspected I hadn't much experience, but a virgin, I wasn't sure. Why did I give it to you? I suppose the better question is, why would I allow you to—," she bit the inside of her cheek, thinking before she continued. "To enter me when I was so unsure. The answer is, I wanted you. I have since the hospital. I decided if I were completely inexperienced, then you were the one I wanted to be with." She refused to look him in the face. "For Zeus' sake, this is an uncomfortable topic of conversation."

She felt him lean toward her, and with one finger, he lifted her chin and demanded she open her eyes. "Look at me, gorgeous. You have nothing to be ashamed of or bashful over. Nothing. Last night was the best night of my life, well, until you woke in agony from your head. But our time together in my bed was—more. You are more."

"More?" Jane questioned.

"More than I could ever want. The last two weeks have been a roller coaster. But, amidst the ups and downs, you inched your way under my skin. When I woke up, and you were in so much pain, I thought I was going to lose it, and I blamed myself for what we did—thinking it was too soon. I even asked the doctor," Warrick searched her eyes for—what—she didn't know.

"You asked the doctor if you harmed me with sex?" Mortified, she covered her face with her hands. "I cannot believe you did that. What did he say?" *Did I just ask him that?* She most definitely didn't want to know what the doctor thought about her losing her virginity just hours before her head began its torture session.

"I told him we were together—and it was your first time." He shifted around on the sofa. "I was worried since it hasn't been long since you were in a coma and hooked to machines. In fact, I felt pretty damn shitty for it. A medical opinion was necessary. Morally, the guilt already weighed heavily on me. He told me that the first time for a woman was most always painful, but the intimacy went a long way in helping you heal from the trauma. Since you no longer have bruising, and your head injury is completely healed, he gave us the go-ahead to continue."

She watched his tongue dart out to lick his lower lip just before biting it, obviously waiting for her response to the doctor's permission. It was his turn to squirm. He returned to rubbing her feet. Uncomfortable conversation or not, he was a master at foot massage.

"So, what you're saying is," she moved her feet from his lap to the floor, "I'm clear to be in compromising positions with you again?"

A mischievous grin split his face. "You're good to resume sex, and I would love for you to choose me to experiment with and possibly master a few compromising positions. In fact, I would consider myself the luckiest bloke in all of Europe."

She laughed at his wit and watched him go from serious to playful as he rose to meet her. All she could muster was a nod, and before she had another thought, he tossed her over his shoulder like a sack of grain.

"You brute!" Jane laughed at Warrick's antics. He slapped her ass. Once in his room, he gently lowered her to the floor where they stood toe-to-toe at the end of his bed. Goosebumps rose over her entire body when he brushed her hair over her shoulder and latched his mouth onto her neck.

"That feels wonderful," her head tipped back, and he ravaged her neck and the swells of her breasts with tiny licks, open-mouthed kisses, and a few nibbles.

"You like that? He pulled back and looked her straight in the eyes."

"Yes." She took in his reddened lips from where he pillaged her upper body. His pupils were blown with lust, showing he was as turned on from touching her as she was from being touched.

"Arms up," Warrick demanded, just before pulling her top over her head. Cupping both of her breasts, he leaned his head down and rolled his tongue around each nipple.

She tugged at the hem of his shirt. It wasn't fair that he was still fully dressed, and she was not. Her hands itched to touch his warm, tanned flesh. Divesting him of his t-shirt gave her the opportunity to crawl onto his bed. She didn't get far. Mid-crawl, he tugged her back to the edge.

"Not so fast, gorgeous."

Jane looked over her shoulder and saw pure, unadulterated lust and awe on Warrick's face. She watched him lick and bite his lower lip as he traced her back, ass, and legs with his eyes.

"Stay like that," he demanded, then grabbed her sleep shorts to roll them off her ass down her legs.

Helping him, she lifted each knee, and once they were removed, she was utterly naked, ass in the air, where he had the most intimate view of her. She just thought she had seen desire on his face. Nothing could match the look he was giving her pussy.

His nose flared, and he didn't blink. Trying to wake him from the momentary trance she seemed to have put him in; she shook her ass. His eyes flicked to hers.

"Gorgeous?" His eyes were wild with need, and that made her clit burn, needing to be touched.

"Yes?" Jane's eyes stayed locked onto him.

"I'm about to devour you. Any objections?" Warrick reached for a condom, tossing it beside her.

"None," she watched as he removed his pants and boxer briefs, then as he gave himself a couple of lazy strokes before lowering his mouth to her core. He flattened his tongue and licked her from clit to asshole. *Fuck me!* The euphoria from that single act outweighed her mortification of having his tongue in her ass. *Oh, dear gods and goddesses.* It only took two more passes with his tongue over her slick pussy to have her muscles bunching tightly, followed by a release of pure ecstasy, leaving tingles all over, with her muscles feeling heavy like she had wrestled with a sphinx or an animal equally as large and not one man's tongue.

Jane dared a glance behind her once her vision had righted itself to catch Warrick rolling the condom over his length. She shook with anticipation. Never had she needed something so bad. One would think an orgasm like the one she just had would have sated some of her need, but it was the opposite. The ache in her core was almost unbearable.

"Please, Warrick."

"Please, what, gorgeous?"

"Fuck me, Warrick."

Still looking over her shoulder, she saw him smirk as he pushed into her. This time, it was only a momentary burn that faded as soon as he pulled back, just before he pushed deeper. With three strokes, he was seated to the hilt, and she was moaning his name.

Chapter Twenty-Eight
Audience with Zeus

Themis

With a thought, Themis called for the two Fates left on Olympus and told them to meet her at their father's mansion. There was no time to dwell; the angel had done something that was changing the course of everything, and Zeus needed to know.

Materializing in the atrium of Zeus and Hera's home, took a lot of self-restraint and humility. After thousands of years, she still hated how Hera maneuvered her way into Zeus' arms. After six daughters with the god-king, she was relocated to a life without him. Her only saving grace was that her six daughters were more formidable than any he had with that bitch. Helping to ensure Hera left her alone. Since Ares had gotten himself locked away for a thousand years, it was time to indulge in a bit of mischief herself. *Within the law, of course.*

She wasn't inside the hall for a second before Clotho and Lachesis were beside her. It took only a second more before a daimon greeted them.

"Moirai, Themis, what can we do for you today?" The daimon formally asked, as if she had not been the one to place him in his station.

"My daughters and I would like an audience with Zeus—and only Zeus." Themis narrowed her eyes at the servant.

"He and the queen—," Themis felt herself stiffen. *How dare he throw that fact in my face?* "—are in the throne room. I will let Zeus know." The daimon turned on his heel and left them standing in the king's entryway.

"The arrogance of the help. I placed him in his position here," Themis spat out as soon as the demigod servant left them. "How can he forget so easily?"

"Remember, Mother. Hera rules through fear. Even her staff regard her power—they know not to betray her in any way. And might I remind you—other than Zenovia, you are most hated amongst her enemies," Lachesis spoke as she looked over the statues lining the walls.

"True, I suppose. However, Zeus and Zenovia were never married," Themis said as Zeus materialized before them. He still took her breath away. Other than a couple of lonely nights over the last ten thousand years, she had seen little of the only man she ever loved. Seeing him standing before her in the home she made for them, stung. Those lonely nights had been recent but still months. The longing she felt vanished the second Hera appeared behind him. She heard herself growl and felt her daughters stiffen at the sight of the goddess who ruined their mother's life. Zeus' lips twitched—*bastard*. He was probably thinking about the last time he was in her bed, and his queen had no idea. Not that Hera didn't have her own affairs. Apparently, things were different when you lived forever—or so Zeus told her when she caught him and Hera together. Thousands of years later, she would never get that moment out of her head. He had shattered her heart, and now she hoped karma would pay a visit to his wife.

"Daughters, Themis, how can we help you?" Zeus splayed his hands out, palm up, feigning nonchalance when everyone in the atrium knew her presence was all but innocuous. It had run through her thoughts that he would think she was there to even the score with his current wife. Enlighten Hera that the god king, taken from her, was back in her bed. But that had never been

Themis. Thinking of revenge and seeking it were two different things.

Themis took a step forward. "We are here seeking an audience with you," she flicked her eyes behind Zeus, then back to him. "And only you."

"I am your queen. What you want to say to *my* husband can be said in front of me," Hera said, her words arrogant and demanding.

Themis raised a single brow at Zeus, conveying her lack of consideration toward his wife. He cleared his throat.

"Hera, obviously, this is a matter regarding Themis and our daughters. Wait for me in the library."

She watched Hera's eyes flash red right before she stepped forward and ran her hand over Zeus' chest. "Whatever you say, my dear." She then kissed him as if they were newly married, right before turning to leave. At least the bastard had the decency to look uncomfortable.

"Now that the drama is over, let us discuss *our* missing daughter, shall we?" Themis stepped around her lover and made her way to his throne room with Clotho and Lachesis following closely behind her.

"What did you say, Themis?" Zeus appeared before her just inside his royal chamber.

"The night of Phantasos' and the Nephilim's wedding, Atropos went missing. We," she gestured to her daughters, "concluded, over the last fortnight, that the war angel either did something with her or knew who had. So, I went to visit him. He admitted that, under the authority of the Most High, Atropos had been taken to set things right and that she would be visiting other realms. He said that you could do nothing about it, and in years to come, all would understand. Alaric then raptured me back to my home on Olympus." The more she spoke, the redder Zeus' pupils became. Lightning sparked between his fingertips, and the throne room shook.

"We will find her, Father," Lachesis said. "We know she is in the mortal realm. It shouldn't be hard to find her signature."

"Can you girls not feel her?" Zeus asked.

"No. That is why it has taken us so long to gather any information. Our telepathy has a colored line between each of us. Atropos' is—was—gold." Clotho said.

"It's no longer there. We can see only ours," Lachesis picked the rest of the thought up and spoke it—a trait Themis was used to when with The Fates.

"What about Atropos' threads. Who will sever the threads that need to be cut?" Zeus asked.

"As of now, only the beings other pantheons have been directed to end will occur," Lachesis answered her father's inquiry.

"I want my daughter found. I will command every Greek god to search for her and every creature to hunt her." Zeus said through gritted teeth as he shook with anger. "Tell me every word that angel said to you."

Themis began reciting Alaric, and her conversation then stopped. Wide-eyed, she said, "I think I know what country she's in."

"How?" Clotho asked.

"The angel is always meticulous with his words. He mentioned that we *would* find her, but not to interfere. And before he raptured me back here, he referenced a meeting he was about to attend—in Monaco."

All three women turned when thunderous crackling sparks went from between Zeus' fingers, up his arms, and to his shoulders. Themis had never seen him so angry. He called on the same daimon who had met them in the atrium. "Bring Artemis to me."

Calling for someone to fetch the goddess of the hunt revealed how angry the god-king was. All he had to do was summon his daughter with the wave of his hand. Instead, he crackled with rage.

Unlike Hera, Themis didn't detest Zeus' children with the Titan Leto, with whom the king had had an affair while married to Hera. Actually, Themis felt justice was served. She couldn't help but smile amid all that was going on. She knew the bitch queen would be angered, having her and Artimus, his daughter, with a goddess he slept with behind her back, in his throne room without her.

"You called for me, Father?" The stunning huntress arrived moments later.

Themis was amazed at how much the Huntress and Atropos resembled each other. Where Atropos' hair was auburn, Artemis' was strawberry blonde and hung in long waves down her back. Each had ivory skin and emerald eyes that seemed to penetrate your thoughts. Both were tall with refined feminine muscles that looked elegant in satin but lethal if crossed.

Artemis looked from her king to her half-sisters with concern. "What's wrong?"

"Your sister, Atropos, has been taken. We know she is in the human realm, and we believe she's in Monaco. Beyond that, we have no other leads. We need you to go with Clotho and Lachesis and look for her."

"Who took her, and why? I mean, she is the Inflexible One. Many would want her gone from her station." Her curiosity wasn't rude, just straightforward. "Where did you get your information?"

The Moirai and Themis told the story, starting with the wedding. Zeus listened but paced throughout the account. His arms were back to normal, but his eyes continued to flash lightning bolts.

"When you go, take the Colchian Dragon with you." Zeus stopped his pacing and looked at Artemis. She can disguise herself

as any other creature, and her heightened senses let her know`
everything. With a War Angel involved, I want my daughters to
have the perfect watcher at their backs. Everyone was speechless.
The dragon watched over the Golden Fleece and had always done
so.

"What about the Golden—," her father cut off Artemis' words.

"You let me worry about the Fleece. Gather your maidens just
in case. I want to know where she is. When you find her, come
tell me. Do. Not. Go. In. For. Her. Do you understand?" he said
to all three of his daughters.

With a nod from each, he turned to Themis. "You will stay here
until Atropos is found."

"I don't think your queen will appreciate me staying any longer
in her mansion," Themis raised her chin in a sign of defiance.
No one but she and the king before her knew of their affair. She
needed the comfort of his arms, knowing he hurt as she did. Their
daughter was missing.

"This is my mansion, and I am the king," Zeus' brow lifted,
daring her to argue. *He must need me too.*

Chapter Twenty-Nine
The Gala

Jane (Atropos)

It had been days since their shopping trip, and most of those days had been wonderful. She had only experienced a few slight twinges of pain while awake; in sleep, she found herself out of sorts. No longer sleeping in the guest room, she had moved everything into Warrick's space. The one time she tried to sleep in the guest room, she found herself encased in his arms, being carried back to his bed. He then curled his large frame around her, and they both fell back asleep.

She slept well until around three most mornings. Warrick would wake her by shaking her while whispering calming words. He told her she would call out in a language he'd never heard spoken and thrash about like she was trying to free herself from someone. She remembered nothing.

Anna and her date came over a few days after Jane and Warrick's relationship had become more intimate. The four had more fun than she could have imagined. Enjoying herself that night went a long way toward making the anxiety over the fundraiser more bearable. The best part had been Anna's resignation to her and Warrick's relationship and gaining a friend.

It had taken Anna some time to relax around her. Jane caught her squinting and shaking her head when she thought Jane wasn't looking. Warrick never changed the way he was, even while receiving death glares from his assistant. He constantly touched her, tucking her into his side when they sat on the sofa, kissing the top of her head when they stood around the kitchen eating off the charcuterie board, and winking at her whenever she wasn't within reach. Anna must have seen enough of their affection for one another that she finally let her guard down. After that, the four of them laughed and joked all night.

Smoothing her palms down the front of her satin emerald dress, which matched her eyes, she did one last check in the mirror. She had to admit, the dress was stunning, and it went a long way toward making her feel sexy. She left her hair down to tumble in waves over her breasts.

"You look stunning, Jane," Anna said. Since the dinner, Anna spoke to her often, calling to check in and chat about the television shows they both enjoyed. When she asked if she wanted company getting ready for the gala, Jane jumped at the chance.

Warrick entered the bedroom twice to supply them with flutes of champagne. The two of them tried to help her with the anxiety consuming her. It was the first time since waking up in the hospital that she worried about what other people would think of her. She had no memories to draw on for conversation, and the last thing she wanted to do would be to embarrass the man who was becoming her everything.

Anna left after putting the final touches on her own hair and makeup, leaving Jane uneasy. *I look the part of his date, but I am far from the woman I need to be this evening.*

Two light raps pulled her from her internal beratement of the fraud wearing the beautiful gown and trendy makeup. When she looked for the cause of the noise, she saw the large onyx bird with a smaller, similar version of the huge, winged creature beside it. She would think the feathered beasts could read her mind if she didn't know better. Carefully, Jane moved toward the glass doors. Together, the two birds tilted their heads as if joined by a string. She stopped when the largest bird shook its head. *Shook its head? What the fuck?*

"Gorgeous—are you ready?" Warrick's voice from the hallway startled her, and her winged watchers took flight.

Calming herself after the craziness of the last few moments and from the anxiety crawling through her, Jane took two deep breaths and answered. "On my way."

Jane's first time in a limousine, or so she assumed, took her breath away. Blacked-out windows, a minibar, and enough room that if you didn't desire to be near someone, you didn't have to be.

Tucked into Warrick's side, soft leather seats and the dim glow of blue lights, she finally felt at ease. She sensed that whoever she had been before her fall had the money and importance that few others possessed. What she couldn't understand was *if* that was true, then why wasn't someone looking for her? Where were her family, friends, and helpers? Why didn't the TV have her face all over it? *Who am I?*

The large car stopped in front of the Salle Belle Époque. It was a place for royalty—a place she belonged. The arrogant thought ran through her mind before she realized it. "This is lovely, Warrick." She slid out of the car, taking his proffered hand.

"It is, but not half as lovely as you," Warrick winked, tucking her hand into his elbow and leading her up the red carpet lined by velvet ropes, keeping those not invited to the fundraiser away from those who were. Many called out to Warrick, asking him who he was escorting, and some asked where Allison was. *Who is Allison?*

Warrick lengthened his stride, causing Jane to stumble a little. He grabbed her elbow, and she hoped the loud onlookers hadn't noticed the slip. "Sorry, Jane. I despise the pops."

Pops? Not knowing who the pops were, Jane steadied herself, and they continued to the ballroom. Her breath caught when they entered. *Zeus. Father.* Words that popped into her mind.

Giant marble pillars held up the entire room. Breathtaking art surrounded by thick gilded trim encompassed the curve of the ceiling. A magnificent crystal chandelier hung from the middle of the 6.9-meter ceiling. Grand was an understatement. The room felt familiar, but she had no idea why; its familiarity calmed her.

Servers came by with flutes of champagne and heavy hors d'oeuvres. Tucked on the left side of the silent auction, in the corner, the string quartet played. Warrick explained what to expect throughout the evening, including waggling his brows at his suggestion of a *fun-filled* ride home. The women were all stunning in their formal attire, but the only man she cared to even look at was the one whose arm she was on.

He was handsome, no matter what he wore—but in a tux, he stood out in a crowd. He looked godly—the only word that could come close to describing him, and every woman in the room thought so too. Some were even prudent in their ogling by looking away when she caught them lusting over him. Others were heedless enough to smirk and shrug. *Human women.* The unbidden thought came out of nowhere, and what it meant, she had no idea, other than it was a slight.

"All the women are looking at you," Jane whispered.

"They aren't looking at me, dear. They are looking at you, wondering who the stunning redhead is on my arm," Warrick whispered back as he took a long sip from his flute.

"Well, that woman beside the stuffy-looking man whose laugh sounds like a bellow is staring daggers this way. Do you know her?" Jane smirked and sipped from her glass. She watched as Warrick turned to see who she was talking about and felt him stiffen.

"Fucking hell," he said. "I heard she was going to be in Italy visiting her mother. I suppose the gossip mill got that wrong."

"So, you do know her. Should I arm myself in expectation of her trying to *off* me?" Jane acted as if she were looking at the gilded statues instead of staking out the competition.

"Well, well, well, look who has added American slang to their linguistic repertoire," Warrick smirked.

"Avoiding my question? That's not very becoming of a gentleman." She worked hard not to smile, trying to seem stern in their banter.

"Oh, if I must. Yes, she is my father's business partner's daughter, and they want nothing more than for us to find ourselves in a relationship. But—she is the last person I would ever aspire to be in a relationship with, so I try hard to avoid her."

"She is rather pretty. Long black hair and big, round eyes," Jane suggested in their intimate conversation.

"But she's not stunning." Warrick turned to face her and looked straight into her eyes. "You, Jane, are stunning." Then, he gently pressed his lips to hers in a chaste, but hot kiss. When Jane looked up, the woman shook her head and left.

Warrick gestured to the tables, where beautiful centerpieces added grandeur to the donations splayed out for auction. "So, I write my name and the amount I am willing to part with for the object or vacation spots," he explained how the silent auction worked.

"And this ritual helps people?" she asked.

"That is correct." Warrick's eyes were focused only on her.

"That's wonderful, but I have no money, and at the moment I'm going by a name given to me less than a month ago. So, you do it." Jane grinned up at her date. She noticed his flinch and didn't know whether it was due to her lack of money or her lack of name.

"Jane, Warrick—I was looking for you when Lucia stopped me and asked, and I quote, 'Who the hell is Warrick with and why the fuck did he kiss her?' end quote." Anna cocked her head to the side with a grin that bordered on evil.

"She saw that, did she?" Warrick answered. He then pulled Jane and Anna aside so the next couple in line could make their bids.

"I had the privilege of seeing her stomp off after his display of affection. I suppose she hadn't left as I thought. Where's your date?" Jane looked around.

"Here she is," Anna said, looking past Jane, having her turn to meet Anna's date.

The slender bombshell who slinked up beside Anna was not who or what she expected. First, it wasn't Melissa from the other day. Second, she was taller than Anna, with dark, buzzed hair and delicate features—*like an elf. Where did that thought come from?*

"Astrid, meet my boss, Warrick, and his lovely girlfriend, Jane," Anna said. Warrick and Jane looked at each other before greeting Astrid. Anna had just slapped a label on them; she was now his girlfriend.

Jane felt the tension in the woman's body, and when they shook hands, she felt a shock of fear. Not her fear—Astrid's. "It's nice to meet you. Have we met before?" Jane asked her.

"I don't believe so. Anna, I'm not feeling so well. Do you mind if I get some air?" Astrid asked.

"Here, let me go with you." Anna walked toward Astrid.

"Oh, no. Stay and mingle. I think I had one too many flutes of champagne. Give me a few minutes, and I'll be fine." Astrid quickly maneuvered her way to one of the many terraces overlooking the city of Monte Carlo and the surrounding sea.

"Shall we look over the auction table?" Warrick suggested, taking her by her elbow, leaving Anna to follow.

Chapter Thirty

Irish Illusions?

Warrick

Diamond-encrusted platinum wedding bands, signed rugby jerseys, two cars, and extravagant vacations were among the two hundred items donated to charity. Warrick had no use for any of them, but he wanted Jane to have fun and bid on whatever she liked. So, they scoured the tables looking for anything that caught her eye.

"Didn't you tell me that you donated something?" Jane asked, not taking her eyes from the donations.

"I donated two trips—three weeks in Bar Harbor, Maine, and a month in Napa Valley." She shivered under his touch when he stealthily ran his hand from its resting place on the small of her back to her ass and back up.

"It's been a while. I'm going to look for Astrid," Anna interrupted, placing her empty glass on the tray of a passing server, looking at the terrace she had seen her date go to.

"We will be around." Warrick smiled. "Do you think she saw me?" He whispered in Jane's ear.

Jane elbowed him. "Shame on you." She turned from the table and looked up at him. "For some reason, I think I've always wanted to travel."

"We can definitely do—," Warrick didn't finish his sentence. Instead, he stared over Jane's shoulder at the wall to the left of the quartet where two women stood, tall, exquisite, and undeniably familiar. The dark auburn-haired woman reminded him of Jane. The raven-haired lady looked like—*no*. Flashes of the black-haired woman looking down at him while crying shot through his mind like a memory. The champagne flute he was holding slipped through his fingers, and the sound of shattering glass snapped him from his trance.

"Warrick," Jane sounded panicked. It must not have been the only time she had called his name. "Warrick, what's wrong?"

"No worries, sir. You are not the first to drop a glass tonight, and I'm sure you're not the last." A server gestured for him and Jane to move to the side where the staff could clean up the broken glass and spilled champagne.

"Do you see those women next to the wall?" Warrick nodded in their direction for Jane to follow.

It happened as if in slow motion. The second Jane looked to where he was pointing, her head exploded in pain. One hand flew to her left eye, and the other to her right temple, right before her knees gave way. Before he could catch her, everything stopped. All the patrons froze in place. Jane's knees were in a buckled state, even though she remained upright, and all chatter ceased. As if a veil came down over his eyes, fog closed in; he could see only a small patch in front of him. Within the section of clarity, stood the two women who had caught his attention. They now stood directly in front of him. He blinked, desperately trying to shake the craziness going on inside his head.

"What the fuck was in that champagne?" He said aloud.

"You are well, my son." The dark-haired woman in the blue Celtic dress had just called him "son." The woman he'd just visualized crying over him. *What the actual fuck?* Warrick ran his hand through his hair.

"We must talk, Alasdair," the similarly dressed, except in green, redhead announced, calling him by someone else's name.

That's it. They have me confused with someone else. He thought.

"We do not. We know exactly who and what you are—or were. More so than you do. My name is Adair—and I am your birth mother."

The room tilted. *Birth mother?* "My birth mother is in France, on holiday. I don't know you. And what do you mean you know what I am?" *Did she just read my mind?* Whatever was in his drink must have been potent because he was now conversing with them. "Where's Jane? What have you done with her?" He said, rambling to the illusions and to himself.

"We will answer all of your questions, but first, you need to sit and take a calming breath. What you are about to hear is a lot to take in, but because your course and the woman you call Jane's path converged, we had to come forward. Something we never intended on doing," Adair, the dark-haired woman, said, then out of thin air, manifested three chairs.

"Fine." Warrick couldn't believe he was about to give in to his mental breakdown. "Say what you need to and bring my girlfriend back to me." He pulled the bowtie loose, trying to dispel the choking feeling.

"Please sit. This will take time." The woman calling herself his mother motioned to one chair.

"I think I'll stand, thank you." Warrick stood with his arms crossed, creating a barrier between him and his crazy illusions.

"Suit yourself." Adair sat, and the redhead moved behind her instead of taking a chair for herself. "Twenty-nine years ago, I gave birth to a beautiful baby boy. Our world was dangerous, and after a vision of his future, I knew I would have to let him go. No matter how much it would wreck me. I named him Alasdair, defender, and protector of mankind."

Warrick stiffened at the manifestation's words. They had called him Alasdair just moments prior.

"Yes," the woman answered the question he had not verbalized. "You are that babe. When I was in my sixth month of pregnancy,

I had a vision of you and a goddess having a child so powerful, it would upset the balance of every realm."

"Excuse me. What the fuck are you talking about? Visions, goddesses, pantheons?" Warrick rubbed his temples where a dull ache had begun.

The redhead took her turn. "You are the grandchild of two royal Irish gods: myself, The Morrigan, and the king, Dagda. Adair," she pointed to the dark-haired woman, "is our daughter, and you are her son."

"I rarely drink, and never to get drunk. I haven't done drugs, ever, and I have a couple of glasses of champagne and go off the deep end." Warrick took up pacing in front of the figments of his imagination. "Say, I don't believe I've gone completely insane. Why would you give me up?" He directed the question to the woman called Adair, who had a single tear running down her cheek. "I mean, you have a dream and say, Fuck it, I don't need him, just in case my dream comes true? Who does that to their child? What kind of nonsense is this?"

Adair brushed her thumb across the lone tear and visibly worked for composure. "It was not a dream like you are accustomed to. I am what we call an oracle, a seer, and the most renowned second-sight user to ever exist. I don't need to manipulate stones or scry with water; I am the stones, I am the water—and I have never in over six thousand years been mistaken. When I saw what you would help create, I had to try to alter everything. The Morrigan warned me that my attempt would not work because of fate, destiny, and fortune, but I had to try. So, she," Adair looked behind her to her mother, "helped me."

"My daughter wanted to protect mankind and her youngest child from a fate she knew could be unbearable. Her intentions were always good; however, the pain of losing you caused her irreparable emotional damage. Even the gods are not immune to such things." As The Morrigan spoke, she moved with a flowing grace that Warrick didn't know was possible, to the second chair. Since he was the only one still standing, he gave in and sat too.

"You know this is insane. I don't believe in pantheons containing gods from different regions. If I were adopted, I would know." And all the while, he knew the adoption part made sense. He looked nothing like either of his parents or any of the family. Not to mention, he always saw himself as an outsider.

"Your human mother carried a child to term, and she never knew that the babe had died the day before childbirth. I stopped time and replaced the baby girl that had died in the womb with you, my son. When the human healer and his staff regained time, they announced the birth of a healthy baby boy. Your mother believes you are the child she carried; however, your father has wondered if she had an affair."

As much as Warrick didn't want to believe in the absurdity, it made his relationship with his father make more sense. His father had always been hard on him, and he could never remember a time when his dad played with him or coddled him. Warrick rubbed the sudden ache in his chest. This also explained why his parents acted more like disgruntled roommates than soulmates. Between the pain in his head and the one in his chest, he wondered if the imaginary conversation he was having would kill him.

"So, I am supposed to find a goddess, have a baby with her that will change the world, possibly for the worse. Not to mention that my mother is an oracle, my grandmother is The great Morrigan herself," He looked at the shock on her face. "Yes, I know the mythology. And my grandfather—well, he's the king of Irish mythos. And the two people who raised me, with whom I have no blood ties, believe I am the child my mother carried to term. My *adoptive* father believes I'm a bastard and my mother is a cheat. Not to mention their baby girl died, and they have no clue." Warrick stood and paced. "I have a feeling we are not done with this tragedy that is my life. What next?"

"No, we are not." Adair, at least, had the decency to look ashamed.

"Well, I can't bloody wait. Let's hear it," Warrick's sarcasm always appeared when agitated.

"You call the woman who is with you, Jane. Why?" The Morrigan asked.

"I found her severely injured. She was in a coma. When she woke, she had no recollection of who she was, so the hospital called her Jane Doe—a common name given to people who lack identification. That's the only name she knows for now." Warrick stood in front of The Morrigan and asked. "Where is she? Actually, where am I?" He hadn't noticed the fog had disappeared, and all that was around him, and the two self-proclaimed deities, were three chairs and never-ending blackness. There was a floor, but it held no defining characteristics. Just black all around.

"You are in a dimension often used for questioning. *Jane* is still in the ballroom where we left her, but don't fret. When you return, you and everyone else will pick up from where you left off. Time and space work differently on every plane." The Morrigan explained, and he couldn't help but notice how much he looked like both women.

"Is she alright? She clutched her head, and before I could grab her, you took me." Warrick narrowed his eyes at them, clearly blaming them if Jane wasn't okay.

"When you go back, you will catch her. If you still want to." The Morrigan said. He could tell she was rougher—more war-like—than her daughter. Which made sense, given that she was the harbinger of death on the battlefield.

"Wait. According to lore, you can shapeshift. You two are the raven and crow I've been seeing. You flew away when Jane appeared. "Why don't you like her?"

Adair spoke in a softer tone; he supposed to keep from angering him any further. "She is not this *Jane* you call her. She is not at all who or what you believe her to be. Jane is the Greek Fate, Atropos. Deity, Bringer of Release, Goddess of Death, the Thread Cutter—one of the Moirai." After revealing the information, she sat back and watched Warrick.

What did she think he was about to do? "I see." That was all Warrick said. He thought about the words Jane used, like Zeus' sake and Hades. When she woke, she spoke in what he thought was an old Greek dialect. She understood and spoke any language spoken. Adaptability came easily, and she held herself like royalty. Had he been sleeping with an actual goddess? *No, all this is my mind playing tricks on me.* Next, these women would tell him that vampires and Santa Claus were real.

"Are you okay, my son?" Adair reached for him, and he flinched away. She pulled her hand back as if she'd been burned.

Perhaps his rejection had hurt her. After all, she thought he was the infant she had given away. "I wouldn't say that I am. Everything you have told me seems insane. In fact, maybe I need to look into psych wards once you release me from this darkness. What now? I go back and ask Jane, or Atropos, if she's been lying to me?" Warrick asked.

"No. You watch her. She means you no harm. In fact, I saw that you two love each other deeply. It is up to you to decide if your feelings for her outweigh the risk that being with her will cause," Adair said, sadness radiating off her. "You must know. There hasn't been a day since I left you that I haven't thought about you—I dare to say every hour. I hope one day you can forgive me." Adair wiped under both eyes where many tears flowed. "Go back and make your decision. We will be watching, but if you need either of us, all you have to do is call our name."

"I sense Greeks," The Morrigan said.

Warrick's mind went dark.

Chapter Thirty-One
Found Her

Lachesis

Cloaked, Lachesis, Clotho, and Artemis arrived on a cliff-side in Monaco with the Colchian Dragon. It was Lachesis' first time to be within touching distance of the enormous red, four-legged reptile. Its raptor-like eyes, slanted nostrils, and spines made the giant seem even more menacing up close.

Before rapturing to the mortal realm, the sisters went to get the dragon. When they arrived, the dragon's serpentine neck swayed, tracking their movements. Sensing they were three of the god king's daughters, the dragon went from being defensive to overly cordial, causing them to look back and forth at each other in confusion.

The dragon slipped effortlessly into their minds and spoke to them. *I mean you no harm, just as you mean no harm to me.* After a brief mental conversation among the four of them, they decided that working together to find Atropos would not be as problematic as the sisters had first thought. All three goddesses had recoiled when Zeus told them to take the Colchian Dragon on their hunt for answers to Atropos' whereabouts. Conversing with the being cleared any misconception that the beast wasn't a sentient creature. She had exceptional intelligence and a willingness to help Zeus, and the dragon would never do any harm to one of his children. If she could truly disguise herself and sense everything as their father said, she would be quite the ally.

The four devised a plan before leaving the mount. Once in the human realm, they would split up to comb the small area the humans called Monaco. Artemis' maidens would wait for her to call for them if needed. The plan was to stay cloaked, where immortals could not see them, and invisible where the mortals wouldn't care that they were there.

"Clotho and I will take the two eastern quarters, and you two take the western two. If you sense *any* signature, let each other know. Do not engage with Atropos. We have no idea what is going on," Lachesis said to her companions. Her father may have meant for Artemis to lead them, but Lachesis was more formidable than even the goddess of the hunt, and she would lead them to her sister.

It had not taken long for Lachesis to catch the signature of an Álfar, more commonly known as an Elf. She let everyone know through the telepathic magic Zeus had cast over his daughters before they left his throne room. He said they needed to communicate properly, then snapped his fingers. While on the mission to find Atropos, they could speak mind-to-mind.

The elf stood on the balcony of a large building, where music played, and the low hum of mortal chatter hung around the structure. No other being stood with the female dark elf. Finding dark elves among humans was common; they often chose the mortal realm because the elven society deemed them lesser. But Lachesis would watch her for a while to ensure the elf was alone.

The Álfar pressed her fingertips to her temples and was mumbling something. Odd, but elves were peculiar beings. Dark elves were exceptionally intelligent and cunning, with morally grey ethics, as far as Lachesis knew. They could live thousands of years, but still die of old age, making them what the gods called mid-mortals.

Watching the female closely, she realized the elf was speaking with someone who wasn't corporeal. What would cause a mid-mortal to use magic with so many humans around? Something was amiss.

No sooner had the thought left Lachesis' mind than two very strong signatures revealed themselves inside the large building where the dark elf stood on the terrace.

"The signatures are Irish and royal," Artemis' voice echoed inside Lachesis' head.

"What are the Irish doing in the Mediterranean?" Clotho asked.

"The Irish never venture down this far. They stay around the Emerald Isle," Artemis answered.

"I will get closer—wait here," Lachesis told her sisters and the dragon.

"We should go with you," Clotho and Artemis rang out in unison.

"I will stay cloaked. I must see if Atropos is in there. Watch that elf. Something isn't right about her. She's being bold, especially now that we know there are other deities around. If we sense them, so does that Álfar." Lachesis knew Artemis would not take kindly to seeing other royals. Unlike her and her fate sisters, Artemis was loyal to their father, to a fault, even when he was clearly in the wrong. If land bordered the Mediterranean, Zeus considered it his. Not to mention the many other parcels of land in the human realm he claimed as property of the Greek Pantheon.

Speaking for the dragon and Artemis, Clotho spoke up. "Fine, we will stay, but if you're gone more than what we deem necessary, you will feel us at your back." Clotho nodded toward the open terrace doors above them.

Without further ado, Lachesis vanished and reappeared in the banquet room, cloaked and ready to fight if necessary. As soon as she entered the striking gold-adorned room, a twinge of familiarity hit her in the chest. Her eyes zoned in on where the faint signature was coming from, and there stood her sister in a beautiful gown on the arm of a handsome man. Atropos repeated the same movements over and over, as did the rest of the patrons. *What is happening? Who is that with her?*

So surprised by the faint signature of her sister and the oddity before her, she had overlooked the greater signatures of the two Irish goddesses standing beside Atropos, and with whom the mystery man was speaking. Her gasp when they looked in her direction had the redheaded Irish deity squinting in irritation. The goddesses and the man were operating outside of time and space. *How am I seeing this?*

I have lent you my senses as a momentary gift. This is not safe. Come back. Lachesis heard the dragon in her mind.

At that moment, Lachesis realized who was looking back at her from across the room—The Morrigan. The Irish queen and the Moirai's equivalent. *What the fuck is going on?*

Knowing the Harbinger of Death had seen her, she quickly returned to her sisters and the dragon. "Time to leave." With a flash of light, they returned to Olympus.

Chapter Thirty-Two

Possible Deception

"Jane," Warrick grabbed her around the waist as her knees gave way, and she whimpered in pain. "Let's find a private room."

Keeping his arm around her, Warrick guided her from the ballroom into a side chamber across the hallway. There, he found a seating area where women often removed their shoes and sat during parties to relax from all the standing. More often than not, a place where men and women went to be alone.

He placed her across the settee and removed her heels. "Are you okay?" he asked, still kneeling at her feet, running his palms up and down her calves. Worry had replaced irritation until his memory stopped his movements. Two women. One called herself his mother, the other his grandmother, and both deities. Then their entire conversation hit him, and he couldn't help but wonder about the woman who was just in his arms. The one who lived in his home and slept in his bed—the one he was finding himself fiercely protective of and who he was *falling for*.

"It's my head again—such pain. Do you have any of those pills that help it?" she asked, sounding tiny and vulnerable in her state.

"I'm sorry. I do not. Would you like me to take you back to my apartment?" Warrick realized he had been referring to the apartment as their home when conversing with Jane. Just then, he called it his—an unconscious wedge placed by the Irish women.

"I don't want to ruin this night. Give me a few minutes, and maybe it will go away on its own."

Warrick looked at her slight figure, splayed out before him, one arm slung over her eyes. She couldn't see him clenching his jaw or the flare of his nostrils. Anger flickered inside him—everything he had done for her. *Has she been playing me the whole time?* He took in the curve of her waist and her slender shoulders. Through the slit in her gown, one naked leg was on full display, causing his dick to jolt to life. *Didn't you get the memo?* He mentally scolded his cock. The woman before him could be a Greek goddess, conning him from the beginning, or he could be going completely mad. The thought of her deceiving him made his chest ache.

Nothing that had taken place over the last half hour made any sense. As he thought about it, the likelihood that he was going mental was more probable than conversing with mythical beings who claimed him as their own. Is it possible that he was adopted, switched—*whatever?* He stood and paced the small room.

Everything about not being a blood member of the Harding family made sense. His father's hatred, his mother's distance, and that he looked nothing like either of them—he could very well be adopted. As he thought and paced, running his hand through his hair.

Jane's odd behavior, her unexplained ability to switch between all the languages she encountered, the way she confidently carried herself—she was definitely different from anyone he knew—but all of those things could have explanations. The illogical part of the night was the mysterious women and the stories they conjured. He didn't believe in the paranormal, fantastical, or mythological; whatever they were. Yet, what he just went through was as real as anything else that had ever taken place in his life.

"I would hate for you to miss the gala because of me. I'll be fine. Please—go enjoy yourself," Jane murmured from under her hands, where it looked like she was trying, unsuccessfully, to massage the headache away.

"No. I'd rather be in here with you." Warrick said.

What he would rather do is find out what the hell happened. But how could he? Ask the woman lying just feet away if she was a goddess and playing with his emotions, call for the two women who dropped the bombshell on him, and see if they are real, or ask his father if he thought his mum had an affair because he found out he was a substitute? Of all those scenarios, calling the deities back for answers—yet he had no clue how—was the only thing he could do without someone thinking he lost his mind.

"I'm feeling better. It's just a dull ache now. Let's return to the gathering." Jane said as she slid her feet back into her heels.

Warrick watched as Jane swung her legs over the edge of the couch. When she stood and wobbled a little, he realized he was being less than gentlemanly by not helping, so he jumped to her side and offered her his hand, despite his instinct to berate her. Just the thought that she could be engaging in some coup for his money or worse, his sperm, had him reeling inside. The Irish didn't think Jane meant any harm, but he wasn't so sure now. He didn't know who or what to believe. Just four months ago, Allison did a number on him, and he declared he would never trust again. The thought that the person who was wrapping herself tight around his heart could be lying was enough to fracture the strides he had made in the trust department.

"We will make one last trip around the ballroom, then we'll leave," Warrick responded.

Jane raised her hand to his left brow and rubbed it with her fingertips. "Are you okay? You don't seem yourself."

He couldn't help but lean into her palm when she slid it to his cheek. This woman had turned his world upside down. For years, he had dodged falling for the fairer sex, never knowing if the woman had ulterior motives. Even the rich just wanted his money. Jane had been the first person to ever make him feel more than just the sum of his bank accounts. She had been loving, down-to-earth, and couldn't care less if he had money. He thought someone finally saw him—the man, not the billionaire. The thought of her not being who he thought she was had him spinning out of control. He may not know her real name, but he sure as fuck thought he knew her.

They had no sooner reentered the ballroom than Warrick heard his name. *You have got to be kidding me!* Warrick rolled his eyes, then turned to see Anna trying her best to stop the blonde beauty from approaching him and Jane.

"Who do we have here?" Allison asked, gesturing to Jane.

"Allison, this is Jane. Jane, Allison. How have you been?" Warrick wondered if the night could get any worse; now he knew the answer.

"I've been well. Do you still have my clothes?" Allison smirked. He knew what she was doing.

His ex wasn't looking at him. She looked between Jane's face and his hand wrapped around Jane's. He wasn't beyond being a royal dick, so he unclasped their hands and wrapped his arm around Jane's waist. That gesture granted him a snarl. *Serves her right for what she did.*

"You left them, so Anna was kind enough to remove them. I'm sure they are of use to someone. Where's Dick?" His tone was pleasant and dripping with kindness. Mirroring Allison, he used tone and body language to cut deep. She forgot he could play the game too.

"Richard had to take a call. Jane, how are things with Warr? I hear you live with him?" Allison's words came out with a bite.

"Warrick has been wonderful," Jane answered.

"Give it time," Allison said. "Good to finally meet you." She turned on her heel and left him to answer the questions written all over Jane's face.

Well, fuck.

"I take it that was your girlfriend," Jane said.

"Was—she *was* my girlfriend, but hasn't been in over four months, and the last four before that were horrible," Warrick answered, with a little more venom than necessary.

"I see," Jane said. "If you don't mind, I would like to go now." She turned away from him and began walking toward the exit. Before she got to the door, she looked around as if looking for someone, shook her head, then resumed her trek to the valet.

Chapter Thirty-Three

Otherworldly Visitors

Lachesis/Jane (Atropos)

She expected to find herself and her sisters back in their father's throne room. What she didn't expect was that the dragon wasn't with them.

"Where's the dragon?" Lachesis asked.

"I don't know," Clotho and Artemis both answered.

Their father materialized and responded, "She was told if she ran into something unusual, she would stay and find out more. Apparently, the beast learned of something important. Don't fret daughters, she will be back soon." Zeus walked up the dais and sat on the throne, engraved with the story of his beginning.

"Why didn't she tell us?" Lachesis asked.

"I don't want any of my daughters in harm's way if I can stop it. The Colchian Dragon has abilities no god or other creature possess. She can sense cloaked signatures and hear whispers from miles away. She sees beyond what any mortal or immortal can. So, tell me. Did you find my daughter?"

Jane felt something she couldn't describe as she was leaving the gala. A cold tingle ran up her spine, creating a fight-or-flight response in her. She felt both a sense of danger and familiarity. Whatever watched her was not normal, at least not of this realm.

Realm? What? Jane shook her head, wondering what craziness she had just come up with. Her mind bounced around as she and Warrick waited for the limousine.

"I'm sorry about Allison. She wasn't always a bitch. Or, perhaps she was, and she hid it for a year of our relationship. Once she became accustomed to money, her entire demeanor changed. She became rude to my staff and then to me. It wasn't until she slapped me that I finally had enough. As it turned out, she was a day drinker, and while I was at work, she enjoyed her addiction. I believe she was indulging her habit tonight; otherwise, she would not have willingly approached either of us."

Warrick looked so forlorn. All she wanted to do was wrap him in her arms and make him feel better. Since they were in public, she didn't want to dishonor him. So, she waited until they were in the limo with the partition raised.

After getting settled into the car, Jane turned as much as her gown would allow, toward Warrick, and took his hand. He looked from the window to her, then down to her hand wrapped around his. *What I would give to know what he's thinking.*

"Don't apologize for the actions of others. You don't have control over anyone but yourself," Jane said.

Warrick responded with a light squeeze of her hand and a slight grin. "How's your head?"

"It's well. What's wrong, Warrick? I can tell something's troubling you, and don't say it's that Allison woman. I could tell while we were in that tiny room you took me to."

He turned his head again and stared out the window. She took it as a good sign that he continued to hold her hand, even while ignoring her question. Unwilling to pry any further, Jane leaned her head against the seat and closed her eyes.

Once in the apartment and still no word from Warrick, Jane went straight to the guest room where she used to sleep, leaving him standing in the foyer. At first, she was only going to remove the gown and then go to his room, but something about their last interaction felt off. She couldn't shake the thought that he was upset with her. To give him space, she would stay overnight in the guest room. She got ready for bed and crawled beneath the covers. She waited for what felt like forever for him to pick her up and carry her back to his room and toss her onto his bed. He never came. Sleep finally took over.

Jane was between sleep and wake, the moment in rest when a being doesn't fully understand what happened, nor do they care. A place of peace and partial dreams that can be manipulated since you are half-conscious and half-asleep. When the bed dipped down, she thought, in her dreamlike state, that Warrick was letting go of whatever kept him away.

"It's about time you came," Jane murmured, and rolled toward the dipped mattress without opening her eyes.

"I doubt you were waiting for me," a deep voice responded with a chuckle. Somewhere in her subconscious, she realized the voice did not come from her lover. *If not him, then who?*

"Of course I was. Are you going to take me to your room, or are we going to curl up here?" Jane asked as she tried to peel her eyes open. They wouldn't budge. *What in Tartarus?* A shudder ran down her spine.

"Goddess, I'm not who you think I am. I'm Aengus, the Irish god of love, youth, and occasionally, dreams. My half-sister, Adair, sent me to check on you and her son—and to help you understand. You see, I am one of the few who know of the prophecy about her son, Alasdair, and you."

Who's Alasdair? She thought.

"You know him as Warrick."

Aengus answered her unspoken question, making her tremble even more with fear.

"He was made mortal at birth and told of his lineage just this night while at the human gathering you attended. He is the son of Adair, grandson of The Morrigan and of King Dagda."

What in Hades' name? Wake up, Jane! She fought to open her eyes. *It's a nightmare,* she told herself, yet something deep inside her made his words ring true.

"Don't struggle, beautiful. You are well. No need fret, just listen."

She felt the so-called Irish deity smooth her hair from her eyes, which stayed firmly shut to her dismay. All of her other senses took on a mind of their own, and she could practically see the Irish countryside from the smell of him. The vanilla and caramel scent of sweetgrass mixed with the earthy smell of moss. The voice was deep and sensual, with a pronounced Irish lilt, completing the picture her mind created. She felt her muscles relax. *This is only a dream.*

"You don't seem to know who you are—interesting. I can see your recent thoughts concerning my nephew. You're falling in love with him. Oh, darling, you need to wake from this misguided state you are in. Life and death hang in the balance, Goddess. I need you to concentrate on who and what you are. Remember your legacy. Remember your station. Know your lover as the prince he is and you, the powerful goddess you are. The prophecy has begun, and you must be kept safe."

That was all he said, as strange as it was, just before she felt the mattress rise back to its original position, and the aroma of land and man no longer invaded her nostrils. *What is happening?* She stopped struggling and trying to open her eyes while the self-proclaimed god spoke, still blinded by the dark of her eyelids and only listening to his words. She continued to lie still just in case he lingered about.

After a few moments of nothing more, she opened her eyes without issue to find the most frightening thing she had ever remembered seeing. Jane opened her mouth to scream—nothing. She felt her eyes widen and moisture flow. Scrambling to the farthest side of her bed was her only recourse, yet it would not be far enough. *Nightmare...this is a terrifying vision,* was all she could think as she desperately tried to concentrate on what to do instead of the tears streaming down her face from the sight of the beast before her. *I'm going to die!*

You are not going to die. Well, not by me anyway. The creature hovering over her spoke, mind to mind. *However, that minor Irish god may, if he shows himself in your bedchamber without invitation again.*

You're in my head. How? Nightmare. Jane responded the only way she could, since her voice was not working—first her sight, now her speech.

I suppose many think of me as such, but I am merely a soldier in your father's arsenal—the Colchian Dragon, and protector of The Golden Fleece. I am here to find you, protect you, and, if you will let me, bring you home.

A vision of a giant of a man on a carved throne surrounded by marble walls and floors flashed through Jane's head. She could sense he was powerful. She grabbed her temple, and this time sound came from her throat as a pained gasp.

Goddess, what is wrong with you? Why are you in pain?

Jane felt the hot breath of the humongous creature on her face; however, the pain in her head was so bad that she could not control her response.

Don't know—so much pain. It was the only thing she could think of as an answer to the reptile's questions.

It felt like fingers were crawling through her head and manipulating her mind just before the pain subsided. She blinked twice to clear the aura from her vision. Clarity showed the creature was mere inches from her face.

Please, I implore you not to harm me. Jane mentally begged the dragon not to hurt her.

Again, goddess, I could never harm the daughter of my king. I have just put an end to your suffering. Why would I hurt you after taking the agony away?

You took my pain away? My father is the king? What are you talking about? She directed her thoughts and questions to the reptilian creature. *This is a dream spurred on by my injury.* Jane tried to convince herself.

What injury? The dragon questioned, conveniently not answering any of Jane's.

Jane squirmed as far from the beast as she could get before she tried her voice. To her shock, she could speak. "I woke in a hospital where healers took care of the head injury I sustained."

Head injury? You? That cannot be. The creature still spoke through her thoughts. *Explain.*

"I only speak the truth. Warrick found me on his property, unconscious, bleeding from my head. When I woke up, I didn't remember anything. I spoke and thought in ancient Greek, even though I understood all the languages spoken in the room where I woke. English was what Warrick spoke, so I mimicked him." She felt herself relaxing as she told her story. "They said I had been in a coma. Once awake, I healed incredibly fast. Not having a place to live, no identification, and no name to speak of, Warrick brought me here to live with him. We've become very close." She hung her head, ashamed as she described their relationship. Her emotions were all over the place since he never came for her during the night.

When she raised her eyes, the dragon was watching her, its head slightly tilted as if gauging what to say.

"Now—explain what you meant by my father being a king. You know who I am, and you can make my pain disappear. Not to mention you are a fucking dragon." She needed reassurance that she had heard the creature correctly.

Jane found it endearing when the enormous creature sat back on its haunches, readying itself to speak. As scary as the monster looked, it seemed gentle. *This was a very elaborate dream.*

Atropos, you are not dreaming. I am here—as for being a gentle creature—I am to my king and his children, even the one locked in the jar. You, my child, are the daughter of Zeus and Themis. I mean you no harm, now or ever.

A twinge of pain shot through Jane's head at the monster's words. A moment of memory, or what she thought was memory, of her facing an angel on a field of battle, along with the same man she saw on the carved throne, plus the two women she envisioned by the sea. Fortunately, the pain vanished as soon as it surfaced, leaving the vision to play out, as if she were watching a television. The difference was that she was in her memory, and she couldn't recall the people with her.

The angel looked at her and told her he had something special in mind for her since she had upset his daughter's life. *That cannot be me?* Jane struggled to let the vision go, her senses telling her she didn't want to know.

As she fought for control, the memories surged on. Flashes of her and two women on thrones of their own. Next, she was in a bedchamber, smirking at a handsome man, telling him the demigod was off limits. She could feel the jealousy running through her veins toward the demigod she spoke of. Then the thread held by her sisters started to fade, her scissors poised to cut, just before it completely vanished. She had been about to cut the thread of a demi—no, of a Nephilim. The daughter of the angel on the battlefield.

Memories of her easily cutting the thread of her nephew and so many others over the millennia. With that thought, she turned her head and retched on the floor by her bed. Dry heaving as the goddess she once was passed effortlessly through her mind. *Make it stop, please.* She clasped her temples, trying to end the memories.

She wasn't the person she thought she was; she had been borderline evil at many points in her life. For the first time since she woke up in the hospital, she didn't want to know anything else about herself.

"No more—please no more." She didn't know who she begged; the dragon before her, the man on the carved throne, or maybe the angel who looked at her with disdain for what she had done to *his daughter? Amanda. His daughter's name was Amanda. She was the Nephilim.* Jane retched again. Her head was no longer in pain, but the rest of her body was in agony. Clarity hit. She was the Pantheon's thread cutter. It was she who dealt the death blows—a Fate. So many dead by her scissors. *I'm a monster.*

Daughter of Zeus, Inflexible One, Atropos—you need to hear me now. Come to terms with this before you harm the babe. Yes, you are death; you are fate, but you have free will to be a better being. Your station does not define you. Stop this and listen, princess.

Chapter Thirty-Four
Gone Mad

Warrick watched as Jane left him to go to the guest bedroom. Part of him broke at that gesture. Had she got what she wanted? An unfamiliar burn started behind his eyes. Shaking the unwanted feeling away, he went to the bar cart and poured himself a tumbler of twenty-five-year-old Macallan and tossed it back as if it were a bottom-shelf glass of whatever was handy. Setting his glass down, he retreated to his room, changed into running gear and earbuds, and left to pound the pavement and clear his head of the unstable thoughts that plagued him.

For his first few kilometers, he blared heavy music that allowed no thoughts—just his feet striking the trail to the beat of the bass in his chest. He felt everything but refused to think about anything.

Once his body grew tired enough not to react violently to his thoughts, he turned his music down. He bounced back and forth between thinking himself mental and contemplating the words of two unstable women who believed themselves to be royal deities.

I'm not my parents' son. He was a god. That had him laughing so hard he stopped running and bent over, struggling to breathe. Jane was a goddess—his laughter was loud enough to cause nesting birds to take flight.

Standing straight, he locked his hands behind his head and walked. His thoughts were on Jane, the woman who had stolen his heart and the one the Irish called Atropos. Memories of her lying on the ground beside the steps with blood pooled around her head, body limp and pale from blood loss, came unbidden. She was hooked to machines that screeched when she stopped breathing. Nurses, as they ran to her room, closed the shades so he couldn't see as they tried to save her life. The fear on her face when she woke. Strange behavior toward electronics and the world around her. Not that she had forgotten, but as if she had never known. Everything about Jane's situation was strange. And everything the Irish said made more sense.

Warrick was so caught up in his head, he didn't notice the outline of someone ahead of him, standing with one leg propped against a tree, until the figure spoke. "Isn't it a little late for a run, Warrick. Or should I call you, Alasdair?"

His words made Warrick stop. The voice sounded familiar. The large, shadowy being pushed off the tree and started toward him. Warrick wasn't afraid; he was adept in several martial arts, not to mention he, too, was a large man. However, as the being drew closer, wings burst from the silhouette, and a tremor of anxiety flooded his senses.

What the fuck? He waited, trying to come to terms with what he was witnessing. He rubbed his eyes—*still there*. Three more steps and the man would be in the light from the sidewalk lamp. Warrick finally saw why the *man's* voice was familiar. He had just sold him an apartment in a building not yet finished.

"Alaric? What—what the fuck is going on here?" Warrick looked from side to side, wondering if there were others with the strange man who approached him. They seemed to be alone, but nothing was as it appeared. The two women had already obliterated everything he thought he knew. The creature before him resembled the man he'd done business with, but this being looked like a warrior with wings whiter than snow, leather vambraces, and armor. His blonde hair was down to his shoulders, where just a few weeks prior it had been short, and he wore an expensive business suit.

"It is time you know who you are, and who the woman you call Jane is," the winged man said.

The being whom Warrick knew as Alaric stopped two meters from him, with his hands out, palms up, as if to convince him he had come in peace.

"If the Irish woman sent you as evidence of her royal status and my adoption, then save your breath," Warrick took a step back with his left foot, giving himself a better fighting stance if needed.

"I wasn't sent by anyone, tonight anyway. There is nothing you say that I don't already know," Alaric tucked his wings behind him, but left them on display a half a meter above his head and down his back.

"What are you?" Warrick asked the man. "Am I going completely mad?" He rubbed his face, hoping to wake from a dream curled with Jane in his bed. *Nope, no such luck.*

"More years ago than you can comprehend, all beings lived here on Earth. All the creatures and gods you learned about in history and art once walked together in this realm, on this ground. Unfortunately, not all immortals can be entrusted to get along with humans and mid-mortal beings. The powerful started abusing the powerless and used them as pawns. So, after centuries of this, God Almighty split everyone into separate realms. Your family belongs to the Irish Pantheon and, to this day, takes care of mortals when called upon. Your mother, Adair, broke the rules and hid you in the mortal world so well that no one would ever know of your birth. She took your godhood, your station in life, and left you as a mortal. At this moment, you possess no immortal signature." Alaric gestured in the direction Warrick had been walking. "Walk with me as we talk."

Warrick did as the *man* said, but didn't take his eyes off the being. "Thank you for the history lesson. Why should I believe that you and those women are anything other than my imagination?"

"You may no longer have a signature, but your physical make-up, what humans call your DNA, is still that of the gods. You hold no power other than that of your blood, your lineage. Give in to your senses. Deep within yourself, you know who you are," the winged being said as they walked side by side.

"Let's pretend that I don't believe I've gone mental, and I believe all that you have said—why are you here? And don't think I haven't noticed that you never answered my question. Who are you? Fuck—what are you?" Warrick stopped their stroll and faced Alaric.

The winged man chuckled. "I'm a Warrior Angel, sent by the Almighty. I am the one who sent the Fate to you. It was time the prophecy was set in motion. Time for the two of you to meet and your destiny to come to fruition."

Warrick stared at the man, waiting for him to elaborate. When Alaric just stared back, he knew the only way he would know more than the history lesson just given would be to ask. "Why? If I am now *human*—you know how crazy that sounds, right? If I'm now human, why am I needed for some prophecy? Also, wait—you're the bastard who hurt her? The one who hurt Jane?" Warrick felt his blood boil. "Why did you hurt her?"

"I did send her here; however, her injury was unintentional. The memory loss is not a result of the injury. You saw how fast she heals. She's a goddess. Atropos had to forget who she was so she could start anew. All she understood was her station and power. She was and is still Death to those under the Greek Pantheon's watch. The most important thing for you to realize is that the Moirai in your home did not know who she was until now. As I speak with you, another is speaking to her. She is learning of her lineage as you learn of yours."

"What are you going on about? Who's speaking with Jane? Atropos, whatever." Warrick's protective nature showed when he took a step toward the angel and demanded answers. The thought of someone in their home without him there made him sick.

Alaric grinned, obviously not intimidated by Warrick's posturing. "Her father sent one of his minions to find her. That *being* is speaking with her as I speak with you. When you return, she will know her true nature. I won't lie. This will be hard for her. The goddess she was before is not the person she has become since she was sent to this realm. Let's hope she sees the error of her ways. Just because her station is that of Death, does not mean she has to take pleasure in the power that comes with it." Alaric said.

"The prophecy. It states we fall in love and create a life that changes everything. What does that mean exactly?" There was so much to take in that Warrick struggled to make sense of it all.

"An infant will be born to start the coming together of all beings. There will be more, but yours will be the first. God will have things the way they were intended," Alaric looked past him in concentration. "It's time I go. Take care of The Thread Cutter. She will need you. After all, you are the only one who can change her nature."

With those final words, the angel vanished, leaving Warrick standing on the running trail with the sun peaking over the horizon and more questions than when he started his run.

Chapter Thirty-Five

Revelation

Atropos

"Babe? What are you saying, dragon?" But she knew. As soon as the dragon scolded her for her meltdown and mentioned the baby, she knew. It was true—she was with child.

The dragon shimmered and, before Atropos' eyes, shifted into a human woman, just a little larger than herself, with long black hair and golden eyes still slightly slanted. She was human but looked otherworldly. Atropos blinked rapidly.

"How—what just happened?" She asked, stumbling over her words.

"Our time is up. Your mate is on his way back, and I have yet to convince you to leave with me," the dragon answered.

Tears still dripping down her face, she clutched her belly and spoke. "I'm pregnant. What does this mean for us? My sisters—what will happen? Mated?" She remembered everything and needed to come to terms with the goddess she had been and the woman she was now. How will the two halves of her ever become one? "Warrick is my mate? A true bonded mate?"

She was one of three who worked as a unit. All virgins, all Fates, all with a job to do. With that realization came a tickle in her head. It was the Moirai bond. They would be able to hear most of her thoughts. She was not prepared.

"You will always be The Inflexible One, no matter that you are with child or that you have a bonded mate. Virginity was never required of the Moirai. Yes, it made your unique bond easier to wield, but it wasn't necessary. So much is about to change, but know this, child—you will always be one of The Fates Three. That will never change, nor will the job you are required to do. You will learn what to share with your sisters and when to block them."

Wiping her tears away, Atropos stood from her bed and looked at where she had gotten sick on the floor. With a wave of her hand, it vanished. With a snap of her fingers, she no longer looked like she had been crying. She looked into the mirror and saw Jane, the woman she wanted to be, not the goddess she was. It was up to her to change. Atropos' hand went instinctively to her abdomen. How was she going to tell Warrick?

"How will any of this work? I cannot live here in the mortal realm, and Warrick may be of divine blood, but he is human and incapable of living on Olympus. Plus, the blood that runs through his veins is of the Irish gods. Never has a deity from another pantheon lived on the mount. Why is this happening to us?"

"Living arrangements will be decided by Zeus and Dagda," the dragon said.

"There is one thing you are very correct about, Dragon. I will not be going back with you. The most important thing right now is my child." She thought for a moment before revealing her request. "I know it will do no good to ask you not to speak of where I am or that I'm with child to my father, for my sisters will soon know, but can you at least give me a few human days before you do? I need to speak with Warrick, and I'm not sure how he will take any of this." While speaking with the disguised beast, Atropos wandered over to the glass doors to watch the sun start its ascent.

"I can give you that—two human days. Until then, I will disguise myself when anyone is around—until you tell your mated about me." The beast grinned, and as a woman, she was even more distressing. She forgot to change the shape of her teeth.

"That may not be for the be—,"

The shifter raised one long, nail-tipped finger to stop her. "I agreed not to go flying back to my king with the news he is desperate for—you will agree to introduce me to Warrick. That is what I require in return. If there's nothing else, I will be watching over you—closely. I sense him close by." With those parting words, she vanished, leaving Atropos to her own devices.

Atropos walked back to her mirror and stared at her reflection. She turned this way and that, taking in all sides of herself. It was strange to see the goddess standing in a bedchamber of the mortal realm—no golden adornments or silken finery—merely dressed as Jane, the human she had grown to like. There was no change in her features, no cosmetic transformation. It was all internal. She felt completely different.

The desire to be better, to be the mortal she thought she was, had her hanging her head in reflection. How would she ever go back to that life? One where she craved more power and so-called justice for what she wanted rather than what should be. How would she ever look Warrick in the face after knowing the things she had done? Would her sisters shun her? Until the moment she opened her eyes in that hospital, her sisters were everything to her—extensions of herself. They will never be as close again.

She remembered the dinner where she had tried to explain to Warrick that it wasn't just memories she was missing. She was sure she had botched it, even though he couldn't have been any kinder. So many things finally made sense; however, she might have preferred going mad rather than being the goddess of death.

The Moirai were among the oldest Greek gods of Olympus, and from the beginning, chastity was a given. All three were innocent in the ways of the flesh, and until the last hundred years, she was never tempted—until the dream god, Phantasos—her first infatuation. Envy hit her when he brought a human into their world. When the woman took her own life, Atropos no longer coveted the Oneiroi or any other being until the same dream god met Amanda.

Atropos wasn't even sure whether it was the mate bond the dream god shared with the seraphim or the fact that the half-breed's thread vanished, taking her ability to sever it that made her jealous. Either way, envy drove her behavior. Having a mate bond herself now made her sick to think she had desired a mated god—one meant for another. How petty she had been.

Her soul sought Warrick almost immediately when she opened her eyes from the coma. It differed vastly from the feelings she once had for Phantasos. Her feelings for Warrick were not driven by jealousy, envy, or boredom, but by love and affection for the man himself. Whatever was going on with them was destined, per the Irish dream god, who visited her. Despite the protection Warrick had sought to provide, she was still with child. How was she going to tell him? For the first time in her existence, she felt like she had crossed a line from which she could never return.

The tingle in her head intensified the more she thought of her sisters and her godhood, and she knew she had to act fast. She fought to suppress the link her subconscious was trying to forge with her sisters. Her pull to them was instinctual. Oh, how she missed the Moirai, but she needed more time. Too much had taken place over the last few hours, and finding out the Irish Pantheon was involved made everything more complicated.

Of course, she knew of the gods her intruder, Aengus, had spoken of. There had been a time when all pantheons gathered intel on their counterparts. When all beings resided together on earth, it was imperative that they could outwit one another. The Morrigan was not only the Celtic equivalent of her and her sisters—she was as formidable as Athena. The Great Queen could shapeshift and cut through a battlefield as if it were nothing. She was the Harbinger of Death and Warrick's *grandmother*. His grandfather was the king of the Irish deities, just as Zeus, her father, was the king of the Greek gods. Warrick's mother was not just any seer; she was the best in any pantheon and had the power to shift her outward form. Warrick's lineage was just as powerful as hers. No wonder Aengus thought she was in danger. The child she carried would have the blood of the most formidable divine beings in two pantheons—*too much power.*

The dire situation she and her baby's father found themselves in was epic. When, not if, the other pantheons found out she was carrying a child who could only be bested by seraphim, well, they wouldn't stand for it. Atropos clutched her flat abdomen, and a tear of fear slid down her face. They would kill her, her baby, and Warrick when he tried to protect them. What will the Irish Pantheon do to her and her baby? Would they take them in, or side with the pantheons who will want them destroyed?

Stop fretting, child. I told you. No one will harm you or the babe you carry. The dragon's voice rang through her mind as if the creature were standing beside her.

Mentally conversing back, Atropos said, *I thought you were gone, dragon.*

You will not be alone while you carry such a precious gift. Now, I can hear your mate entering the building below. Tell him.

Atropos geared herself up to retort, but before she could, a mental picture of smoke wafting from the Colchian Dragon's nostrils played in her head, and she decided to keep her thoughts to herself.

Chapter Thirty-Six

No Love for Death

One last glimpse at herself, making sure her emotions were not displayed across her cheeks, Atropos donned what Anna had called leggings and an oversized t-shirt. She wanted to present herself as humanly as possible, so when she gained the courage to address the baby in the room, Warrick would see her as the Jane he hoped he still cared for. With a thought, she pulled her hair into a ponytail and applied a light dusting of makeup. There were things about being a goddess that she had missed. Quickly getting dressed was one of them.

When she heard the front door shut, she knew it was time to face whatever was next. Unfortunately, without her sisters, her seer ability seemed to lack life. She splayed her palm over her flat belly and spoke. "No matter what he says, you will always have me."

When Atropos entered the kitchen, Warrick's back was to her. He faced the sink, downing a bottle of water. She took time to appreciate the sight he made with arms and legs on full display and a vee of sweat from the neck of his shirt, almost all the way down his back. *He must have run far today.*

"Good morning, Warrick," Atropos said and watched as the sound of her voice made him go still. Slowly, he turned, and she wasn't prepared for how he looked. She had removed all traces of her tears—Warrick had not. She could see that he had shed a few of his own. *Why?* He looked grim, and the light in his eyes before the gala was gone. No teasing grin on his lips, no sweet endearment, and he hadn't taken one step toward her. He had not seen her since they came home last night.

"Warrick? Are you okay?" Atropos took steps toward him, but the kitchen island lay between them, and from the look on his face, he wasn't willing to close the distance. He continued to stand in the same spot—water bottle now at his side. No words. He just blinked. "You don't look so well. Can I help in any way?"

He continued to stare at her. *Would you like me to show myself? I bet that would get a reaction from him.* The dragon was holding to her word. She was still present but invisible.

For Hades' sake, no. He's human. That might kill him.

Atropos slowly walked around the island. Toe-to-toe with the Irish prince, the father of her unborn child—a human. "We need to talk."

Finally, a movement—he cocked his head to the side. *Better than nothing, I suppose.* She thought for the dragon's sake.

"You remember," was all he said. Head still cocked, assessing her.

It wasn't a question. How he knew was beyond her. Ever so slowly, she nodded; so much for keeping her emotions under control. Those two words from him made her eyes sting, warning her she was about to cry.

"When?" Warrick's voice was deeper, gravelly, possibly a little angry.

"During my slumber, it all came to me. When I woke, I knew." Atropos was afraid she would lose what little control she had over her emotions if he continued to look at her with such distance and pain in his eyes. "Can we sit and talk?"

"What do you remember, *Jane*?"

Why did he sound so angry? Atropos thought.

"Why are you so angry with me? What have I done?" Her voice was low, barely above a whisper.

"Did you know? After you woke. Did you know?" Warrick spoke nonsense.

"I don't understand what you are asking. Did I know what, Warrick?"

"Have you known the whole time that your name is Atropos?" There, in the kitchen, a few steps from the sink, was where the woman that she hoped always to be, in his eyes, died. If he knows her name, then he knows her position.

A tear ran down her cheeks, replacing the sting with visible hurt. She felt numb, except for that spot in the middle of her chest. It felt like the fissure that started when she remembered who she was just completely cracked apart. She wiped the tear away with her thumb.

Tell him, child. The dragon spoke without her usual sarcasm.

I need you to get out of my head or leave. Atropos sent the thought to the dragon, and then, as she had done with her sisters, she barricaded the signal.

This time, she shook her head as she desperately tried to gain the composure and strength she would need. "I did not. Not until I was woken after you went out for a run today." Her hand went to her abdomen, and with all the strength she could muster, she lifted her chin. "We need to talk, and standing in the middle of your kitchen is not the place."

"Oh, I don't know, *Jane,* seems like as good a place as any, since I'm sure you're dying to get back to—where is that place again? Oh, yes. Olympus."

"I see." Atropos knew they had to talk, and he was going to be an ass. So, she stilled herself to do what was necessary. With a mere thought, she and Warrick were sitting side by side on the sofa—she with a steaming coffee mug in her hands and a blanket over her legs, and he with another bottle of water and fresh clothes.

"What the hell, Jane?" Warrick jumped from the sofa and spun toward her. At least that time when he used her mortal name, he did it with shock and not disgust as before.

"Since you already know who I am, I thought I would make us more comfortable." She held up her hand, palm facing the mortal ass when he looked like he was going to interrupt. "It's my turn to talk. What we have to discuss will take more time than a quick conversation at your kitchen sink. Now," she took a sip of coffee, "I just found out who I am. How long have you known?"

"Are you trying to intimidate me with your power display?" He asked with one eyebrow raised. At least he wasn't afraid of her.

"Of course not. You know I can perform many magics—I believe that's the term humans use—so I cut to the chase. Don't divert the question. When did you find out?"

"Last night. At the gala." Warrick took the seat he had just vacated. "Just before I took you to the other room because of your headache."

"I sensed you were upset, but I don't understand how—,"

"When I asked you to look at the two women, your head exploded with pain. That's when it happened."

Atropos thought back. "They were your biological family. Apparently, every time I got close to remembering anything about myself, my head would start hurting." Atropos thought for a moment. "They stopped mortal time, didn't they?" She asked Warrick.

"That's what I gathered. I suppose it could all just be that I've gone insane instead. It's a lot more plausible that I have." Warrick leaned his head back and looked at the high ceiling. "The dark-haired woman called herself my mother. The red-head, my maternal grandmother. Considering I never knew I wasn't my parents' child, they started from the beginning. Adair, my *mother*, said she saw me fall in love with a Grecian goddess, a Fate, and we would have a very powerful child. No other pantheon would allow such a thing, so she begged The Morrigan, her mother, to help hide me in the mortal realm."

Atropos listened as Warrick spoke. He never looked at her; he just kept conversing with the ceiling. He looked utterly defeated. "I don't know what to say. I was told during my dream state that The Morrigan and Dagda were your grandparents, and Adair your mother."

It didn't take an immortal to know that Warrick was on the brink of what mortals called a meltdown. Too much information, too fast. Her fingers itched to touch him, to console him.

"Were you told of the prophecy they spoke of?" Warrick finally turned his head to the side, still not lifting it, and looked at her, waiting for his answer, practically curled into himself.

Here was her opportunity. The prophecy. "Yes. I was also told of your lineage. I found out from an Irish god who invaded my dreams. Ironically, he wouldn't tell me of my lineage, only part of yours. He knew I had a problem remembering and that I was in love with, and I quote, the Irish Prince." She enjoyed the bit of shock she could hand back to him. Apparently, he had never thought of himself as a prince, or even Irish, since he grew up English. Or was it her declaration of love that had him wide-eyed?

"Can you honestly tell me that you had no idea who I was. Who you were. What you were—and what would happen if we continued to be so—," he broke off his sentence.

Atropos felt her questioning brow jump to her hairline. "So—?"

"Intimate," Warrick finished, his voice slightly raised.

"Wait. Are you suggesting that I wounded myself, nearly died, all to lose my innocence to you? The entire time, claiming amnesia. You cannot be serious." Atropos' heart cracked a little more. She wasn't sure if her immortal heart would continue to beat if she endured much more. If she told him about the baby, he would definitely think it all planned—and just like that, she changed her mind on what she needed to do. *Protect our baby.*

"I honestly don't know what to believe anymore," Warrick said. "None of this seems plausible. I have a hard time believing you knew nothing. No matter what anyone says." He sounded so angry and forlorn.

"I see. Well—," Atropos stood and slowly folded the blanket that had been covering her legs. She felt his eyes boring into her profile as she worked to keep her emotions at bay. "It seems that we have hit the end of whatever this was. Thank you for taking me in. I will take my leave." She rounded the sofa, working hard not to completely break down in front of the only man who, in thousands of years, had ever taken a piece of her. At least he had given her a life to replace it.

Atropos walked out of the room. He made no move to stop her, and with a mere thought, called for her sisters. It took seconds, and she was back on Olympus.

Chapter Thirty-Seven
Olympus

Atropos

Never were the Moirai affectionate, even with one another. So, it took Atropos by surprise when, before she could tell what room of the mansion she was in, Clotho and Lachesis wrapped their arms around her, sobbing into her shoulders. Minutes ticked by before they let her go. She could see her parents waiting for them to part so they could have their turn. When her sisters released her, her parents took their turn. Themis hugged her as she had when she was a child, and Zeus kissed her forehead and muttered something that sounded a lot like, *Thank the Almighty.*

When she looked past her father's frame at her mother, who had backed away to let him have his turn, she could tell that her mother knew. Call it a mother's intuition, or that she was not just Divine Law and Order, but an oracle. Whatever it was, Themis knew she was with child and no longer pure. She could see it in her eyes, and as soon as she thought it, her sisters gasped in unison. *Well, fuck. I forgot to block them in this realm.*

"What's wrong?" Zeus asked whoever would answer.

"Nothing. We are just so happy to have Atropos back with us, that's all." Themis explained. She looked shocked and weary, and so did her sisters.

"I want to know what happened to you?" Zeus bellowed. Apparently, the daddy's little girl phase was gone, and now the broody, she-is-mine, king of the gods wanted answers.

"I'm exhausted, Father. Can I come to you tomorrow and recount my time away? I need a long, hot bath, and my bed."

Zeus looked from her to her sisters, then to Themis. With a resounding huff, he relented. "At first light, come to my throne room. We have much to discuss. Bring your mother with you." Never one to wait for acknowledgment of his orders, Zeus vanished.

Three sets of eyes were trained on her, each with the same question. A mixture of wide eyes and furrowed brows spread across her sisters' faces as if they were shocked but unable to process the information. Themis' eyes were sad, and, unlike her, she was biting her cheek, revealing a vulnerability. *Goddesses should be perfect*—a mantra instilled in them from conception.

Finally, her mother cleared her throat and gestured toward the sitting room. "Please, daughter, let us talk."

Atropos looked at each deity, closed her eyes, and braced for the inevitable. When nothing came, she reopened her eyes to see Lachesis wave her hand, producing glasses of ambrosia and cakes between them. The goddesses took up three of the four gold-trimmed plush chairs that circled a carved, gilded table. Each sipped their nectar and waited for someone to start the uncomfortable conversation.

She was upset with herself for letting the three of them find out the way they had. It had been weeks since she stretched her powers, and when she saw her sisters' faces, she realized her mistake. Coming to terms with who and what she was proved difficult. Throw in that she fell in love with a man who last looked at her with disdain and the baby in the womb from that man, and she wasn't sure she would ever think rationally again, let alone remember to be on constant guard with mental intruders. *That was the first time I ever thought of our bond as intrusive.* Atropos covered her mouth at the realization and strained to keep her hormonal emotions under control.

Stilling herself to be the one who broke the silence first, she placed her cup on the table and straightened her spine. "I woke in a human hospital. A mortal male found me on his property, injured. Somehow, I ended up hitting my head and almost died—well, I suppose I would have died if I had not been divine. Anyway, I was in what they called a coma for a few days, and when I woke up, I knew nothing. Not who I was, what I am—nothing. All I knew was that the world felt off, and nothing made sense. Warrick, the man who saved me, had been the only one to visit. The healers felt I should stay with him while my brain healed and my memories returned."

"I see," Themis said. "How did your condition come about? Did the human harm you?"

That was her mother. Divine Law and Order, always thinking she needed to bring order to a situation. Most of the time, she was all for the humans. Often, she and her five sisters thought she loved mortals more than her own daughters, but Atropos could see it written all over her mother's face. She was ready to unleash all the power of Olympus on Warrick.

"No, Mother. He and I fell in love. I didn't know I was a virgin when it happened. I had guessed I wasn't overly familiar with such intimacy, but I had no idea I would turn out to be a celibate goddess. We guarded ourselves against pregnancy, but destiny will have its way." She was struggling not to show the emotion the subject of Warrick and their unborn child brought out in her. *Goddesses should be perfect.*

Lachesis and Clotho both gasped. Atropos hung her head. Keeping her sisters out of her head for any length of time proved hopeless as she tried to guard against her emotions taking over.

"Who prophesied this?" Her sisters spoke in unison, as they often did. This time, it was just the two of them, and she was on the receiving end of the mind meld.

"That goddesses are meant to be perfect?" Atropos knew that wasn't what they were asking about, but why not?

Again, in harmony, her sisters spoke, "No, who prophesied your destiny?"

Irish deities and the story of Warrick's past spilled from Atropos. She was glad they let her get everything out before making any abrupt decisions. *Will they want me to stay in the Moirai mansion? What if father won't allow me to stay on Olympus? Do I want to?* Her mind reeled as she spoke.

She watched her sisters sit stoically, ears tentatively pricked. It was the bond that gave way to their true feelings. Both ached for her and were saddened only by where she and Warrick left things. *That's odd.*

Whenever the subject of the unborn child came up, she could feel warmth and happiness emanating from her sisters. Everything coming through the bond was unexpected. She thought she would glean disgust, rage, and even sadness from their minds, but it was quite the opposite. She felt them embrace her.

We love you, came down their mental channel from Lachesis.

Once her tale was complete, her mother stood and motioned for her to stand with her. She grabbed both of her hands and stared into her soul with her gray eyes. "You are my child. I know we aren't a family of affectionate beings, but you will always be my baby girl." Themis placed her hand over Atropos's hand, which was fixed to her belly. "This baby is my granddaughter. Keep her safe from all who might harm her. Your sisters and I will be with you—the Moirai and the Horae."

"Thank you, Mother." Still holding Themis' hands, Atropos bowed her head and gave her a slight curtsy. Not only was she their mother—she was once their queen and deserved the honor.

"I will be in Zeus' throne room early. He will know your story before you enter. I guarantee that he will fight to keep you safe here on Olympus. No other pantheon will take your child or mine. Now, go rest and enjoy being back with your sisters. They've missed you something fierce." With one last kiss on her forehead, her mother dematerialized.

Slowly, Atropos turned to her sisters, and, for the second time in thousands of years, they embraced her as if she were their world.

Chapter Thirty-Eight
Mouthy Dragon

Warrick

Still sitting on his sofa, Warrick rubbed his hands down his face, completely exasperated by his actions. He could not fathom why in the bloody hell he sat back and allowed the woman he was in love with to walk out. He hadn't thought when she left the living room that she would immediately leave. When he heard the odd crackling sound, he knew. The apartment felt empty.

"I'm such an idiot," Warrick said aloud.

"That you are human," a voice came from behind him. Warrick bolted upright and turned to see who had let themselves into his apartment. To his astonishment, it was a middle-aged woman with larger-than-normal nostrils and dark golden, slightly slanted eyes. She wasn't dreadful, just unusual, much like what he imagined an alien to look like.

"Who the bloody hell are you and how the fuck did you get in here?" Warrick now stood a mere meter from the stranger, and she made no attempt to flee.

"She warned me not to show myself in my proper form because it might kill you—something about heart failure." The bizarre-looking woman scratched her chin with one long fingernail. "So, I'm here in this human skin. Why didn't I just scare you to death after your earlier display? It's beyond me. Anyway, human—I'm Atropos' guardian. You may refer to me as Drakaina."

"Okay. Drakaina. How did you get into my home?" Warrick's voice lowered an octave, and he felt his hands pumping into fists at his sides. Two signs he had enough.

"And here I was told that humans were inclined to be clever creatures. I should check my sources better. Did I not just tell you that I'm Atropos' guardian?"

"You did." Warrick's neck grew hot.

"Does it not stand to reason that I was either already here or that if I'm the guardian of a goddess, that I might be able to materialize and vanish as I wish?" Drakaina demonstrated by doing just that. Except she popped to the far corner of the room.

"What the fuck? How'd—?" Warrick was having trouble forming sentences. Pointing and grunting was all his brain would allow at that moment. Every hair on his body stood at attention from the chills that plagued him. "She just vanished and reappeared on the other side of the room." He was talking to himself, but the woman commented on his musings anyway.

"Ah, there's that human intelligence, I see." He watched as the strange lady rolled her golden eyes—of which he had never seen such an eye color on a person before.

"You are nothing like Jane. What are you?" He could hear the unease in his own voice. Every muscle in his body tensed, readying to run from her.

The woman took a few steps closer to him, and he fought his instincts and planted his feet, refusing to give away any ground. "Finally, you ask a question that is not ridiculous, human."

"Stop calling me human. Again, what are you?" His voice sounded a little more stable that time. *Good.*

"Want me to show you—hum—Warrick?" Her grin was borderline maniacal. "I mean, I could just tell you, but what fun is that? You choose. Show or tell?"

"Just tell me, for gods' sake. I don't have all day. I need to find Jane."

"Oh, you're no fun. Sit. This will take a while. No, you are not going to look for Atropos. That's her name, by the way. Say it, human." The woman pointed at the sofa, directing him there while demanding he say Jane's real name.

With a deep inhale to settle his anger, Warrick did as the woman said. "Atropos." Then he sat, wondering why he was allowing a woman who had yet to answer his question to tell him what to do.

"I can see and hear your reluctance to accept what you have learned over the last twenty-four human hours. Until you are ready to admit to yourself that humans are amongst the minority in this world, you will not be worthy of Atropos or your station." Drakaina conjured a large, cushy chair in the corner of the room, where she sat and snuggled in.

Warrick jumped to his feet from the adrenaline sparked by the magic. "What the bloody hell? How did you do that?"

"I see. It's the show that you understand, no matter the words spoken. I just told you that mortals are the minority, and you focused on the chair."

Warrick watched as she rubbed her hands back and forth over the arms of the plush monstrosity. "Well, it seems you and I are going to take a trip together. We will see if Atropos was correct about your human heart." The strange woman prattled on as he continued to stare at the chair.

Before the woman could perform another act, the thin hairs on the back of Warrick's neck stood on end. He felt her as soon as she spoke.

"Not so fast, egg layer," came a familiar woman's Irish lilt.

Out of thin air, the woman who called herself his mother appeared between him and Jane's, *shit Atropos'*, guardian. No longer was she dressed in the finery from the gala. She wore an ancient black Irish bog dress with a tight-fitting bodice and full-length skirts covering her feet. Her onyx hair made it difficult to tell where her long locks ended and her dress began; they bled seamlessly into each other. She was beautiful, and Warrick could see the uncanny resemblance. Same blue eyes with inhumanly long lashes and perfect bow lips.

Perched on top of her right shoulder sat a large crow. When he gave the bird his attention, it squawked and asked him, "Whatcha lookin' at?"

"Well, well, well. Has Mama decided her son needs her attention? As you can see," Atropos' guardian gestured between herself and Warrick, "we don't need your assistance. I promise not to eat him."

"What did you just say?" Warrick knew the shock of her statement had to be all over his face. "Eat me? What in the bloody hell are you on about?"

"You haven't even introduced yourself, Dragon?" Adair asked, not looking at the strange woman still seated in the conjured chair but straight at him.

"D-Dragon? What do you mean, dragon?" his eyes were jumping between the two women and occasionally the crow. He knew neither of them very well, including the Irish who claimed to be family, so his flight instinct was on high alert, and ways to escape their presence played through his mind.

"Not that it is any of your concern, Raven Queen's daughter, but I was asked by Atropos not to expose myself to him due to his fragile mortal essence. If you insist, I could change right here. I will adjust my stature to the room around me, so no need to remove furniture or the roof." The smirk on the weird woman's face was priceless. She gave new meaning to the adage—*If looks could kill.*

Warrick watched as the women verbally sparred, trying to piece together what they were saying and what they weren't. Unable to take the bickering any longer, he interrupted. "Someone tell me what the hell his going on." And to his astonishment, the crow on Adair's shoulder shrieked and then repeated him word for word.

Adair took pity on him and gestured to the sofa. He was getting damn tired of people telling him to sit down, but he reasoned that if he wanted answers, he should do as she asked.

To his surprise, after he sat, the woman who called herself Drakaina was the one to start. "Your mother is correct; I am a dragon from the Greek Pantheon. Have you ever heard the tale of the Golden Fleece?"

"Yes, although I'm not well-versed in it. I remember that a dragon—No! There's no way." Warrick answered.

"That is precisely what I meant by you have to acknowledge your heritage so you can appreciate hers."

He knew the woman meant Jane—*Atropos,* internally correcting himself again. "Are you telling me that you are actually a dragon and not an odd-looking woman?"

Drakaina leaned her head back and laughed. "Good thing I've had many a century to learn not to be offended by such things. Yes, I am the Colchian Dragon. Zeus sent me on a mission with three of his daughters to find Atropos. When we discovered her, she was with you and the Irish goddesses in that gathering of your nobility."

"You're an actual dragon," Warrick said aloud, trying to wrap his mind around the fact. He then turned to his biological mother. "And you are truly my mum?" When Adair nodded, he leaned forward, placing his elbows on his knees and his head in his hands. "And I suppose Alaric is really an angel. It would be so much simpler if I were mad than knowing immortals and creatures of legend exist," his hands muffled his words, but when the dragon answered, he knew they heard.

"Angel? You saw the Angel?" Drakaina asked.

Warrick sat up and prepared to absorb a great deal of information. "A couple of times. The first time we met, he purchased an apartment from me. The second time was during an early morning run after the gala. You and your mother had just told me about my lineage and the prophecy," he addressed Adair, "and I was upset, trying to come to grips with everything you told me and what that meant for my relationship with Jane. Anyway, Alaric, he called himself, came and reiterated everything you had said. He also elaborated a little more on the prophecy."

"That angel took my master's daughter, and she was injured in the mortal realm. He's high on my list of creatures that need to be eaten," Drakaina said.

Warrick watched Adair roll her eyes at the eccentric woman. "As I told you before, I asked The Morrigan to help me hide you after I witnessed the prophecy. The only proper way to conceal a godling is to strip them of all their god signature and turn them mortal. You have to understand—the life of a god is not what one would think. Yes, we have riches and power, but true love tends to wane over time, and when that's all you have, you become bitter and complacent. I felt like turning you mortal was far better than you awakening the prophecy and being hunted by every pantheon." Adair's confession sounded a lot like a plea for forgiveness. "I begged The Morrigan to help me. She told me it would not work. I knew better—but my love for my child outweighed any sense."

The crow on Adair's shoulder stared at Warrick the entire time she spoke. It turned its head sideways a few times, as if it were trying to read his mind. *Maybe it can.* Warrick thought right before the ebony bird cawed and flew from Adair's shoulder onto his.

His spine went rigid. He'd never been that close to a live crow before. It looked straight into Warrick's right eye, bending its head from one side to the other. He could have sworn he saw The Great Queen in its pupil.

"What is this bird doing?" he asked Adair. "Is this my grand-mother?"

"And here I thought our pantheon was peculiar," the dragon said under her breath.

"No. However, she can take hold of the bird's essence and see through its eyes while controlling some of its behaviors," Adair answered.

"That must be why I saw your mother in its pupil," Warrick replied. "Please take it." He walked to Adair and turned so she could remove the creature.

"I am sorry. She wants to make sure everything is going well. I've been asked to bring you back to our realm. Before you say anything, it's just for a visit, and as soon as you want to return, I will bring you back," Adair said.

"I'm not sure about that," Warrick replied.

"Oh, goddess, before you interrupted our day, Warrick and I were going on an adventure. I think he would be better off with the Greek Pantheon. I mean, that is where Atropos is," Drakaina said, grinning so wide all of her pointed teeth were on full display.

"Look, dragon. I'm not going to say that I understand why you want my son to go with you, but whatever your reason, good or bad, it will not happen. Even if he doesn't want to go with me, he will not be going to Olympus."

"For now. Mark my word, Adair. He will go to Olympus at some point—if not sooner than even you can see. That will be the safest place for them." With those final words, Drakaina disappeared, leaving Warrick alone with the woman who proclaimed to be his mother, a goddess, and a seer.

Chapter Thirty-Nine
Secrets Must Be Kept

Atropos

Atropos slid her fingers across the enormous four-poster bed made of olive wood, remembering her first time in the guest room at Warrick's apartment. No television decorated the sixteen-foot walls of her bedchamber. Instead, it was adorned with paintings by artists who lived centuries prior. Lachesis acquired the infamous paintings of The Fates Three from The Gallery of the gods and divided them. Hers hung above her bed. Looking at it, Atropos thought about the goddess she had been before and the woman standing before the piece. Her face sat center stage and proved who was once most important—she had thought she was. She decided while standing before the large painting of Death that she would rather hang anything other than a painting of herself in her chamber. The goddess she was now would be the deity she would strive to be forever—the one in the painting was no more. She needed to tell her father that she wanted to be with Warrick—or have him live with her on Olympus. Either would do; however, living without him would not. *I should not have left. I should've fought for him.*

It was time, so with a mere thought, Atropos stood in her father's atrium surrounded by statues of the Olympians. Every god and goddess was on full display in white and gray marble. Before, she only saw the ones on the far right—The Fates—herself. Now she saw all the gods.

"Goddess, our king, and your mother are waiting. Follow me," the young nymph said as she turned.

Was it her, or did the walk from the entryway to Zeus' throne room feel so much further than ever before? She supposed it was the anticipation of his reaction when she told him of her ultimate decision. Even if he was her king and her father, he knew, and so did everyone else, that whatever a Fate wanted, they got. All beings were afraid of the ones who held the threads that bound them. Even a god's thread could be severed. It took a special set of scissors, but it had been done many times—Phobos' face flitted through her mind. Even though his thread needed to be separated, she did it with no remorse. That was unacceptable. *One should never kill and remain unaffected by it.* She thought.

The nymph stopped and gestured for her to enter the vast room with its equally large owner. Zeus was very tall and extremely handsome. He sported a graying beard and the body of a thirty-year-old man who paid daily homage to the gym. All the gods of Olympus were beautiful, so it stood to reason their king was magnificent.

Entering the room, Atropos noticed that another, besides her parents, waited for her. Zeus sat on the carved throne, and her mother stood at the base of the dais, to Zeus' right. The Colchian Dragon sat to the side, further from the dais, her size taking up a lot of space. Well, this should be even more interesting than she thought it would be.

All heads turned to watch her approach the king. She, like all of his subjects, curtsied before the throne—she didn't need to give him another reason to be angry with her. No matter who held the power, it was the respect that came with his station that made her lower herself.

"Approach," came the baritone command from her king.

She obeyed and moved to stand by her mother. Movement came from behind them, and she figured the dragon had ventured closer. Atropos clasped her hands in front of her and did not look at Zeus until he began; even if it took forever, she would hold her tongue. More proof she had grown on her trip to the mortal realm.

"Be thankful, child. Your mother came before you and begged for an audience. She told me of the dilemma you find yourself in—but I'm unsure you understand the extent of what you have done." Zeus stood from his throne and walked down two of the five steps that made their way to the dais.

Oh, she knew, but she would never tell him that. It wasn't the loss of her virtue or the fact that she was with child. It was that the child belonged to two pantheons and could very well be more powerful than any god before. The daughter she carried was an enigma—the first of her sort. Like the Nephilim, her daughter would be one of a kind; unlike the Nephilim, she would be an infant—a babe born of royals from two powerful pantheons. A newborn to a Fate of one realm and the great-grandchild of the triple goddess who decided the death of warriors. The grandchild of one powerful god-king and the great-grandchild of another. Not to mention the granddaughter of the most powerful seer to have ever lived. The power of law and justice ran through her baby's veins with the potential to influence metamorphosis. No other pantheon would allow such a child to be born.

"Yes, father," Atropos looked up at her father. He might be the king who once treated her mother harshly, but he had always respected the Moirai. Was it the power they possessed? *Possibly.* But no matter the reason, he demanded they always call him father instead of your majesty or king.

"A child is never a burden. However, this one will be a danger to you, to herself, and to anyone who loves her or tries to protect her. Once this child is known, every pantheon will be terrified. She will be the first of such power, and from what Drakaina whispered in my ear, she is the first of more. She is a prophecy come true, and now it's our Pantheon's responsibility to keep her safe until she can do that for herself."

"I understand. May I speak to you about her father, Warrick?" Atropos asked.

"May I interject, your majesty?" To Atropos' surprise, the dragon had morphed into a woman and interrupted.

Not smart, Dragon, Atropos telepathically chastised the beast.

"I do believe what you have told me needs to be said. You have the floor, dragon; however, don't take too long." Zeus acknowledged the interruption with grace and walked back to his throne.

Atropos closed her mouth when she realized that her shock at the disruption had her father agreeing. *How close is he to this reptile?*

I heard that, Thread Cutter. Remember who I am.

Atropos jerked her gaze to the eccentric woman, who smiled widely as she tapped her temple. *Well? Answer the question.* She refused to be intimidated.

Oh, I will. But for now, I have information you need. It may help you get what you want. Yes, dear, I can see everything in your head.

"I know the two of you are conversing," Zeus cleared his throat. "If you are going to speak, do it aloud so we can all enjoy the banter."

"I'm sorry." Drakaina looked between Themis and Atropos as she spoke. "After you left, I spoke with Alasdair, the man you call Warrick. He is still struggling to believe in what he considers impossible. After some verbal sparring, I come to understand that he is more of a show-me kind of man. I was about to rapture him when his mother, the goddess, not the mortal, showed up. She knew what I was and refused us our trip to Olympus. She is taking him to the Irish Pantheon. I did not tell either of them that the prophecy was triggered, and you are expecting."

Atropos felt her heart speed up. Warrick was in the realm of the Irish gods. How would she ever get to him? "If they don't know the prophecy has been set in motion, how do we know they will allow him back into the mortal realm? Keeping him would ensure the prophecy didn't start."

"No matter what, Adair and The Morrigan know one cannot extinguish a person's destiny," Themis interjected.

"The Irish will not keep him from going back if he wants to. My opinion is to give him a few days to come to terms with the strangeness he found himself in, and to have someone watch for his return. Until then, you remain here and stay safe," Drakaina spoke without her usual sarcasm.

"Daughter," Zeus' booming voice made her jump. "Your mother told me everything, and while I'm not pleased with the fact that you and my granddaughter will be in danger, I hold no ill will toward you."

Atropos knew her father's approval was necessary, but to what extent she had not considered until his words brought hot tears to both eyes. Zeus' first time to see the Death Dealer cry, and it was the approval of her and the baby she carried. And for the second day in a row, her mother wrapped her in her arms and let her feel.

"The news of Atropos' baby will be kept between your Moirai sisters and us. Do not speak of this to the Horae or any of your half-siblings," Zeus demanded.

"What if the Oneiroi find out?" Atropos asked.

"They know better than to tell your private dreams to anyone—including me," her father answered. "Now, leave us." Zeus looked pointedly at her and Drakaina.

Chapter Forty
Irish Realm

Warrick

It took Adair just over seventy-two hours to convince him to return to the Irish realm with her. To Warrick's surprise, she stayed after the dragon left, asking to see his world. Deep down, he knew she was trying to get to know him, but he wasn't so sure he cared. Whenever he entertained the thought of her being his mum, the thought of her abandoning him and wiping him clean of all magic made his chest ache. How can you miss what you never had? He also found himself indulging her wish to find out more about him. It took some convincing for her to leave the crow behind. Apparently, where she came from, it wasn't odd to have a crow on your shoulder.

First stop—the construction site, where he found Atropos injured; then his office, where he introduced her to Anna. He was fairly sure his PA didn't buy it when he told her that the new woman with him was a cousin from Ireland. During those couple of days of being Adair's tour guide, he watched her when she wasn't aware. He could practically see the wheels turning in her head. Deep thought and worry creased her brow. Only once did he ask if she was okay. After seeing her in that state several times, he had to know. Faster than he thought possible, her demeanor changed, and all signs of distress vanished. Clearly, she was hiding something, and that something troubled her. Hopefully, her burdens were not because of him. Upset as he was with the woman, he didn't want to be responsible for her troubling thoughts, so he gave in to her invitation.

That's how he found himself standing outside a stone circle in the middle of who-knows-where, Ireland. One second, they were standing in his living room. The next second, they stood on grass reaching above his ankles. Making a journey of almost two thousand kilometers in mere seconds. It stood to reason that he was a little stunned.

He heard Adair the first time, or so he thought. She was telling him what they needed to do to cross over to the realm of the Tuatha Dé Danann, but apparently it was the third or fourth time she had repeated herself, because the exasperation in her voice pulled him from his thoughts. When he looked at the seer, she had a hand on her hip, and frustration wrinkled her brow.

"Since you are with me and the blood in your veins runs royal, you will pass through without issue. Now, hold my hand," Adair held her hand out to him and wiggled her fingers.

He took the proffered hand but noticed blood on the palm of her other hand. *Where did that come from?* He wasn't about to inquire because the look on her face was that of annoyance. It seemed goddesses weren't accustomed to repeating themselves—much like billionaires.

"It's just hard for me to believe that mortals don't stumble into other realms all the time," Warrick said as he took her hand.

"The stones know our blood. Even yours without your powers still hold the essence of the god. If you so desired, you could do this without a deity. Now, prepare yourself. The first-time crossing realms can be a little overwhelming." With that last warning, Adair skimmed her bloody palm over the roughened stone and closed her eyes.

Dizziness engulfed Warrick. It felt as if his insides were being left on earth while his feet followed Adair. At the onset of the nausea, he closed his eyes. Hell, he wasn't sure what was happening, but it felt vastly different from leaving one country and finding himself in another. When prompted, he opened his eyes to what he could only describe as an ancient land. The air smelled of earth and sea. Few people milled about, but those who were there wore ancient Irish garments, and several were covered from head to toe in battle armor as if they expected a war to break out at any moment. He stood outside an enormous castle that looked far newer than the ones he toured as a teenager.

When he saw several women and a couple of men walking around with onyx birds either perched on their shoulders or forearms, he cracked a smile—of all things to snap him out of being awestruck.

"I guess you were right," Warrick nodded toward two women talking, each with a bird perched on their shoulder. "Owning a crow is a thing here."

Adair laughed. Her singsong laughter hit him differently. Maybe it was their surroundings, but one thing was for certain. In that moment, he knew—*she is my mum.* The realization made him stumble.

"Are you well, son?" she asked.

"I am—and I'm not. This is just so much to take in. A few days ago, there wasn't such a thing as mythological gods and strange creatures actually roaming the Earth. Divine beings weren't walking around with crows on their shoulders, boulders couldn't take you to faraway lands, and I knew who my parents were. I'll be okay. It's just going to take time."

"I understand. It's my fault this is happening to you. Please know that if I could turn back time, instead of predicting it, this wouldn't be how your life would go. This," Adair gestured around them, "would be your legacy since you would help rule one day, and you would not struggle with an unknown heritage with a family of strangers."

"I've had a wonderful life. It was complete until Jane, I mean Atropos, walked away. Before her, I enjoyed everything a human being could ever ask for. Now—," he looked off into the distance as he thought about Atropos. "—I feel like I was somehow cheated. My feelings are ridiculous, I know this. Here I am, one of the youngest billionaires in the mortal realm with my whole life ahead of me, and before the redhead entered my life, I was content with that. Happy even. If I could have her back, I would give it all up."

"I know. I've watched you grow up, and so has your grandmother. Your adopted father wasn't always my favourite person in your life, though he did provide for you well. Humans have incredible senses when they allow them to flourish. It's when they suppress them that misplaced anger and irrational reactions take place. If your earthly father had just spoken with your mother, he would have known she hadn't had an affair, though he was correct, you were not his son, nor were you hers."

"What will happen from here? I do have a very productive life at home." He didn't look at Adair. Instead, he looked out over the green moors of ancient Ireland, wondering what they expected of him now that he knew of their world.

"You are mortal, Alasdair."

Hearing her use his given name made him jerk his eyes toward her. "I understand that is the name you gave me. I respect that, but I've had enough shock, and if it's not too much to ask, I want to be called by Warrick. That's one thing I can control when it feels I control nothing."

"That's fair. What I was saying was that you are mortal. Your place is the mortal realm; however, until we know what Atropos plans on doing about the prophecy, a permanent home will be left up to fate."

"She left me and went back to Olympus. Maybe the prophecy was miscommunication," Warrick mumbled. The irony was palpable. Just two days ago, he blamed her for trying to make the prophecy come true by getting pregnant. Now all he wanted was to be with her forever and fill her belly with babies.

"Son, I have seen how that goddess looks at you. She's not done with you yet. Now, before my father sends out a hunting party for us, we'd better get into the castle."

Surprisingly, it took longer than expected to get to his grandfather's throne room. Trepidation had all of his senses on high alert. He could still smell the clean sea air and the earthy scents of moss and grass deep inside the castle. Being immersed in the fortress, with its damp stone walls, gave him a chill which countered the clammy hands he wiped down his jeans. Finally, coming to a stop, Warrick couldn't help but admire the ornately carved double doors before them. Their wooden structure was amazing, and as a construction master, he appreciated its beauty. The doors stood closed, so tight that no light seeped through from the other side. The carvings were so intricate that he wondered how unaided hands could produce such flawless work.

What lay behind them was the heritage Adair had just spoken about. Mere inches of heavy wood stood between him and the king of the Irish Pantheon, The Phantom Queen, and a world he wasn't sure he wanted to know. His palms were still damp, so once more he rubbed them down the sides of his jeans.

"I can feel that your heart picked up rhythm. There is no need to be so uneasy; no one in this realm would ever seek to harm you."

"It's not that I'm afraid of what's about to take place; it's that behind those doors, the life I've always known will come to an end. This," Warrick looked around at the dark, damp walls with battle armor hanging as if they were Sadler paintings, "I can say was a dream. Behind there," he pointed at the doors, "are people I can never chalk up to an overactive imagination. You were in my world. You by my side is an extension of that. In there—that's your world. And only your world." Warrick sucked in as much air as his lungs would take. "I'm ready."

Warrick watched as Adair slowly curled her fingers, then rapidly opened them up, flinging the heavy doors wide. Warm candlelight glowed all around the vast room, flickering off the giant man and the red-headed woman from the gala—*The Morrigan.* From the tension in the air, whatever happened before Adair flung the doors open had not been amiable. Both god and goddess tried to hide their irritation, to no avail. It hung too long in the air to be defied. Warrick felt Dagda's contempt, and from The Morrigan, he deemed her sentiments more regret and sadness. *Am I feeling their emotions? Weird.*

Adair's head swiveled between him and her parents. He briefly wondered if she had seen their meeting before she opened the doors. "Warrick, this is my father, ruler of the realms of the Tuatha Dé Danann, King of the Irish Pantheon, and your grandfather." Dagda nodded in greeting. "And you have met my mother, The Morrigan, The Harbinger of Death, and your grandmother." She also nodded. "Mother, Father, meet Warrick, who was born Alasdair, Defender of Mankind, your grandson."

Instead of nodding, he turned his head and looked at Adair with a raised eyebrow. "Defender of Mankind?" He was positive he broke protocol, but damn. The surprises kept coming. "I've never heard that before."

"That is your title, here." The deep, heavy brogue boomed in the somber atmosphere. Dagda came from behind the table and stood less than a meter from him. He was a beast of a man, highlighting his own size, which was much taller than that of the parents who raised him.

"Father, he has asked that we call him by Warrick, his human name," Adair revealed.

Warrick could tell the god wasn't pleased with his refusal to be called by his birth name. So, as any good business mogul would, he took charge of the situation, not giving Adair a chance to answer for him. "It's for now. With all the recent shocks, I find it unnatural to be called by a name I only heard a few days ago. I hope you understand."

Each gave a slight nod and moved on from the topic of his *title*.

"I'm glad you decided to embrace your true nature. Here, you are the royalty you were born to be." Dagda's words were kind and at odds with his size.

Warrick supposed they were trying not to give him any reason to refuse them. All three gods seemed eager for him to be a part of their family.

"Even though I possess no godly abilities?" Warrick asked.

"Your blood makes you sovereign, not magical ability. You carry the blood of the King of Great Knowledge and the Phantom Queen. No one will question your lineage. They will sense it." The Morrigan walked around and stood by Dagda as she spoke.

The three deities stood so close that Warrick could touch any of them and not extend his arm all the way. A profound sense of respect roared through him, and he fought to stay upright, but he lost control of his head. Involuntary reverence had him looking at four sets of feet, head bowed.

A booming laugh released his forced response. "You are definitely our grandson. A human in form, a god in blood, you are the first to withstand the compulsion of our station. Some may resist one of us; a couple have resisted two of us. You are the only one to resist hitting their knees when in the presence of the three of us."

In that moment, Warrick felt the hum of his blood. There was a difference he couldn't fully place, but he was no longer just a human man.

Chapter Forty-One

The Prophecy

Warrick

Adair became someone Warrick could count on to tell him the truth—or so he thought.

They had been in the Irish realm for three days, and she had divulged much of her past and the actual history of her parents, not the human mythos from books and television. He sensed she was desperate for him to understand her world. Unfortunately, it would take time to come to terms with her abandonment of him to mortals whom she didn't know. After many conversations, he understood she thought she was keeping him safe, but that didn't stop the emotional war going on inside him. Many trips around the castle and several around the lands had Warrick wondering why she thought he would be safer anywhere other than in a realm full of gods ready for battle. Everywhere he looked, immortals walked freely with weapons strapped to their backs. The castle seemed impenetrable, with its vast walls and the magic that surrounded it. Once they were more comfortable with each other, he would ask. For now, he listened, absorbed what she told him, and took lessons in wielding weapons from his grandfather.

Late in the day, Adair invited him for a walk along the shoreline. Usually, while on their walks, he remained engrossed in their conversation, but being on the edge of such a large body of water had him thinking of home. The salty smell of the sea permeated the whole of the land, but there, with the cool water splashing over their feet and the thick scent of the sea had him missing

Monaco—missing her. It was the tall cliffs hugged by the ocean that made him realize how far he was from the warmer waters of the Mediterranean.

Internally, he warred with himself, knowing she was no longer in Monte Carlo, and if he were there, he would still miss her. *Maybe I should've gone with the dragon.* Lost in thoughts of what could have been, Adair's raised voice grabbed his attention, snapping him back to reality.

"I'm sorry. I was immersed in thought. What were you saying?"

"I was asking if you were okay. You've been distracted all day," Adair bent and grabbed a rock. "What has your mind so consumed?"

"Nothing. I'm fine." Warrick didn't want to talk about Atropos. He wanted to see her. Discussing her would only make everything real. For now, he could pretend she was part of his imagination—just a dream. Regrettably, he wasn't very good at lying to himself.

"You asked if I was okay when we were in the human realm, when I was melancholy. I claimed, as you just did, that I was okay. When we don't want to burden anyone, we tell a trivial lie. You knew I wasn't being honest, just like you aren't being honest now. So, I'm going to tell you what I was upset about, and I want you to do the same with me." Adair waited for his answer.

"Deal. What had you upset that day?" Warrick asked.

"Not wanting to sound ridiculous, I didn't tell you that something the dragon said had me wondering. It was too early for me to see, even then, but as of two days ago, I should have been able to," Adair nervously stroked the tail feathers of the crow with one hand and turned the rock over and over in the other.

"Am I supposed to understand what you are talking about?" Warrick could feel the apprehension radiating off his mother. That was the first time he thought of her as his mother and meant it.

Adair gave him a half-hearted smile. One that in no way gave off happiness. "When The Morrigan became pregnant with me, she foresaw my ability. The fear of my power drove her to flee with me, trying to protect my father from what she foresaw I would see. She, in her own right, is a powerful oracle, but I am the best seer ever to live—that includes all realms and every pantheon. When I found out the reason, my mother wouldn't allow me to meet my father, and I was angry. We both knew she couldn't stop destiny, but she ruined my relationship with my father anyway. When I saw your fate, I was wracked with fear and sadness. I knew better, but panic took hold of me, and all I wanted was for the vision to be false. I called for my mother for the first time in thousands of years. I did the same thing with you that she had done with me, knowing deep down it would never work. Destiny will prevail, but my love for you was too strong to think rationally.

After the dragon said you would go to Olympus, possibly sooner than even I could see, I wondered what she meant. The only thing I could fathom was that the prophecy had begun. Atropos must be with the child, and Drakaina knew you would go with her to keep them safe. So, I scried and looked into my theory. I saw Atropos through the water, but it was too soon to tell if she was with child. Yesterday and again today, I looked by scrying with rocks and water, and again without anything but my divinity. Each time, I couldn't see Atropos. She is no longer accessible to my sight."

"What are you saying?" Warrick asked. He felt unease spread through his body. "What's happened to Atropos?" Not thinking, he grabbed Adair's shoulders and demanded. "Is she alive?" His hands trembled.

"This has never happened. I can see whatever I set out to view, even in other realms. I can feel her life force; she is alive and well. There is only one explanation. Atropos is with child—your child."

Dizziness, then the sour taste of bile hit Warrick. It wasn't until the first inclination of fear left him that he took in exactly what Adair said. Only once had he experienced a pregnancy scare—he was only nineteen. *How can this be? I used protection, hell, I even explained it to her.* Warrick paced in front of Adair, running his hands through his hair as he tried to process her words. He finally came to a stop and stared at the sea while he spoke aloud.

"I'm to be a father?" He felt his grin spread. His smile was so large that the corners of his lips ached from the strain. "Are you certain?"

"It was part of the prophecy. 'Only three can see the child before its birth,'" Adair recited.

"Why would that be?" Warrick asked.

"The Almighty doesn't want the child seen. If the babe cannot be seen, then the truth of it cannot be proven. Your baby has protections even without our interference."

"Wait. You never told me that part of the prophecy. Is there more you aren't telling me?" Warrick felt her fear and watched her hesitation.

"Yes. There is more. I don't believe you are ready for it in its entirety. I'm surely not prepared to deliver it." Adair turned and started the trek back toward the castle.

"Adair," Warrick called after her. She continued without turning around. "Adair, stop!" Still nothing. Forward she rushed. "Mother!" Warrick yelled in a voice as commanding as his grandfather's.

Adair stopped and slowly turned to face him. She had made it several meters, but he could still see the tears dripping from her face.

"Please do not make me recite the complete prophecy. I beg you. Just let this go." His mother begged loudly enough for him to hear over the breeze. The crow's piercing caw filled the air, as if it felt its owner's distress, clearly agitated.

Warrick jogged to her. They were now toe-to-toe, cool waves still splashing their feet. "If you don't tell me, I can't prepare for the outcome."

"If I tell you, you will spend time trying to prevent things that cannot be stopped. Just as my mother did and as I did with you. Destiny will prevail, no matter your interference."

"Please tell me," Warrick begged.

"That prophecy had me so upset, I never tried to see it again. Let me look; whether the outcome is the same or different, I will tell you. Only the Almighty can change one's lot. Just let me see if He has altered any of it. I promise, I will tell you." Adair's face wore fear and the tears of sadness. Whatever she was hiding was beyond troubling.

"When will you know?" Warrick asked.

"Give me a couple of days." She pleaded with her eyes.

"Forty-eight hours. No matter what." Warrick said.

Adair nodded, looking at the tiny pebbles at their feet. "No matter what," she repeated.

Warrick retired to his room in the northern tower of the castle. Adair told him when she showed him the room that it would be his for eternity. And there lies the question he's been afraid to address. How long is eternity for a god turned human? Is he immortal, or, as his lack of a god signature would suggest, mortal? Several nights after he was told of his lineage, he lay awake for hours, contemplating how life would unfold if Atropos came back. She was forever; he might only be given seventy-five to eighty years. Even though that would be a long life for a human, it would be a slight drop in the vessel of time for an immortal god from the royal line. Could he break her heart that way? Would their child be a demigod? How long do demigods have?

In the darkness of a castle in another realm, Warrick could only worry about his baby and the goddess he loved. Are they okay? Will she have to live a god's lifetime without him and their child? How can he get to her? What about the prophecy had Adair so worried?

He fell asleep with the thought of Atropos holding their tiny bundle with love radiating from her eyes as she watched their child sleep.

Chapter Forty-Two

Sisters

Atropos

Atropos had two constant companions—her unborn baby and exhaustion. She hadn't slept since arriving on Olympus. Granted, it had only been one night, but knowing she would face her father, she tossed and turned as if it were an Olympian sport. Her mother must have woven some magic, because Zeus was taking her situation extremely well. Her fear was that he was right. Few, including some gods of Olympus, would want her child to be born. She had one thing on her side—she was the Thread Cutter, the Inflexible One. After being in the earthly realm, she had thought the weight of her station a burden. Now she believed the title was the greatest protection her child could have. Every being knew she would exact revenge if they harmed her or her baby—and many knew from the past that she didn't have to cut a thread quickly—threads could be shredded, slowly, with the right amount of resentment.

She closed her eyes and prayed to the Almighty—something she had never done before—for the protection of her unborn child and Warrick.

Gradually, she peeled her eyes open. After fighting off her sisters and that damned dragon, Atropos finally got some much-needed rest. It seemed the babe in her demanded sleep and food over all things. She was ravenous. Ironically, she craved human food—Ambrosia only satisfied her hunger for a couple of hours. The thought of human anything made her heart ache. *I miss you, Warrick.* She thought.

After bathing, she snapped her fingers and donned clothing to face her family and the lizard whose presence she could feel. The dragon was in the throne room; she guessed it was waiting for an audience with her. *Well, she can wait a little longer.*

With a thought, she materialized in the kitchen, looking through everything for sustenance. Usually, her server brought her food. Just another change after raiding Warrick's pantry in the human realm. She found herself capable of such tasks. Now that she thought about it, this was the first time she had been in the kitchen since she was a girl. A smile pulled at her lips as she remembered their cook making special things for her and her sisters. That was so long ago—millennia in fact—finally, a memory where she wasn't a monster—one she would enjoy telling her daughter.

"For Zeus' sake, Atropos. What are you doing?" Lachesis stood in the entryway, gawking at her.

"Looking for food. What does it look like?" Atropos responded, then turned back to her exploration.

"Any reason you didn't have Damon get you something?"

"I can get my own. Why are you in here?" Atropos asked, not looking at her eldest sister as she hunted and gathered her meal.

"I felt you wake and come down. When I came looking for you, your signatures pointed me here." Lachesis was now at her side, helping her place food on the large island in the center of the massive room.

Atropos' eyes flashed to her sisters'. Mind to mind, she spoke. *Signatures?* Atropos placed her hand over her abdomen.

"Yes, she is projecting a god signature far stronger than I would have imagined her capable of at this stage of development. She's strong, Atropos. I would wager stronger than anyone truly expects."

A surge of fear ran down Atropos' back. *No, she can't be even stronger. How will I protect her?* Panic spread through her mind and body.

"Not just you, sister. We will keep her safe. My niece will stay strong and be safe. That you can count on, now, stop the worry. Come to the throne room. That dragon of yours refuses to leave until she speaks with you." Lachesis smiled and led her out of the kitchen. "I'll have Damon bring you food. He will have it to you far faster than you can conjure it."

As usual, her eldest sister was right. When they entered the grand room, a table full of food sat closest to her throne, and in the center of the room sat the massive dragon.

Atropos' eyes widen at the sight. Drakaina had no qualms about presenting her actual size in the room as large as their stateroom. She had to be at least one and a half times larger than she was in her bedroom on Earth.

The reptile's scales were brighter with hints of greens and soft blues on Olympus. Atropos noticed and marveled at the beast's beauty—until she spoke, and then she remembered the creature's sharp tongue.

She could have sworn the dragon smiled just before it shrank into its human form with a menacing grin.

"Hello, Thread Cutter. You look well-rested. We should talk—," the dragon stopped what she was about to say and just stared at her.

"What?" Atropos held her hands out, palms up, telling the beast to continue.

"I feel the babe. Her signature is strong." Drakaina's eyes held awe and a trace of concern.

"Yes, my baby is strong, just like her father. What is it that you want to say?" Atropos held her belly, giving the little one what felt like an extra layer of protection.

"I came to let you know that your father ordered me to be your daughter's protector."

Atropos and her sisters glared at the shifter. "For how long?" she asked.

"Until she is old enough to protect herself."

All three Moirai gasped in unison. What her father had done was unheard of. The Fates lived by themselves. No one had ever seen them use their full powers. Together, their powers made them what they were. Their servants didn't live in the mansion with them, as in other gods' homes. They lived in smaller dwellings on the land near them. Same for the Horae. How would having the dragon constantly around affect their abilities? Their bond?

"Why would my father do that? She is safe here, in our home on this mount." Atropos paced before the thrones where her sisters sat. Finally, she stopped her stride between her sisters and Drakaina, facing the creature. "Why, Drakaina. What haven't you or my parents told me?"

"Hera knows. She overheard part of the conversation between Zeus and Themis before we entered this morning."

"Are you sure?" Atropos asked.

"Unfortunately, yes. And that's not all. Apollo spoke with your father while you were sleeping. When everyone was looking for you, he saw through scrying that you would be with child before you returned to Olympus. Today, he saw through your sisters that you had returned—he could no longer see you, proving you are indeed with child," Drakaina said.

"This cannot be happening," the Moirai said in unison.

"Apollo is a moral deity. Plus, he knows his mother would rain down all sorts of pain if he ever harmed an innocent. It's Hera your father is weary of," Drakaina had concern etched in her reptilian eyes. That alone had Atropos spiraling.

"I should have cut her thread centuries ago."

"We know how you feel, sister, but you cannot speak such aloud. Even in our home," Clotho reminded her. Zeus never made it easy on those who spoke against his wife, even if they spoke the truth.

Atropos sounded feral when she responded to her youngest sister, "I don't care. This is my child, and I will kill anyone who even contemplates harming her. I don't give a fuck who they are married to or the power they wield. I control the scissors, and to save my child, I will use them."

She saw everyone flinch at her declaration, but no one spoke against her. The goddess she had been before her time in the human realm was synonymous with fear and petty vengeance. When you could exact death on any being within your pantheon without remorse, everyone kept a wide berth. There was no need for them to know that her thoughts on her station had changed, unless it came to the safety of her unborn child; she no longer believed in the idea of killing without regret.

Lachesis cleared her throat and, as usual, jumped in and guided the conversation. "We will set up a place for you to sleep. Which form do you prefer while in the mansion?"

"In my bedchambers, I would prefer to be in my dragon form. When around the inside of the mansion, I will be in this form. I will feed elsewhere; no need for me to eat with you," Drakaina answered Lachesis, but her eyes stayed trained on Atropos.

Atropos was glad her sister stepped in since she couldn't shake the anger surging through her veins. The thought of that bitch queen knowing she was with child enraged her. Hera was a menace, and ever since the Nephilim locked Ares away, she had become even more unpredictable.

"Does she know of my baby's lineage?" Atropos asked the dragon.

"I'm not sure. I believe Apollo does, but I'm unsure about Hera. You should speak with your father." Drakaina answered.

"Does our mother know that Hera has been informed?" Clotho asked.

"That I don't know either. Zeus can reach me telepathically, but he only told me what I conveyed to you. He shut our connection down afterward. I am sure he's having a discussion with Hera. Now, if you don't mind, I'll be in my bedchamber working." The woman turned back into her dragon form. Much smaller, so she could be shown through the castle.

After eating, Atropos sat in the council room with her sisters and discussed how they would make up for the time she had been missing. With a plan in place, they retired to the sitting room, where they could discuss the more intimate topic of her unborn child and the human realm she returned from. Her sisters were interested in everything. They wanted to know how humans interact with each other daily. Warrick was a topic that caused her pain, but one she wanted her sisters to know about, just not so soon. He looked so broken and angry before she left him. Of all the times they shared, it was that moment she could not escape.

"Will you tell us about him?" Lachesis asked. "We get glimpses from your mind, but very little. You have his memories locked away, beyond our sight."

Atropos squirmed in her seat, clearly uncomfortable with the subject of Warrick. "He changed me. I know you have an idea of how I feel. It's hard for me to speak of him—my heart feels like it is breaking apart."

"So, it is true, then," Clotho said, her head slightly tilted as if she were trying to see more than through their bond. "You are in love with the mortal god."

"If this pain is true love, then why does everyone strive for it?" Atropos fiddled with her fingers in her lap, not looking at her sisters, afraid of seeing pity dancing across their faces.

"I suppose while the love is good, it is wonderful, and when it isn't, there's nothing worse. Pick the poison you would rather drink," Lachesis said.

"As I told you, he found me injured. He read stories to me while I was unconscious and gave me a journal to write in when I needed to make sense of my surroundings. My head would pain me so severely that I would scream and pass out. He cared for me each time. The first time he made love to me was the most passionate experience of my life. Yes, I know sexual passion is not something we've been privy to, but loving someone is more fantastic than anything I've experienced while watching it play out for others. I never doubted his affection for me until he was faced with my reality. He thought he'd gone mad or that I lied to him." Through her tale, she looked everywhere but at her sisters. When she was done, she looked up and felt hot tears dripping down her face and onto her hands. Both of her sisters had tears running down their faces. They felt her anguish and, in return, showed their vulnerability by allowing her to see their tears.

Chapter Forty-Three

Unlikely Prisoner

Warrick woke on the fourth morning in his ornately decorated bedchamber. Curtains draped over the rails of his four-poster bed, large paintings showcasing the Irish countryside lined the walls, and crown moulding trimmed in gilded carvings. As a man of means, he'd stayed in the most lavish hotels and homes around the world, but nothing compared to the ambience of his room in the realm of the Irish gods.

Like every morning since arriving in the Irish realm, he woke, looked at his surroundings, reminding himself of where he was, then immediately began thinking of Atropos—and now—their baby. One thought led to another, eventually leading him to the prophecy and Adair. His mum was keeping the full prophecy from him, so the only part he could fixate on was what he knew for certain. He loved Atropos and knew they should be together, and their child would grow up knowing its father. That's it—he knew what to do. Within minutes, he washed, dressed, and wound his way through the castle to Dagda's throne room. He needed to return to his world and figure out how to find the woman he loved. It was time for him to leave, and he needed a god to take him back.

"Good day, Warrick. How are you this morn?" Dagda sat before a feast, alone.

"I'm well. Do you know where Adair is?" He asked his grandfather.

"I do. Sit. Eat. Once we've talked, I will tell you where your mum is." Dagda took a bite of eggs and rashers.

Warrick stiffened when the god referred to Adair as his mother. He knew who she was, and sometimes in his own head referred to as such, but she was not the one who raised him. Besides, he was still upset with her; even though he tried to be understanding, there was pain knowing she left him, no matter the reason.

Pulling the chair out to sit, Warrick gestured to the chair next to his. Someone had been there. "Who's sitting there?"

"No one. They left after their meal." Dagda continued to eat, but Warrick saw a slight grin from around his fork.

So much for being nosy; the king gave nothing away. Though he suspected it had been the Morrigan who occupied the spot.

As Warrick spooned food onto his plate, Dagda cleared his throat and sat back in his chair. He knew the god waited for him to finish, but he continued as if he had no clue. A brief thought went through his mind that maybe he shouldn't keep a god waiting. Once he finished loading his dish with all sorts of food, he gave the deity his attention. The smirk across Dagda's face told Warrick all he needed to know.

"I know you are angered by Adair leaving you with mortals," Dagda began, "but until you have a child of your own, you will not understand. She loves you. We all do. No matter if you lack magic, you are my grandson. The last one, since all of my children refuse to have more babes. This realm, these lands, and this castle will forever be your home."

"Maybe one day I will see her as my mum, but she isn't the one who raised me. My mother cared for me as a child and, in her own way, still does. I don't want to betray the woman who took care of me, that's all. Am I hurt by Adair's actions? I'm human, so of course, the knowledge crushed me. She left me in a realm she knew very little about with humans she knew little of." Warrick didn't realize he was shaking until he looked down at his fork; the food he was about to eat was back on his plate.

Dagda nodded in understanding. "Just please, give her the benefit of the doubt. One day, she will show you her heart, and you will see her love."

It was that heartfelt conversation with his biological grandfather that had him appreciating why they called him the *Good god*. The divine man was the Irish god-king, yet he advised him on how to properly brandish a sword and wield a dagger; now he was giving him advice. He was becoming closer to Dagda than he had ever been to his human grandparents.

"Will you tell me where Adair is?" Warrick asked.

"She left just before you woke. She was going back to the human realm to look for something. I'm not sure what, but it seemed necessary. She told me to tell you that she would be back shortly." The two ate the rest of their meal in companionable silence.

Once finished with breakfast, Warrick requested his leave and took off for the shoreline, where he felt closest to home. He sat on the pebbled beach, just out of reach of the water, and contemplated his next actions. The dilemma he faced was finding Atropos. Drakaina said she was back on Olympus. If that were true, how would he get there? The mount had to be like the realm of the Tuatha Dé Danann, with an obscure entryway protected by magic.

Think, Warrick, he demanded of himself. Not even a divine realm out of reach to mortals would keep him from his baby or the woman who owned his heart.

He watched the sun as it traced a path from one side of the sky to the other, still without an answer to his problem. Once Adair returned from his world, he would question her. Maybe she knew of a way to Olympus.

As he stood and brushed the dirt away, resigned to return without answers, he heard his name called from a distance—or he thought he had. Searching, he looked up and down the water's edge for the caller. He saw no one. *Weird.*

On his trek back to the castle, he heard the caller again, and he was sure it was his name being yelled out. Still muffled, he was positive it came from the direction of the castle.

When the castle came into view, he saw an unusual number of guards stationed atop the curtain wall. *Something's wrong,* he thought, then turned and looked at the gatehouse. The portcullis was down. *Seriously wrong.* Fear rushed through his veins as he ran to find his family.

Warrick was panting by the time he reached the throne room and woefully unprepared for the sight that awaited him when he entered Dagda's council. *What the hell?*

"Anna? What the actual fuck is going on here?" Warrick's mind raced as his eyes took in the scene before him. Anna and the woman she had brought to the gala stood at the bottom of the dais, their hands bound behind their backs. Dagda sat on his throne, a meter above the constrained women, with Adair on his left and The Morrigan on his right. Warrick shook his head in confusion and anger, his mind reeling at the sight.

"Warrick," Adair spoke, "I went to your realm for answers. I have an ability we have yet to discuss. It's the power to turn back moments while scrying. I can see the past as well as the future.

The only problem is that I must be where the action took place, which is why I left this morning."

Warrick walked forward and stood beside Anna. "Good to know. Now, explain why you have my personal assistant cuffed and in tears." He knew not to address her before he found out what was going on, but it wasn't easy. Anna had been with him for years, and he trusted her.

"When I went to the mortal realm, the first place I undertook was where Mother and I showed ourselves to you the first time."

"The gala?" Warrick asked.

"Yes. The night we spoke to you, I sensed the signature of an Álfar, which is not unusual. For the dark ones especially." Adair explained.

"I don't know that term. What is an Álfar?" Warrick asked.

"You would know them as elves," Adair said.

Warrick's brows shot up. "You felt the presence of an elf? At the gala?" He questioned Adair.

"Dark elves are commonplace amongst mortals. They don't always fit into their own world but blend well with humans. You see them mostly in your entertainment industry." Adair clarified. "That is why I didn't think it a problem when I sensed one at a human gathering."

"Again, good to know, but what does that have to do with my assistant standing in *this* realm?" This time, he looked at Anna and asked, "Are you okay?"

All he received from his employee was a slight nod and a few more tears. His anger built. "I demand you release her. She knows nothing of this world or any other than her own."

"We were just about to get to the bottom of that when you arrived. If she is, as you say, we will return her, and she will not remember her time here. The only problem will be the exhaustion when she wakes. She will feel as if she hasn't slept in days." The Morrigan said.

"I followed the Álfar's signature from where we met you, and it led me to Anna's home. She and the elf were in a deep discussion. Actually, it sounded like an argument. So, I listened. From what I gathered, coming into the conversation a little late, your assistant was ready to call their relationship quits. The elf," Adair pointed to Astrid, "was not going to let that happen."

Warrick looked to his right at Astrid, whom Adair called an elf. He noted she was remarkable, even with buzzed hair; she was stunning and just an inch or so shorter than he. It was when he got a look at her ears that he flinched. *What the hell?* They were pointed. *Someone would have noticed that, surely.*

"Elves are real. What else from my childhood storybooks am I going to find living amongst us?" Warrick gaped at the Álfar.

"That is a conversation we can have later," Adair acknowledged his inquiry. "When I looked deeper into this elf's memories," Adair started down the dais steps and stopped in front of Astrid, "I saw some eye-opening details." She turned and looked at him. "She has what her kind call a double. Meaning she is a twin. It appears she and her double are at odds; ever since she began working for the Greek goddess Hera, her brother grew exasperated. He told her of the goddess' clever and conniving ways and refused to follow her down that path. He also told her that the Grecian deity would not take up for her if she were ever caught. My question is, caught doing what? When I heard Hera's name in her memories and saw that she was a spy for the queen, I brought her and her consort here at once."

"Why did you bring Anna if Astrid is the spy?" Warrick asked.

"I will not leave anything to chance when the lives of my family are at stake. We will question them both. If she is not involved, she will be returned unharmed." Adair spoke to him, but monitored the dark elf.

Chapter Forty-Four

Strongest in the Room

Atropos

Atropos could not believe it had only been four days since her return to Olympus. When she thought of Warrick, it seemed so much longer. The day after she found out that Hera and Apollo knew of her pregnancy, she met with her half-brother. They had never been close, since few aspired to be acquainted with the Moirai, especially the Thread Cutter. Most she knew of him was that he was Artemis' twin, and they both were considered *good* gods. Rarely did either of them play in the grey area.

He spoke of her unborn with awe and seemed to hold no malice toward such a powerful being. She asked if he had seen Hera's inquiry into her condition, and all he said was that the queen knew and thought the father was mortal.

That eased Atropos' worry but didn't entirely lift it. She would never trust her father's manipulative wife.

Zeus finally granted her an audience, and that was where she was going. Her mother told her that while she was in Zeus' mansion, he learned of Hera's knowledge and was dealing with her. Every time he chose the bitch who came between the Moirai's parents' relationship, it didn't go well. Often, they lashed out, and more often, they refused to speak with him for years. She had no choice but to talk to him this time. Hera was the one god she never wanted to know about her child, and her father was one of the few who did.

When she entered the vestibule of her father's mansion, she felt a shift in the air. Something was different. The daimon, who came to see her through the palace, looked her up and down and snarled—she smirked.

"You know, daimon. If I want, I could have you dangling by a thread. No, pun intended. If you ever look at me that way again, know that you will have to tell your master that you will be incapable of serving her for months. Now, show me to my father and pray to your queen that I don't change my mind and exact my anger on you when I return to the Moirai mansion."

The daimon's eyes grew wide, and his forehead peppered with sweat. He took great care to change how he looked at her, then turned and escorted her to see her father.

Once Atropos and the servant stood at the entrance of Zeus' council room, she turned to the daimon and said, "If you know what is good for you, you will change where your loyalties lie." She then turned and gestured for the double doors to open.

By the time she stood before her father, Atropos had gone through several emotions. Denial, she was sure, once she spoke with her father, that it would all be a misunderstanding and the bitch queen would know much less than she expected. Fear that her evil stepmother would sell her out to every pantheon and cause war. And as she took in her father's appearance, eyes lined with anguish and distress—she knew—Hera knew everything. With that revelation, anger started coursing through her veins, and her second sight took hold of her. It showed an elven female, who looked familiar, speaking with Hera's lapdog—the daimon servant she had just threatened. It had been a long time since she felt her eyes spiral with rage.

Zeus stood when he saw her enter, and they met at the base of the dais. "I see by your swirling red eyes, you know."

"Know what, Father? That your wife knows about my baby? Or is it that my dear step bitch knew where I was the entire time?" Atropos' words came from deep within her chest—guttural and intense. "Could it be that she knows who and what the baby's father is?" The marble floor trembled beneath their feet.

Atropos was fully embracing her epithet—Death, as so many called her. Gone was the Jane Doe hopeful; she was now the most powerful god in the room. With a wave of her left hand, a golden thread appeared. Her grin must have been one carved from the Underworld, because Zeus' eyes went wide and his fingertips sparked. "Do you know whose life hangs by this thread, Father?"

Zeus took a step back. "I will not allow her to harm you or your baby, Atropos. You must know that."

"This is not Hera's life thread. It's yours." She felt feral as she began to laugh. "For my baby, I will destroy the world." With a flick of her left wrist, the golden thread disappeared, and a pearl colored one took its place. "Now this is Hera's thread. Look at it closely, Zeus." With a wave of her right hand, her scissors appeared. "You and I both know that you could never control her, but I can. Why you insist on continuing the facade is beyond any of your children's comprehension. If your evil wife comes near my child or Warrick, I will sever this thread without consulting you. That is a promise—She. Will. Die." Atropos knew her father wouldn't help her. From that moment on, she would have to rely on her mother, sisters, and Drakaina. She turned to leave, thought better of it, and returned to him. "Also, if Hera hires, coerces, or compels another being or creature to harm my child or Warrick, she will still die alongside her minion. You should tell her, so she is prepared." Then Death turned from the king and vanished.

Atropos shook as her sisters embraced her. They had seen everything through her eyes and knew that she was well beyond the limits their father had instilled in them regarding Hera. Zeus had always intimidated and sometimes even threatened them when they were younger, never to lash out at his wife. She and her five sisters blamed the goddess for destroying their mother's life, and revenge was always at the forefront of a god's mind.

Even though he wasn't faithful to Hera—few deities were—he was fiercely protective of her. She had caused the deaths of people and gods that he once loved—the alienation of his one true love and the daughter they had together. It was less than a decade ago when he learned he had a granddaughter and laid eyes on both his child and his granddaughter for the first time. Hera was the reason Ares became so rotten. She waged wars and connived, yet Zeus still shielded her. *Why?*

"We stand with you, sister," Lachesis and Clotho said in harmony.

"I meant what I said. I will split her thread in half and not care that I did. She is a horrible deity and deserves a cell in Tartarus." Atropos' body relaxed in her sisters' hold, and she could feel her eyes returning to normal. The red haze was gone, and her voice no longer rumbled. "Thank you for standing with me. I should inform the Horae. If it's up to us to protect my child, I will need all my sisters."

"You should speak with Mother before you do," Clotho said.

"Do you believe they will side with Zeus? I know they despise Hera, but do you think they will stay out of this to keep from angering Father? Surely, they will protect their innocent niece."

Atropos searched her sisters' minds to see why the suggestion. All she found were memories of the six of them with Zeus.

"They detest Hera as much as we do; however, having Father mad for centuries is always an issue. We both believe they will side and fight for your baby, but Mother sees more of them than we do. Having her input may help," Lachesis explained.

"It is strange seeing things from my personal perspective instead of cumulatively. There is nothing I won't do for my baby. Nothing. I will become a worse Death than ever before. I'm not against retribution."

Chapter Forty-Five
Iron and Threats

Warrick

Dampness seeped into Warrick's bones as he and Adair interrogated his personal assistant and the dark elf in the lower chambers. When Dagda told Adair to take the captives to the dungeon and question them, he thought his words were to instill fear, which they did. Both Anna and the Álfar trembled the entire way down to the dark, dank chambers below the fortress, where hay-filled cells with a bucket in each lined both sides of the passageway. There had to be at least twenty in total.

Warrick moved to walk beside Anna. "Did you know she was sent to spy on me?"

"No. I'm not so sure that this isn't an elaborate dream. Other realms, gods, elves—I've lost my mind." Anna's monotone reply convinced him. She parroted his sentiments when he discovered otherworldly beings and realms existed.

"This is all new to me, too. I had no idea until a week ago that any of this was even possible," Warrick said as he took in the dreary cells under the dim lighting and the pungent smell of mildew and fresh hay.

A jarring sound came from the Álfar that drew his attention away from his assistant. The elf's eyes were blown wide, and under her breath, he thought she was repeating, "no." She was sensing something.

It was when a chair made of solid iron, in the farthest cell, came into view that the dark elf started begging for her life. Warrick's mind started turning over. *Could the folklore be true?* Could elves not bear the touch of iron? He would soon find out.

"Please. Please, don't put me in that chair. I will tell you anything you want to know." Astrid begged, while stiffening her legs to keep them from progressing toward the metal seat.

"You see, Astrid. I'm normally a gentle soul, even when provoked. However, my grandfather and my mother are whatever they need to be." He noticed Adair's head snap toward him when he referred to her as his mother. "Like them, though, once you conspire to harm my family, pleading just pisses me off. You see—if that chair were like all the others down here, you would not be begging. I find that unremorseful. You don't give a fuck about my—" Warrick almost called Atropos his family, "the Greek Fate, Atropos. You only care for yourself. Why aren't you begging for Anna? That makes you vile in my eyes. How could you know such a brilliant person and not beg for her life over your own?"

"I swear to you, I would never try to harm anyone," the elf continued to beg for her life. He noticed the dim light in Anna's eyes completely extinguish as she watched the woman she was dating forget all about her.

"What did you tell Hera?" Adair asked the dark elf, standing mere feet from the iron seat, she holding one side and Warrick the other, as the Álfar thrashed in fear.

"Set me down in another cell, and I will tell you everything. If you place me there, I will be unable to speak through all the pain."

"No," Adair said. "You will sit here." She pointed to the ground where they stood. "Anna, you may sit beside your girlfriend."

Warrick noticed Anna sat beside the elf, but not close. He could see the revulsion on her face for the woman. He also saw the disbelief as she stared at Astrid's ears. Anna was in shock, betrayed, and scared. And he knew from her actions that everything she found herself in shook her to the core.

"Now, tell us what you told Hera," Warrick demanded.

"I never spoke to the goddess. Apparently, elves are lesser in her eyes, so I only spoke with her servant.

Warrick rolled his eyes. "Then tell me what you told the servant."

"I was to look for the Lost Fate. When I found her, I would receive ten thousand euros. If she were dead, ten times that. During the gala, I felt a faint signature; however, it was her appearance that gave her away. I've seen The Fates Three paintings in the *Gallery of the gods* when they were on display. Her heavy Greek accent confirmed it. I told the daimon where she was and who she was with. My being at the gala was a coincidence. Anna and I had just started dating. I swear."

"What else have you told the daimon?" Adair asked.

"Nothing. I know nothing else. However, I'm not the only being or even the only Álfar looking for her."

"Who else?" Warrick shouted at the elf. "Who else do you know was looking for her?"

"Hera's minions let everyone who took divine tracking jobs know she would pay for information. This isn't the first time or the last. How do you think she's gotten away with so many dark missions? She's been paying beings and creatures from other pantheons to give her information," Astrid said.

Warrick turned to the gallowglass who had followed them down. "Place Astrid in the chair until she gives you names of others who do her type of work for Hera. We need leads." When the order left his lips, Astrid begged.

"Yes, your Majesty," the Norse warrior nodded.

Warrick pulled the shocked Anna up from the floor by her armpits. "Anna will go back with us. She has nothing to do with this. She was with the wrong person at the wrong time."

Adair got on the other side of Anna and helped him haul his assistant back up the staircase as the screams from the elf bounced off the stone walls. When Astrid yelled Anna's name, her legs buckled, and Warrick swooped her up into his arms to get her out of the dungeon faster.

Between exhaustion and realm-hopping, Anna's body could only take so much. She passed out once inside the stone circle, right before Adair brought them back to the mortals' apartment. Warrick had held her all the way from the dungeon to her bedroom, worrying the entire time about his assistant's mental health after what they had put her through.

"Are you certain she is not part of the elf's plan?" Adair asked her son after they had laid Anna on her bed.

It was time he admitted what he was experiencing. "I'm not sure how to explain this. It started sometime after you and your mother visited me at the gala. I can feel a person's emotions. It's been gradually increasing in intensity." Warrick closed the door to Anna's bedroom and turned to face his mum. Adair just blinked at him, as if trying to process his words.

"You're telling me that you can feel everyone's emotions? Or just some?" Adair asked.

"So far, everyone's," Warrick responded.

Under her breath, Adair whispered to herself, "This cannot be."

Warrick answered anyway. "Well, it is. And while we are on that subject. Your parents are still madly in love with each other, and I believe The Morrigan stayed over two nights in a row."

"I know. Or should I say, I knew it would happen. I've seen their futures. Never tell them you know. They honestly believe it's a secret."

For the first time since he met Adair, Warrick saw her smile and heard her laugh. The sight warmed his heart, and he felt a little closer to the woman who gave him life.

He cleared his throat. "I would never." He laughed with her. "Since we are back in the human world, I want to go home and see if she's been back." Warrick knew Adair would know who he meant. "I need to go by the office, too. Anna kept everything afloat during my absence, but now that she isn't there, I need to check on the workers."

"I'll go with you. After hearing that other pantheons are looking for the lost Fate, I don't want you to be alone. It's just a matter of time before other deities start putting you and Atropos together. You are a prince without power, and that makes you vulnerable. You have our signatures all over you now."

Warrick convinced her to walk to his apartment. Dematerializing and rematerializing messed with his head; plus, he needed the normalcy of his world. It would also make it easy to stop by the construction site since it was between his and Anna's place. Once at the site, he spoke with the foreman and explained that he and Anna would be in and out, and that if he had any issues, he should text or email one or both of them. While there, he showed Adair where he found *Jane*, unconscious and bleeding profusely. That sparked memories of her lying in a hospital bed with lines attached all over her body. From there, his memories progressed to better times with the goddess, and sadness flooded his system. He missed everything about her. *I'm such an ass,* he thought.

Knowing that she was carrying his child made him fierce with overprotectiveness. Now that he was back in his world, the need to see her was overwhelming. The human realm was where their relationship began. The warm salt air incited the need for her, and the surrounding city where he fell in love with the goddess roused a passion to possess her. A demand that required him to hunt her down and never allow her out of his sight. Like he told the elf back in the dungeon, he was usually a gentle soul. Things had changed. He would find a way to get to her.

No key on his person, Adair flashed the two of them from the hallway outside his apartment into the foyer of his flat, where ultimate chaos met them. Every piece of artwork was on the floor, several destroyed; furniture turned on its side, dishes broken all over the floors and countertops. Everything was a mess, but the worst of all was the words, meant to upend his delicate hold on reality, written across the mirror in the entryway. ***No one can save your child.***

Warrick shook with all-consuming rage. Anger had never felt alive in him before. He could feel the heat of the wrath as it coursed through his veins with every pump of his heart. A sharp pain hit his eyes, and a red hue replaced his normal vision.

"Son, you must calm down!"

Warrick heard Adair, but she seemed far off. Way too far to be standing next to him. It was when she touched his arm that he realized he had zoned out. He blinked, but the redness was still there, and the trashed remains of his home were levitating. *Am I doing this?* His internal voice asked. What he said aloud came from a different place.

"I will kill the person who did this," Warrick growled.

"Please, Warrick, come back to me. Stop this. You are going to burn yourself out."

With no understanding of the time that had passed, Warrick's internal voice won the battle. "What just happened?" He whispered, still not fully in control.

"A divine signature is pouring off you, Warrick. You must calm down so we can talk."

Chapter Forty-Six

Get Her Back

Was the message meant for him or Atropos? The difference was whether they knew he was an Irish prince or just knew he had been with the Greek princess. To threaten an unborn baby, the messenger had to know Warrick's blood was divine—*but how?* *What just happened to me?* He paced, trying to dispel what he could only describe as power coursing through his veins.

"How are you feeling, my son?" Adair asked, waving a hand to clean up the mess the intruders left behind. All but the message. That she kept.

"I physically feel amazing, but a little out of control. What's going on? Did I just levitate objects?" Warrick looked from Adair to his apartment. She had cleaned up the wreckage, but he couldn't stop seeing everything floating in a red haze.

"It seems when my mother and I removed your abilities, we only barred them. This should not be happening." Confusion creased Adair's forehead. He watched as she looked at him, then at her hands. "I think we need to call for your grandmother. She's lived much longer and would have better insight into this."

A tapping sound came from the living room. With his mother still in shock and him not much better, Warrick went to investigate. Tapping its beak against the sliding door of the living room balcony, a large raven with human eyes waited for entry.

When he opened the door, the onyx bird flapped its wings twice as it glided into his apartment. When his grandmother landed, she did so in her goddess form with her long red hair flowing beautifully down her back. It was a testament to how far Warrick had come in accepting his new life. He didn't question allowing a wild bird into his home, knowing it was a family member.

"I felt Adair's anxiety. Tell me what happened." The Morrigan demanded.

"I'm here, mother," Adair walked into the room.

Her color is a little better, he thought.

"I'm not the one we need to be concerned about." She reached out and touched her mother's hand. When she did, The Morrigan's eyes widened, and she turned to Warrick with fear, concern, and a lot of anger.

"We will get to your power after I see the message for myself." The Queen of Nightmares walked to the foyer to see the mirror that harbored the horrific words. Words that had broken his bonds.

"I cannot see the child or Atropos. I believe it's because she carries the unborn," Adair said, as the three of them looked at the disturbing message. "Can you see who wrote it?" Adair asked her mother.

"I, too, am unable to see them. It seems the Almighty doesn't want us to see the infant," The Morrigan said. "However, when I find out who is threatening my great-grandchild, they and their kin are dead."

"That was my exact reaction," Warrick commented.

His grandmother turned to him. "I can see what happened to you when you read the message, though. It seems your reaction was a little more potent. Your powers are manifesting."

"How's that even possible?" Adair asked.

"Someone as powerful as the descendant of the Irish royal line cannot be held back if they wish to move forward. It seems that goes for their divine abilities as well as their prowess."

"Did you know this could happen?" Adair stared at her mother. Warrick could feel her anger boiling under her skin.

"I did. Had I not known, I would never have allowed you to wipe his power and send him away," his grandmother held her head up, readying herself for her daughter's anger.

"Why didn't you tell me? Why pretend?" The room shook as Adair began interrogating the Queen of Nightmares.

Like mother, like son, he thought.

"There was no consoling you, no reasoning with you once you saw that prophecy. You needed to protect your baby, and hiding him was the only thing you would consider. You kept him from our world to protect him, and I helped you. It was not guaranteed that he would ever become the god he was meant to be," The Morrigan now pleaded with her daughter.

"When did you know?" Adair asked through gritted teeth.

"I tried to see the prophecy several times over the years. It was when he became an adult that I saw the same vision as you did—I, too, was devastated when the future stayed the same. Over the last decade, I watched for any changes. One day, I saw the prophecy change to him fighting to save his child, followed by another scene, his daughter calling him Daddy—she was speaking, and he was with her. He looked much as he does now. I knew at that moment he would be with a Fate of the Greek Pantheon and wouldn't die before she was born. That's when I physically began watching him on the human plane and not just through divination."

"I died—in the prophecy you saw? That's why you hid me and stripped me of my power. That's the part of the prediction you didn't want to tell me." Warrick looked at his mother, who had tears streaming down her pale face. Everything that angered him about her vanished. When she thought she was protecting him, she was genuinely trying to save his life. How could he be mad? "Mum," he spoke to his mother.

Shock registered through her tears. Without words, the mother who bore him wrapped her arms around his waist, and without hesitation, he engulfed her with his. They both cried. When he looked up to speak to his grandmother, she was no longer there.

"Now what? How do I find Atropos, and how do I save my baby?" Warrick asked, still clinging to his mum.

"We need my father to speak with Zeus. If that's where she's gone, we need the kings to intervene.

"So, back to the realm of the Tuatha Dé Danann, then? I need to find her now. Isn't there some other way?" Warrick asked.

"Unfortunately, there isn't. It's rare for Dagda to come to the human realm. Long ago, he came here often, but if he were to now, all the pantheons would talk."

"Which, if they don't already know that he's my grandfather, they would quickly find out," Warrick murmured under his breath.

"Exactly." With a thought from Adair, the two of them were back in the stone circle and a moment later, entering the throne room of the Irish god-king.

Chapter Forty-Seven
Decisions

Atropos

After speaking with Themis, the Moirai decided their sisters should be told of her unborn child and Warrick's lineage. They, too, were triplets. It seemed Zeus and Themis had only girls, and they came in threes—maybe it was a good thing that they hadn't had more offspring. The Horae's powers were smaller embodiments of their mother's, each taking a portion of her abilities and saturating them into one goddess. They were all moral. Morality came easier when your station never called for death or destruction. No matter if they refused to fight with her, they were the gatekeepers of Olympus and would deny passage to anyone who sought to harm her child.

She knew all five of her sisters loved her; it was just that the Moirai were part of her and would help her at any cost; she knew that now. However, the Horae were more like their mother, siding with justice and peace. Keeping the peace would be the only reason they would refuse to rise against their father's bitch of a wife.

"Welcome, sisters," Eunomia, the Goddess of Good Order, waved her and her sisters into their home. "It's so good to see you. Would you like some Ambrosia? We're having some by the ponds out back. Come."

"That sounds nice," Atropos said as they followed the eldest Horae through the palace and out the back, where a gorgeous garden stood, full of exotic flowers from around the human realm and rainbow-colored fish in various ponds. Waterfalls made the ambiance even more tranquil if that were possible. Their sister, Eirene, had to be the gardener. She was Peace, the goddess of all things peaceful and the arrival of spring.

"How beautiful the garden has become since we were last here," said Lachesis. "If I had known it was this amazing, you would find me lazing back here often."

Everyone laughed as they mingled until Eunomia stopped midair with her cup and openly stared at Atropos. "You're not drinking your Ambrosia, and you look kinda green. Are you okay, sister?"

All heads turned toward her, and she felt the Horae's confusion. Seldom did a divine entity feel physically ill, and unlike the Moirai, they were not part of her. "Actually, I'm feeling a little nauseated." Atropos set her cup on the table.

"But goddesses only get nauseated when they're with—," Dike, Justice, representing both human and divine moral fairness, said. "Atropos, you can't be. Can you?"

"When I went missing, I was without my memories. Long story, but in the end, I fell in love, and I'm with child."

All three Horea stood gaping, as they tried to make sense of what she said. Finally, Eirene snapped herself out of the daze and squealed in delight. "Oh, Atropos, that's wonderful. Tell us everything."

Atropos began her tale from when she woke in the hospital and ended it with Hera learning she was with child, laying it all out for them to sift through as they drank their divine wine. Every mention of Warrick made her chest ache, but she held strong and refused to cry.

Several hours later, and many cups of stronger wine for the others, the six of them sat around the Horae mansion discussing the issues a child with so much power could cause. From grand gestures of love to the leveling of realms, it was a scary conversation and an eye-opening glimpse into the depths many would go to in order to keep such power from manifesting.

"From my limited understanding of the prophecy, my child is one of several to be born that will reset the Almighty's plan. They will begin the reconstruction of a better world where all realms will live in harmony," Atropos said.

"That would definitely be a miracle. If the Almighty has started his global shift, then we must all listen," Eunomia, the eldest Horae, said.

"Does that mean you are willing to fight for your sister's child when the time comes?" Clotho asked.

The Horae looked at one another—then, in unison, nodded. "We will fight for our sister, our niece, and the Almighty. Even if Zeus despises us for it," Dike, the middle sister, declared.

"Our Father will come around—he always does. Although it may take him some time. He loves each of us; he needs to stew in his anger for a time," Eirene, the youngest, said.

"Agreed," the Moirai concurred.

Atropos had grown tired and dismissed herself, leaving her sisters to their gossiping. She needed rest. Right as she was about to lay her head atop her pillow, her father's voice boomed around her.

"Daughter, you are needed in my council room. Now."

"What in Hades' name?" She said, rising from her bed, and telepathically beckoned her sisters. *Did you hear Zeus? He needs to see me now.*

We heard, and we'll meet you there, her Moirai sisters mentally responded.

Atropos inhaled deeply, grounding herself. She knew her father loved her, but she didn't think he loved her more than he cared for Hera. That goddess had something over him—whether it was a spell or something truly insidious, she didn't know, but she meant what she had said to him. She would destroy anyone who wanted to harm her baby or the man she loved.

The thought of Warrick made her eyes burn. She needed to see him. She went to the basin in her room and splashed water over her face. Zeus didn't need to see the evidence of her sadness. Fierce, where the gods were concerned, was the only way they would see her. None of them would see that the death dealer possessed the ability to love beyond her sisters.

When Atropos arrived at the king's mansion, her sisters were waiting—all five of them. Apparently, the Horae were serious and decided to make their stand clear before the threat of war. She felt her smile grow as she took them all in.

"Thank you," was all she could muster without giving in to her tear ducts—*damn hormones. Powerful, Atropos...You are fierce,* she mentally recited the mantra.

The daimon from before was the one to open the massive doors. Since her Moirai sisters shared her thoughts, they knew he was Hera's puppet.

"You know, daimon. It's not only our sister who can punish. Each of us can manipulate your life's thread. Clotho can put obstacles in your way, and she has an exceptional imagination. And as for me. Well, I can shorten that string you cling to," Lachesis said, grinning widely at the servant.

"You better change your allegiance, because we will know," Clotho followed up, patting the daimon on his chest as she sauntered past him. "We know the way." All five sisters followed the youngest Moirai to their father's throne room. When the doors opened, they all stood still, gaping at its occupancy.

"Jane—shit—Atropos!"

One second, she was standing there staring at what she thought had to be a mirage; the next, she was being swept up into the arms of the man she had been pining for.

"Warrick? How did you get here? What's going—," his mouth cut the rest of her sentence off. He kissed her with all the passion of a starved man, and she was his first meal in days. Not caring who watched, she wrapped her legs around his waist and returned his kiss, completely obliterating her façade—it was clear she was in love.

She could also get embarrassed. Her father cleared his throat, and she felt the heat rise from her neck to her face. Reluctantly, they pulled apart and just stared into each other's eyes.

"Well, I suppose that's one question answered, Alasdair," Dagda said.

Atropos turned to see who had spoken, and her mouth went dry. There was no mistaking the handsome, godly man who had at least seven centimeters and four stone on her father—*but how?* She knew the deity taking up so much room was none other than the Irish god, Dagda, and the equally beguiling woman beside him had to be Warrick's mother, Adair. She looked closely at the woman. It was uncanny how much Warrick favored her. If her appearance hadn't given her away, the crow sitting atop her shoulder proved her to be the greatest seer to ever walk the realms.

She whispered in Warrick's ear, "What's going on? And did he call you, Alasdair?"

"I know you carry our baby, and I'm here to beg you to come back with me." He placed his right hand across her belly.

"You know?" she questioned, placing her hand over his and continuing their one-on-one conversation, amidst the curious gods before them.

"I do, and I have so much I need to t—," Warrick began and was interrupted by a servant announcing the arrival of his grandmother.

"The Morrigan, my king," the traitorous daimon announced.

With a grin, Warrick looked down at her curiously. "Did you just growl?"

"I'm sorry. He's one of Hera's minions. I'll explain later. Introduce me to your family."

After introductions were made and the kings had sized each other up, it was time for everyone to discuss whatever had the Irish Pantheon on Mount Olympus. Themis conjured a table large enough to seat twelve gods and goddesses comfortably. The kings sat at each end, Themis to Zeus' right, The Morrigan to Dagda's. Warrick sat between his mother and Atropos, his hand atop her thigh, as if he were fearful she would vanish. Her sisters filled in the other spots, with Lachesis and Clotho sitting across from her. She knew it was their way of lending their strength and protection, even if family surrounded them.

Zeus' booming voice began the discussion. "Dagda reached out to me to discuss the unborn child of Atropos and Alasdair. The Irish have been made aware of some disturbing facts. King Dagda, would you like to fill everyone in?"

"Before I do, it seems there are many more present than I'm comfortable with. I believe this conversation should be between the parents and the grandparents, keeping knowledge of the situation to a minimum."

It didn't go unnoticed by her and her sisters that their father liked that idea. He tried to hide the gleam in his eyes when the idea was presented. Themis put an end to the nonsense before it began.

"That's right," Atropos remembered they had met. "Now, why do they keep calling you Alasdair?" Atropos whispered, remembering he still had not answered her.

Warrick spoke into her ear, "That's my name, and while here, it's what I must go by." Everyone glared at them as they whispered.

"As the goddess of Divine Law and Order, I can assure you that my daughters are trustworthy and extremely protective of Atropos and her unborn. They will be the baby's biggest allies," Themis glared at the gods, making sure they saw the conviction in her.

"Don't forget me," came the deep, throaty voice of Drakaina as she materialized in her dragon form.

Atropos tried to hide her grin. She had invited the creature, knowing the throne room she had been summoned to was in the enemy's den. When her father narrowed his eyes at the intruder, she spoke to keep him from banishing her.

"It was I who invited the Drakaina, Father. She is our child's protector, is she not?" After all, he was the one who had sent the reptile to guard her unborn.

Zeus took a deep breath, calming himself. "She is."

"We meet again, dragon," Alasdair said.

"We do," Drakaina said as her dragon form shifted into her human form. With a mere grin, another chair materialized at the table.

"Another being to know of our situation?" Dagda questioned.

"As the mother of my unborn, I trust all those present. Each here would lay their life down for our baby and for me." Except possibly her father, but she would never say that aloud.

With a gavel, her mother interrupted the commotion, "Let's not squabble. It's the parents who decide who will know what is said in this meeting."

A nod from her, and Alasdair silenced everyone.

Chapter Forty-Eight
Irish and Olympians

ALASDAIR

Having Atropos at his side healed something deep inside him. If it hadn't been clear before, it was now—she was his forever. Neither Monaco nor the realms of the Tuatha Dé Danann were home; she was, and the babe in her womb made them a family. He felt a jolt of power run through his veins at the thought. An overwhelming shock of protection for the domestic unit he had started. Every deity sitting at the table, except the damn dragon, was an extension of that family.

"We have an Álfar captive who confessed to taking money for the whereabouts of Atropos. She was among several who had been seeking the missing Fate for profit. They would receive ten euros for whereabouts, and ten times that if they found her dead." As he spoke, he watched Zeus for any indication that he already knew. Either the god was a great actor, or he didn't know the bomb he was about to drop. "She said the person paying for the information was the goddess, Hera."

Everyone at the table gasped, except Zeus. He stood and glared at Alasdair. "The elf is lying. Tell me, was the Álfar you speak of a dark elf?"

"She is, however, one of my abilities is that I can feel emotion and sentiment. The elf did not lie," Alasdair had no recollection of standing, but found himself on his feet. "I understand your dilemma; that is why I'm asking Atropos to return with me, where she will be safe."

Zeus recoiled as if Alasdair had physically struck him. "She will not leave this mount. My daughter is under my protection," the king thundered.

"With all due respect," Alasdair was the one speaking; gone was any semblance of Warrick. "Atropos may be your daughter, but make no mistake, she is mine—and the child she carries is my daughter. You may be a king and I only a prince, but even you would have to go through me and mine," he gestured to his mother and grandparents, "to get to her. As long as Hera lives here, Atropos will not." He felt Atropos flinch.

Zeus' jaw clenched with anger—they were in his home, on his mount, with his pantheon at his back. Maybe he shouldn't have provoked the king, but Zeus needed to understand that as long as Hera was a threat to his family, he had no problem asserting his claim. Zeus' hands twitched and sparks fired from his fingertips. His eyes swirled red. Alasdair snarled, readying for a fight.

"Don't alienate your daughter by starting the war which we are all here to prevent, Zeus. You and I both know she will be safe in our realm. I have the most skilled warriors of all the pantheons, except for maybe the Norse, and as you know, they are beyond vicious," Dagda said, now standing, showing support for Alasdair.

"You highly underestimate the Greek Pantheon," Zeus growled out.

"Maybe before the god of war got himself locked away," The Morrigan chimed in, standing with her eyes swirling crimson. "I have my doubts you have anyone else who would stand against those who want to protect a child, and one of your Fates."

"Let us all take a seat," Adair said, but the four royals either didn't hear or refused to listen.

A steamy roar came from the other side of the room. Drakaina had left her seat and backed far enough away to shift back to her dragon form. She spoke aloud while in her reptilian skin. "Sit, all of you. We are here to protect the innocent growing in Death's womb, or have you forgotten? Prince Alasdair?" she spat his title out like it tasted bad. "The most powerful gods in this room are not the kings, and we all know it. One of those goddesses is the mother of the unborn. Now sit your asses down and ask her what she wants."

Alasdair looked at Atropos. She watched as he lost sight of the goal. *Get her and the baby off Olympus without notice.* He reluctantly sat down beside her, worried he had shown too much emotion. He felt nothing coming from her, her mother, or her siblings. *Fascinating.*

Slowly, Atropos rose from her seat once everyone else had returned to theirs. Alasdair looked around the vast room, and all eyes were on the goddess he once saw lying almost lifeless in a hospital bed—it made him nervous. She glowed with health. *Maybe taking her wouldn't be good for her.* He refused to give that line of thought wings. The mere thought of her being in the same realm with that vile queen made his blood boil.

"I understand both sides. As we know, I would need to return if I left, as a god needs their home to recharge. But I have the same reservations about staying on Mount Olympus as Alasdair. Our child must come first. All of you know what is at stake here. If my sisters can visit regularly, all five of them, and Drakaina can come with me, I will go with the Irish to the realm of the Tuatha Dé Danann."

Alasdair reached for her hand, and she didn't hesitate to take it. They stood as a front against anyone who dared to come between them, even though he knew he had groveling to do and so much to tell her.

"Now that has been settled, let us discuss how the next seven and a half months may go and how we will protect the child when she is born," Themis said.

Adair stood, her eyes swirling white. She was the seer. "I see many angered by the conception of such a powerful goddess. Once, I saw the death of Alasdair to save his unborn, now I see a war where he is fighting to protect his young daughter. As we each know, destiny can only be changed by the Almighty. Even the Fates don't have the last say. Only He does," Adair said. With those final words, his mother's eyes returned to normal.

Zeus' eyes still swirled, but they were no longer red. He tapped his fingers against the table, in thought. Alasdair saw resignation cross his bearded face. "Not only will the dragon go with my daughter, but a hundred Olympian soldiers will be sent. Half will travel back and forth with her. And before you complain about the extra security measures I am instituting, know that I will not waver. I am your King, Atropos. No matter how powerful you are. You will do as I say."

No one fought Zeus on his reinforcements, including Dagda. "You should know that I will use whatever force necessary to protect my realm," Dagda said.

"And, know I have returned to the Irish realm for good. All battlefields will be under my control. Make sure you tell your wife," The Morrigan's grin unnerved him. He wondered what Zeus thought of the Harbinger's threat.

"Hera was asking about Atropos as we all were. Trying to keep her safe," Zeus said. "She will not cause a war over the child."

"You continue to think that, Father, but I'm afraid you will be found wrong," Lachesis said.

"Now that we have an idea of things to come, I would like to ask that until we can no longer contain the babe's existence, we do not speak to anyone, who isn't in this room, about her. Every minute the world is not privy to her is one minute she is perfectly safe," Adair said.

"All in agreement?" Themis asked as she surveyed everyone's reaction. "Good. Unless there is more, I believe having the Irish here will already set tongues speaking; keeping them here any longer will only make it worse."

Alasdair looked around the room to see who agreed when his grandfather spoke.

"Agreed," said Dagda. "We will leave. Send your soldiers to our stone circle, five to ten at a time." He turned to the sisters, "you may come anytime, just let Atropos know and someone will meet you at the gate."

No more was said; each deity vanished to their own realm except for Alasdair and Atropos. He went with her to the Moirai mansion.

Chapter Forty-Nine
Rumors Cause War

Atropos

She couldn't decide if she wanted to kiss or slap the infuriating man. His heavy-handed behavior in the throne room could have caused a war. However, she couldn't deny how devastating he looked when he told her father what she would be doing.

So much had changed in such a short amount of time. One thing being that he was with the family he denied when she last saw him. The other glaring revelation was that he had abilities—godly abilities.

All her questions could wait; what she needed was for him to wrap himself around her. "You know you almost started a war," Atropos smirked, once they were alone in her bedchamber. "Also, what is going on. Last I knew, you were in denial."

"I was devastated when you left. Between that damned dragon and my mum, I became a believer," Alasdair answered.

"Okay, we'll discuss that, but what about your godhood? It was my understanding that it had been stripped as a newborn, and you have been completely mortal since."

"Can you feel my signature? I'm not mortal, never was. It's a long story. Another story we'll discuss at length, but now I need to hold you and know I'm not dreaming."

Alasdair took two large strides and stood toe-to-toe with her. She could feel the heat radiating off his body, and damn, he smelled amazing. With each of her heavy breaths, her nipples grazed his muscled chest, causing them to lengthen and harden, sending a burn of need between her thighs. He was waiting for permission. *Does he not understand that he always has permission?*

"Well, are you going to do something about that or just stand there torturing us both?" Atropos said, nodding at his erection straining against his pants.

In one fluid motion, he had her tossed onto the bed and her clothes on the floor. He knelt between her bent knees, taking her in as she looked at him.

"I was afraid I would never touch you again. Never hold you. Now that we're here, all I want is to make sure I'm not imagining this," Alasdair said as he traced his finger from her knee to her core and back down to her opposite knee. "The second I felt you vanish, I regretted my reactions to everything. It took me losing you to understand how in love I had become. When I found out you were pregnant with our child, I almost lost it. Adair and Dagda held me together so I could get here."

She listened as he poured out his heart. How ironic that the goddess known as The Inflexible One had become completely adaptable with a man. After thousands of years, her life had changed for the better. No matter the struggles she would soon face, she was happy—for the first time.

"I was worried you would never want to see me again. Had it not been for my mother and sisters, I would have returned and begged you for a second chance. They grounded me and helped me wait for you to come to your senses," Atropos said, grinning as he continued to trace his fingers over her naked body.

As she laughed, she noticed he'd become stone-faced. Anger and fear flash through his eyes. "Never go to the human world without that dragon and me. Hell, we'll take soldiers and The Morrigan with us."

"Why?" Atropos asked, suddenly realizing the turn their interlude had taken while she was completely naked. Slowly, she sat up, tucked her legs under herself, and pulled a sheet over her body. Alasdair made no move to stop her. *Something's wrong.*

"That's why my pantheon came to Olympus. When my mother and I took Anna back to her apartment, we stopped by mine. It was wrecked. Broken dishes, artwork worth millions of dollars, destroyed, and a note written on the foyer mirror," Alasdair stared past her as he spoke, as if he relived that moment.

He and Adair took Anna back? What is he talking about? "I have so many questions, but first, what did the note say?" Atropos could sense his anxiety.

He finally looked at her, and when he did, chills traveled down his spine. She knew that whatever was about to come out of his mouth would change the way she thought about her and the baby's safety.

"It said, 'No one can save your child.'"

"No!" Atropos slapped her hand over her mouth and rushed to the bathing chamber, where she retched.

Refusing to stay on Olympus a minute longer than necessary, Atropos opened her mind to her Moirai sisters and Drakaina, conveying everything Alasdair had told her. She now understood why he insisted she go with him to the Irish Pantheon. In her heart, she knew her evil step-goddess had a hand in the message left in his apartment. Only question: was it for her, or did the writer know of *Warrick's* lineage? Goddess or not, she no longer thought for herself. She refused to stay on Olympus any longer.

She returned to the bedroom, dressed in leather fighting gear with daggers strapped to her thighs. "I'm ready to leave."

"Do you not wish to wait for the soldiers your father promised?" Alasdair asked.

"I don't trust my father."

Only minutes after she told him she wanted to leave, they stood inside the stone circle with Drakaina, waiting for him to open the gate to the realm of the Tuatha Dé Danann. She felt Alasdair vibrate with energy as she surveyed her surroundings. It wasn't her first stone circle, but the pulsation that came from the one they stood in was fascinating. She felt both the need to flee and the desire to stay. *It must be the magic to keep humans away.*

That's when it happened. She went from contemplating the emotions stirred by the boulders to seeing everything in slow motion. Alasdair placed the blade of his knife to his palm, and the sky turned dark. The sudden shift in the atmosphere made each of them turn. The second long interruption drew Alasdair's attention from his blade to the sounds the darkening sky brought. That instant of hesitation kept them on the human side rather than the divine. Only a second, and everything went to Hades.

Five meters outside the stone circle appeared several elves of each race, two dire hounds, and a witch, known as a Norse Mare. Each wearing the look of triumph. Atropos grimaced at the blackened smile set in the bloody red mouth the witch displayed. She had seen nothing so gruesome. It looked as if her decayed teeth had just ravaged a gory carcass, and she failed to clean herself afterward. The sight made her pregnant belly roll. *I refuse to retch.*

Drakaina shifted from the human facade she had donned, so as not to scare those in the Irish realm, into the largest dragon form Atropos had ever seen her manifest into. The dragon covered the stone circle in its entirety and came snout to nose with the diverse crew who were there to intimidate, if not to kill. She noted a slight waver in their smirks, but they didn't turn tail. *Stupid.*

"What do you want?" Drakaina asked. Steam rolled from her nostrils, and still, they did not move.

"We are here to see if the rumors are true," the one light elf in the group spoke up. Atropos was surprised an elf of light would stoop to such tactics. It seemed no matter one's allegiance, evil dwelled in all.

"What rumors?" Alasdair asked, standing between Drakaina's forelimbs. Gone was the mortal man; he was now the god she'd seen a glimpse of in Zeus' throne room.

Just before he walked toward the raiding party, he had pulled Atropos behind him and given her a look that made even Death take a step back, but he was right. She knew better than to dive headfirst into a battle, whether with weapons or words. She was carrying his baby, and she didn't need to make the target on her back any larger.

"The ones that tell of a child with supreme power has been conceived, and the parents are those of a Fate and a missing divine Irish prince," the witch said. To the Norse, she was a witch; to everyone else, a demon.

"Sounds like an interesting rumor. I don't know of any princes," Alasdair replied.

"No? Well, I bet she does," said the light elf as he pointed around Alasdair to her.

Drakaina roared, daring them to continue. "If I were you, I would run and never return." A blast of fire from deep inside the dragon's throat shot into the air, followed by a second roar that caused the ground under their feet to tremble. The display was terrifying and should have intimidated their visitors. It did not.

"Whatever you think you know is incorrect. If there is such a child, why would it matter?" Alasdair asked, still between Drakaina's legs, blocking their view of her.

Laughter came from the largest dark elf, who was built like the strongest of her pantheon. She had to admit, his beauty was a waste on such a horrible being. He stood at least two meters, had long, raven black hair in a warrior's braid, smooth tan skin, and if the laughter had not been at them, she would have thought it alluring. She couldn't shake the feeling that he reminded her of someone, though.

"The *rumor* has already cost me a sister. So, I would say it matters," the handsome dark elf said, and took half a dozen steps toward them, flanked by the dire hounds.

"What's your sister's name?" Alasdair asked.

The Álfar shook his head and laughed again. "Do you think that since I'm of the Dökkálfar, that makes me stupid? There is only one reason you would know an elf by name. So, where is my sister? Is she alive?" He took another three steps and was stopped by a row of fire mere centimeters before him.

"Maybe you are stupid. He would never judge your intelligence by your Elven lineage. He's judging your stupidity because you are standing before an enraged dragon, demanding answers with an insidious motley group at your back. That demon alone will get you killed," Drakaina said aloud so the Mare could hear her every word.

"Your sister is alive; however, she supplied information to a vile goddess who gives no allegiance to those she considers disposable. Would you know anything about that?" Alasdair asked, now standing with a dagger in his fist.

That was where she knew him from. His eyes were as vibrant as his double's. The one she met at the gala.

Chapter Fifty

Battlefield

Alasdair

The Álfar closed his eyes and slowly shook his head. "Foolish girl," he said under his breath, but Alasdair heard him even though they were still a couple of meters apart.

Seems my godly abilities are increasing, the thought flashed through his mind. Alasdair took several steps out from between the dragon's legs toward the elf.

"I assume you are Astrid's double. Are you here for your sister or for the rumors?" Alasdair asked, just loud enough for the dark elf to hear.

At the female's name, the elf looked up and straight into his eyes. "All I want is my gullible sister. Tell me where she is, and you can do with the others as you will."

Before he could answer the elf, war cries sounded from the other side of the circle. Someone or something was closing in on them. "It's a trap," Alasdair yelled. "This is no way for you to ever see your double again, elf." Then he ran to the goddess, carrying his unborn child.

Alasdair heard Drakaina roar and felt the heat of her blaze as he zoned in on his world. Atropos was bracing herself to fight, and she was magnificent. He watched as she pulled a sword from thin air and conjured metal armor over her body. Thinking hard, he conjured a dagger in his other hand—the weapon he had taken to best during his practices with his grandfather. He felt himself morph into the formidable prince he was born to be—fire boiled beneath his skin.

Screams from the motley group penetrated his ears as he came up beside Atropos. "Drakaina is taking care of them," he pointed behind him. "I want you only to fight if someone gets past your dragon or me. Promise me!" They could hear chaos all around them and readied for the ones he knew were about to top the small hill.

Seconds later, a band of mixed warriors came into focus. He wasn't sure who or what they all were, but there were at least twenty figures, all carrying weapons, perched atop the hill, watching—assessing.

"I promise," Atropos said, just loud enough for him to hear. "I've called for my—," the other Moirai interrupted her words, as they materialized beside them.

"Thank fuck," Alasdair said, and pressed a quick, gentle kiss to Atropos's forehead. "Stay by her side. Protect them." Speaking to her sisters as he strolled out from the dragon's hind legs and stood fisting his daggers, glaring at the enemies trying to rid him of the two people he cared most about. He blocked the sounds of death behind him, knowing that the dragon had that side covered.

Alasdair's past flashed before him. A couple of months ago, he was a young billionaire. The most extraordinary event in life was the drama of his father trying to fix him up with his partner's daughter. Now he stood, daggers in hand, facing a horde of beings he didn't recognize, readying to keep the woman he loved and his unborn child safe. He couldn't explain the change that came over him. He knew the man who stood in preparation for battle had always been there. A familiar fire coursed through his veins; a slight twitch and burn in each eye made him blink rapidly, and then a red hue focused his sight. The hill was at least fifty meters away, but he could see beads of sweat trickling down his enemies' faces and smell their breath. He would be in awe of his sharpened senses, except his foe smelled horrific.

A tingling sensation ran up his back, signaling the dark elf was coming up behind him—he recognized him as an ally—the Álfar's emotions told him so. Alasdair made no move toward the elf, just waited for him to go to his side.

"Took you long enough," Alasdair said, not turning his gaze from the hillside.

A low chuckle came from the elf. "I was busy ridding us of the Mare. She wanted to kill your goddess. The dragon is dealing with the rest.

"You've earned your sister back, but make no mistake. If she ever takes money from Hera, or Hera's minions again, I will cut her throat myself." Alasdair turned and looked at the elf, knowing his eyes gave away his station. "Understood?"

"Yes. Now, let's get this over with so I can see her."

Growling the words, Alasdair made each one carry to the horde who were inching their way closer, "Each of you will die. I now have your faces and scent memorized. Even if you flee this battlefield, I will hunt you down. No one threatens my family and lives to try again." With that declaration, he and the dark elf took off in a run toward the throng of creatures and demigods.

Once close enough, Alasdair jumped with his daggers poised and cut down the first four foes he encountered. He could hear metal on metal and grunts and cries of pain coming from beside him. He sensed the elf was holding his own. The smell of copper became stronger with every kill. Blood splattered his face and dripped from his knives. Daggers meant he had to be up close and personal with the opponent. He took them in, knowing they each wanted his baby dead. Anger surged through him. When he looked up, he saw more adversaries spilling over the hilltop. *FUCK!*

A sudden flash of heat and screams came from his right. Drakaina must have finished with the elves behind them. Two dire hounds jumped over his head and caught a couple of creatures who were heading for the dark elf. Good to know they were on their side. Those fuckers were huge, with teeth half the length of his forearm.

His world came to a halt when he heard a feminine scream from behind him. *Atropos?* He felt a hand on his shoulder, one of an ally—*Dagda.*

"Go, we have this," Dagda said and gestured toward the Moirai. The "we" his grandfather spoke of was his mother and The Morrigan—both looked pissed.

With a thought, Alasdair was by the Fates' side. It wasn't dead; the Mare looked more insidious with her head hanging to the side and blood dripping from her mouth and nose. *The Norse had it wrong; it is a demon.* The fiend walked toward Atropos and her sisters, and nothing they threw at the creature deterred it. Animation—the witch had become a puppet, but who held its strings? He turned in a circle, looking for its master.

There, next to one of the largest stones of the circle, stood a woman—no, not a woman, a goddess with two doglike creatures at her sides. Her eyes swirled green, transfixed on the instrument of death she wielded.

"Necromancer," Lachesis yelled to him.

"How do I kill her?" Alasdair asked?

"You don't. I do," Atropos said.

"But—," the look with which she cut off the beginning of his objection would have killed a lesser man. "Okay."

Between her sisters' fingers, a thread appeared. Together, Clotho and Lachesis pulled the speckled black string taut, and the puppeteer started to run. Wind swirled around the necromancer, picked her up, and deposited her before the Moirai. The puppeteer kicked and tore at the invisible hands holding her bowed before her executioner. A pair of gilded scissors, like none Alasdair had ever seen, formed in Atropos' right hand. All three sisters' eyes glowed white as Death's voice resounded off the giant stones.

"Hecate, Goddess of Magic and Ghosts, you have defied Hades and tried to kill my unborn. With my shears, I release you from this plane of existence and thrust you into Tartarus, where Hades will sort you." When Atropos cut the thread binding the goddess to the world of the living, a faint cry could be heard, followed by a gurgle, and the puppeteer vanished. The witch fell; her eyes glazed with death and the instant smell of rot.

Alasdair wrapped Death in his arms—her eyes still entirely white. She was the most powerful of them all, but that power came with a price there was no coming back from. To end a life was forever.

"Thank the Almighty," he said as he patted her down, searching for anything amiss. When she slumped heavily in his arms, he knew her eyes were back to normal.

The ground trembled, causing his attention to turn toward the battle he'd left. His grandmother flew above the conflict as a giant raven with swirling red eyes, wielding her mental weapon, striking fear and death across the battlefield, causing the beasts who dared cross the war-torn land to shriek and flee. Adair and Dagda were there to intercept, ensuring no one who meant their family harm left alive. In mere minutes, the land held death, and the only ones left standing were the dark elf and the family he fought to protect.

He picked Atropos up and set off for the stone that would lead them to their new life. "See the cut at my hairline?"

"Yes," Atropos looked up at him.

"Take the blood on your hand and place it on the boulder. Hold it there until the world changes," he grinned. "Let's go home." He felt her soft touch against his battle wound, then watched as an Olympian goddess used the blood of an Irish god to open the portal to the realm of the Tuatha Dé Danann.

Chapter Fifty-One

An Ancient World

ATROPOS

An ancient world came into view. When she blinked, a medieval castle grew from the mist. Clotho and Lachesis stood on either side of them, as transfixed as she was. This realm was so unlike the opulence of Olympus, where everything bled wealth and power. Even though the Irish had both, theirs was steeped in tradition, reaching back to the beginning of time. The Irish reveled in their ancient rituals and primordial fortresses.

This will take some getting used to, Clotho relayed through their bond.

Is it odd that I feel safer here than in our home on the mount? Atropos replied. Her sisters answered with a shake of their heads.

Warrick refused to put her down as he headed to the gothic mansion. Warriors who stood atop the gatehouse nodded at their prince. She would have to remember he was no longer Warrick—he was now the prince of the Irish gods, Alasdair—defender and protector of mankind.

"Wait here, and my mother will see you two to your rooms. I'm taking Atropos to wash up. We'll meet you in the great hall for dinner after everyone has cleaned up and dressed," Alasdair spoke as he continued to the stone steps.

The glint in his eyes had her hoping he meant to do more than wash up for dinner. Living through a battle puts a being's carnal instincts on high alert. Plus, it hadn't been but an hour since their reunion was cut short, and she was dying to get him naked and between clean sheets. Or just naked; she didn't care where at this point. He looked down at her and smirked. Her emotions must have betrayed her intentions.

"Wash first, then we fuck," he winked. Her arousal had her core burning.

"Do you not possess the power to clean us without the extra step of washing?" She knew she was pouting.

Three more steps, and they faced a thick wooden door with iron embellishments. He kicked it open and took her to a large bathing chamber. *Who knew such luxuries existed within a medieval castle?*

"Oh, I possess such power, but trust me, you will enjoy the bath."

He carried her down the steps into the bath, their clothes vanishing as they went deeper. "Nice trick," she said.

"I have many more," Alasdair said, then set her on her feet. The warm water came just above her nipples. With a smirk, a loofah and soap appeared in his hands.

He thoroughly scrubbed himself and then her, making sure he removed all traces of the battle. The water turned red, then, with magic, it became clean and clear again. Once they were scrubbed, he hoisted her onto the side of the bath and spread her thighs wide enough for his shoulders. It only took one stroke of his tongue up her pussy to have her writhing. One more, and she shook violently. When he stood and pushed inside her, she came loudly.

"Fuck," he said in her ear. "If you clench me any tighter, this will be over before it begins."

"Harder." Her command had him thrusting his hips hard and fast, chasing his release and demanding another from her. They both fell off the cliff together. It was intense and wild and exactly what they both needed. For the first time in weeks, she was sated and unbelievably happy.

Unlike what she was used to, the great hall encompassed all the Irish gods. On Olympus, many of the gods were at odds at different times, making a banquet with everyone at once was almost impossible without bloodshed. To walk into a vast room where so many deities mingled and laughter pierced the air instead of angry shouts, settled something in her soul. The community quieted any reservations she had about living in the realm of the Tuatha Dé Danann.

Dagda, Adair, and The Morrigan sat at the front of the hall with two empty seats to Dagda's right. Adair waved them to the chairs just before the king stood, and the room fell silent.

"Today is the day my grandson takes his place at my right, where his mother sat. She decided to vacate the spot, stating she wanted to be only a grandmother." Dagda chuckled. "Yes, you heard that correctly. Alasdair will be a father soon. But, before that, he will be married."

Atropos leaned in to whisper into Alasdair's ear. "What did he just say?"

The bastard smirked and then rose and walked to the front of the massive table. Then, to her shock, he knelt before her.

"Atropos, the goddess of death, Moirai, Daughter of Zeus—please take my hand in marriage. Stay with me for eternity. Bare my children. Allow me to love you unconditionally." He proffered a ring set with an enormous diamond, surrounded by emeralds. Beside the ring were a necklace and a bracelet, both lined with Connemara Marble. "These are the jewels of the divine royal line. Please take them with my truth: I love you beyond measure, I promise to be an exemplary father, and I need you to be my wife."

Chills assailed her body, and the burn of tears began in the corners of her eyes. This man, whom she had only known for a short time, had turned her life upside down and was about to obliterate everything she had ever known. Moisture gathered on the lower lids of his radiant blue eyes. He was so strikingly handsome and impossibly sexy. For Zeus' sake, she was already carrying his daughter; of course, she would be his for eternity.

"Yes!" She covered her mouth and wept in public for the first time in her long life.

Cheers of congratulations and music rang throughout the great hall. For the rest of the evening, they danced and enjoyed life, knowing that whatever came next, they had two pantheons of family standing beside them, protecting what they held dear.

Epilogue
No Room for Mistakes

"I don't trust that elf," Clotho said to Lachesis and Drakaina. The three sat on a thick wooden bench at one of the many tables full of tankards of beer and goblets of wine. The Irish drank and danced in celebration of the victory and their prince's engagement.

"He fought beside your sister's prince and saved your lives from the demon witch. What more do you want from a male?" Drakaina asked as she tore into a large piece of meat.

"No one should look like that."

"Like what?" Lachesis asked. "I see nothing wrong with him. I mean, pointy ears aren't my proclivity, but he can't help that."

"Exactly. Have you ever seen anyone other than a royal god who looked like that? He must be concealed in magic. If he will hide something as trivial as his appearance, he will hide many truths," Clotho said, her eyes locked on the unsuspecting Álfar. "It's not normal."

The goddesses and dragon continued with their meal, and she kept watch over the elf. He didn't look happy, even though the surrounding festivities were boisterous and jovial. They just won a battle to protect her niece and witnessed the engagement of the century, so why did he frown? One wrong move and she would remove him from the realm.

It must have been the suspicion coming off her in waves because once the threat left her mind, his eyes flicked to her. He stared at her with his dark, set orbs.

What colour are they? No one's lashes are that long, not even mine, she thought. "Why is he staring?"

"Maybe to figure out why you are staring at him. Come on. Let's dance with some of these Irishmen. Maybe we'll find one to make passionate love to us and declare their undying loyalty," Lachesis laughed and dragged her by her wrist onto the dance floor, where everyone danced together, some with tankards of beer wrapped in their hands, sloshing it across the floor. She had never seen such.

After two songs, a large, masculine arm snaked around her middle. She stiffened. Never had she been that close to a man, and had certainly never touched so intimately by one.

"I figured if you were going to stare at me all night, goddess, you should know my name."

His deep voice caused a sensation she had only experienced in the dark confines of her bedchamber, alone. Even then, the feeling was never that intense. With his warm body pressed against hers and bodies dancing all around, she quickly became overheated and tried to pull away.

"Nuh-uh. Not so fast, princess. I want to know why you kept staring at me with a look of disdain. Is it possible I've found someone who doesn't want in my pants?"

"You either let me go or die. Your choice, elf," she said.

Where are my sisters?

We are close, but if we intervene, everyone in this room will see us as weak or as needing three of us to best them. You have this. Lachesis said, and Atropos agreed.

Fine. Clotho understood, but having his hands on her was not something she was handling well.

Maybe you should try to enjoy it, Atropos interjected.

"You see, Princess. I'm not afraid of you. Could you kill me? Yes. Do I care? No. Want to know why?"

His hand splayed wide over her stomach, his thumb just under her left breast. The other, *oh Zeus,* rested on her left hip. His heat and the smell engulfed her. She knew better than to ask, but she couldn't help herself.

"Why?"

"Because I can feel you. You tremble at my touch and most of all, this close—I can smell your arousal."

Before she could muster a response, he was gone. When she looked back, he was in the same seat as before, holding a mug of beer to his lips. *Despicable elf.*

She snarled at him. He put down his beer and gave her a half grin, then winked.

The walls of the room shook when the news of the minor battle in Ireland traveled back to him. He had to tell them, even if doing so meant more lashes and possible death. Ever since the goddess' son was locked away, she stopped pretending to be rational. Everyone was her enemy, even her consort. No matter if they were gods or demigods, creatures, or humans, every line that could be traced back to her husband that wasn't produced by the two of them was on her list for revenge. Somehow, she had it in her head that they all conspired to kill her grandson and trap her favorite. While plotting, the queen convinced the Spinner of Clouds that her children would be next. The two were determined and used their love of family to vindicate their actions.

"Tell me exactly what happened."

The light elf before him was only a couple of hundred years old. He stood proud with his white hair tied at his nape and a bow slung across his back.

"They had a dragon and the prince we thought was human, well, the rumors were true. He is not. Dagda and The Morrigan joined the skirmish. There was nothing we could have done. We only had a handful of trained soldiers. Most were just those we paid to be there. Many ran and were killed anyway."

"Do you think you should live?"

"Sir? Why—well, of course. We were not prepared to fight such strength. Now that we know what we're up against, we will win the next one. The child will not make it to its birth."

"Hmmm. Well, you are correct about one thing. That baby will die. But it won't be you who witnesses it."

Before the light elf could react, a blade was sticking out of his heart.

The older light elf removed a cloth from his sleeve and wiped the blood from his fingers. "Bring me Ash and Astrid's father."

Thank you for reading The Lost Fate!

Book I of the Moirai Trilogy

Sign up for L.W. Phillips's author newsletter. This is where she finds her ARC and BETA readers; there are always giveaways!
http://eepurl.com/ii9BAb

L.W. Phillips is a businesswoman who figuratively wrote all day for years. She went through each day thinking of her life and those of others as scenes and scenarios in books. Finally, she wrote her musings down—well, she typed them out. One morning she woke with a full-length novel—actually, it was four months later, after much hard work, she woke up with a very raw, full-length rough draft of Dream Divine. Semantics.

She is married with three children—two grown and one college teenager. She breeds crested geckos and runs a dental company. Not to mention all of her dogs, cats, and fish. When does she sleep, you ask? She doesn't.

Her escape is the world of fantasy. Reading and writing relax her.

Her motto is to never to give up and follow your dreams!

Acknowledgements

I WANT TO THANK God for giving me the gift of gab and perseverance.

Second, JoAnna and Kellie—It takes a lot to tell a friend "no that won't work" while keeping up their spirits, but these two women have done a phenomenal job of it.

Third, JoAnna, thank you for the awesome merch and inspirational words. Editor of the year!

Fourth, Dar for hitting the artwork just right the first time!

Fifth, my daughter, Allison—she is my biggest fan.

My husband—Ty, thank you for putting up with me and the fictional worlds in my head.

Last but not least, my readers! Thank you for helping make my dreams come true!